SAY FOREVER

Something More Book Three

TARA WEST

Say Forever

Dedications

To my husband and little girl. Thank you so much for putting up with my crazy hours and moods while I worked on this book. Your support means the world to me.

Jodi, you are amazing. Thanks for the awesome swag and for motivating my fan club.

To my fan club, thanks for your faith in my books. You are the reason I keep writing.

Special thanks to Carrie, Raven and Tammy for your comments on my manuscript.

Emma Jameson, I humbly bow to your words of wisdom. Thanks for your advice.

Theo Fenraven, I don't know what I'd do without your edits. Thank you!

Chapter One

Christina

It's been three weeks since my screw up. Three weeks. According to the directions on the box, plenty time enough to know if I'm pregnant.

Don't be a wimp, Christina. Just do it!

I'm sitting on the toilet, staring at this damn stick, too petrified to piss on it. What the hell is wrong with me? And how is it that a tiny piece of plastic is causing so much turmoil in my life?

Because if it's positive, my new career is over, or at least it's put on hold. There's that whole issue of me being just twenty-two when I have my first child. Sure, I know other girls younger than me have had kids, but I'm not them. I'm not ready. I'm just not ready.

Then there's this other part of me, this twisted, crazy part of me that thinks about how adorable my little brothers are, and how Andrés and I would have a cute baby, too. My brothers are only three and four-years-old. My child could actually play with them in a few years. Or get into trouble with them, as my brothers are inclined to find trouble wherever they go.

Oh, gawd, how would I be able to cope if he or she turned out like my brothers, or like Andrés tells me he used to be as a kid?

And even though I hate myself for chickening out, I slide that little strip back into the box and hide it at the bottom of my cosmetics bag. I'm better off not knowing—for now at least.

Because if it's positive, I'll have to tell Andrés. Three weeks ago, on the night Andrés and I had unprotected sex (unprotected because I was stupid enough to forget my pill box at my mom's house in San Antonio) he'd shown me the most beautiful engagement ring. Then he'd put the damn ring away and said something about how he didn't deserve to ask me to marry him yet.

I know what's going to happen if we find out I'm pregnant. He's going to take out that ring again. And that's not what I want. When Andrés proposes, I want it to be because he's ready to ask me, not because he feels pressured by the baby news. And if I am pregnant, I don't want Andrés to think that swayed my decision, either. Baby or no baby, I already know what I'm going to say if and when he pops the question.

Even though we've only been together seven months, we're starting to finish each other's sentences. Whether it's eating Mexican food, enjoying the outdoors, going to art museums, or just curling up with a movie, Andrés and I are perfect together. And then there's the way he makes my heart hammer in my chest whenever he comes home from work and wraps me in his arms. When I place my hand over his heart, lean up and kiss him on the lips, I just want to melt into him. He completes me, and I couldn't imagine a future without him. Of course I'd say yes. Yes! Yes! Yes! Now if he'd just ask me.

I could forget old-fashioned conventions and ask him. Why does it always have to be the guy who proposes? But if I do turn out to be preggers, I don't want Andrés thinking that was why I wanted to get married. No, best to wait it out in agony, wondering if Andrés still has that ring, and if so, why doesn't he just ask me already?

I finish my business and pull up my pants. Then I grab my cosmetics bag off the floor and hide it at the bottom of the cabinet, not that Andrés will be going through my lipsticks, anyway.

I stare at my face in the mirror as I'm washing my hands. I look terrible. My normally bright green eyes have a dull haze to them, and they appear to be sunk in their sockets. My skin has this deathly pale pallor, except for my nose. I used to think it was on the smallish side, but now it has swelled up like a balloon about to burst, and it's as bright as a ripened strawberry.

The doctor said I have a case of sinusitis, so she put me on antibiotics. So far, the infection doesn't seem to be clearing, and I've been reduced to a booger blowing zombie all month.

Now that I'm on antibiotics, and my birth control pills aren't as effective (actually, they're not effective at all since I decided to quit taking them until I find out if I'm pregnant), Andrés has to wear a condom. He hates it. I hate it, too, but I'm not taking any more chances. Hopefully, it isn't already too late.

* * *

Andrés

I shouldn't have shown Christina the damn ring. If I thought the weight of those unspoken words, "Will you marry me?" felt heavy before, it is nothing compared to the pressure I am feeling now, like the noose around my neck has been cinched and strung up, and the hangman is about ready to kick that stool out from under my feet.

I stir the spaghetti sauce and lick some of the red juice off the spoon. Needs sugar. Christina likes her sauce more sweet than tart, and I want tonight's dinner to be perfect, in case I get the nerve to ask her to marry me.

The thing is, I want to give Christina that ring, but the timing never feels right. First off, there's the fact that I acted like a total ass three weeks ago, and I don't feel like I've done much of anything to prove to her how much I love her. I've taken her to San Antonio twice to see her family. I bought her new seat covers for her car. I cleaned up the spill from the can of soda she left open in the fridge. Those things hardly count.

I open the sugar container and pour in a few tablespoons. Then I add more chopped cilantro. I always end up using a whole bushel, so I don't know why I add a little at a time. I survived two tours in Afghanistan, and I'm fucking afraid of spice.

I take a swig of beer and stir the sauce. I've been too much on edge lately. Things were tense around here last week after Christina took her finals. We didn't think she'd pass psychology, but she squeaked by with a C minus.

Last weekend her family came up and we held a surprise graduation ceremony at my *tio's* house. I could have asked her to marry me then, in front of our family and friends. But, seriously, what guy does that? What if she said she wasn't ready? Everyone would have thought I was a total dick, and my cousins wouldn't have let me live it down.

I could wait until after Christmas. Or I could wait until next Christmas. She should be ready after a year. Maybe by then I would have done enough to deserve her.

But I don't know if I can stand the noose around my neck that long. And then there's that way I catch Christina looking at me. Every morning when we kiss each other goodbye, she's got this wistfulness in her eyes and in her voice. I keep telling myself it's her sinus infection, but I don't know. There's something off about her, especially when she talks about her baby brothers. Why do I get the feeling she's longing to have a baby of her own?

Just last month she was saying she didn't want to ever have kids. She asked me a totally unexpected question last night when she was sitting across from me at dinner. She wanted to know if my teeth were naturally straight or if I'd had braces. When I told her I'd never needed braces, her eyes lit up. She dropped her hand to her stomach, resting it there for a moment before she picked up her fork and flashed a bright smile.

What was that about?

Is she subtly trying to tell me she's ready for kids? Now?

She's been wearing those earrings I got her a few months ago almost every day now, too. The earrings look a lot like the engagement ring I had made for her, with one diamond in the center, surrounded by a circle of emeralds.

Why does she wear those earrings every day when she hardly wore them before? Actually, she never wears jewelry to her temp job airbrushing cars. At least, until now. What is she trying to tell me?

Does Christina want me to propose? If she does, why doesn't she come out and say it? Is she ready to have kids? How in the fuck am I supposed to know? I wish women came with instruction manuals. My life would be so much easier.

Now I'm debating what I should do. Do I suffer in silence and put it off until next year? Do I ask her soon, like maybe this week, knowing if she refuses, it might ruin our Christmas?

I hate how fucking confused I am right now. If I'd been this indecisive when I was deployed in Afghanistan, I wouldn't have made it back alive. Usually, when I know I want something, I set my mind to it and do it.

Just fucking do it, Andrés. Just ask her.

The sauce is starting to bubble. I turn down the burner and stir the pot real good, so the paste doesn't stick to the bottom. I add a ton of parmesan, wine, and portabella mushrooms. Then I cover the simmering pot.

A small pot of water on the other burner starts to boil, so I add the pasta. Christina sent me a text a few minutes ago telling me she's on her way home.

I pour her a glass of soda water and add some fresh oranges and stevia. For the past three weeks, Christina has refused to drink my homemade sangria. She said the doctor told her alcohol weakens her immunity. Christina is taking the advice pretty seriously. She won't even take a sip of my beer now. Too bad she's still feeling sick after three weeks. I think the stress from finals has worn her down.

After the table is set, and the pasta and sauce are almost finished cooking, I reach into my pocket and finger the drawstring on the velvet pouch—the pouch with the diamond and emerald engagement ring. I wrap my fist around it and clench it tight. My whole body tenses up as determination strengthens my resolve.

Goddamn. I'm proposing tonight!

* * *

Christina

"Mmmm. Smells delicious."

Even more delicious is the sight of Andrés, wearing nothing but a fitted T-shirt and jeans, slaving over the stovetop. I stand back for a moment and admire his physique. He's taller than most guys, about six feet, with thick wavy hair, broad shoulders, and a tight body. Very tight. Even though he's been out of the Army for eight months, and works long hours managing his uncle's businesses, he himself in prime condition, getting up at the crack of dawn at least three times a week to run and lift weights.

I don't know how he does it, but I sure do appreciate it, especially now as I continue to drool at him. Even more impressive than his backside is his front, the real reason I call him my Spanish Adonis. I close my eyes and recall the image of his face, which looks like it was chiseled out of stone, a beautiful square jaw, full, sensual lips, high cheekbones, and large dark eyes, framed by thick lashes.

Why do I torture myself like this? As sick as I've been all week, I shouldn't be horny, but I am. I wrap my arms around Andrés's waist and nibble on his ear while he's trying to scoop our pasta into bowls. I giggle when the big wooden spoon he's holding clatters to the counter. I have the feeling if I keep this up, dinner may have to wait. Even though I came home hungry, sex always trumps food.

"Spaghetti and meatballs, mija," he rasps.

"I'm not in the mood for meatballs," I say to him on a growl, leaving the rest of the words unspoken.

I trail my hand down his abdomen. He's standing rigid, like a soldier at attention, as I slide my hand even lower. As I press my breasts against his back, I don't even feel the rise and fall of his chest anymore, which means he's holding his breath. Good. I've got the boy under my spell.

I deftly unzip his jeans, and when I lower the elastic on his underwear, his erection springs to life. He throws his head back and groans as I wrap a hand around his cock.

Still holding his erection, I smile coyly up at him as I lead him to the kitchen table. I release him long enough to pull out a chair. I tug his pants and underwear past his knees and then with a gentle push, he falls obediently into the chair.

I take a cushion off a nearby seat, throw it at his feet, and then drop to my knees before him. He flashes a seductive half-smile as he stretches his long legs out and leans his head back. His large erection juts out before me, a beautiful display of prime man-flesh, ready to be devoured. I lick my lips as I brace my hands on his thighs and eye him with a feral hunger. I gently swirl my tongue around the tip of his cock, coaxing clear juices out of the slit.

He groans and grabs my shoulders, pressing my face against his groin.

I shake him off and point an accusing finger in his abdomen. "I'm setting the pace."

He responds with the cutest pouty face ever, but he drops his clenched hands to his sides.

But honestly, who am I kidding? I love foreplay, but like I said, I came home hungry, so I wrap my lips around his head and slide his shaft deep into my mouth. Andrés's groans gutturally as he flexes his hips, pushing the tip of his erection against the back of my throat. We set a steady pace, me slurping and suckling up and down his electrified flesh while he thrusts into my mouth. Andrés's groaning is intensifying, and I know if I continue to blow him, I'll be devouring more than just his cock.

My insides are quivering by this point, and my panties are soaked through. My tender flesh is thrumming in anticipation, because as soon as I'm done sucking Andrés, I'm going to mount him right here on this chair.

Andrés grabs my shoulders and pulls me off of him. "Stop," he pants, "Or I'll come in your mouth."

I look up and flash my best wicked smile. The poor guy has been having latex orgasms for the past three weeks. I know he'd enjoy coming in my mouth while my tongue swirls against his sensitive flesh.

"That's okay," I say, as I lean over and lick him from base to head in one fluid stroke. I spit into my hand and massage moisture into his balls, and then I slowly slide him back into my mouth. His balls tense beneath my hand as the head of his cock jars the back of my throat. He cries out, and his hips jerk erratically before his warm juices explode against my tonsils. I swallow while continuing to suckle and stroke him.

He's still moaning and groaning as I slide up and release his shaft. I wipe a hand across my wet, swollen lips and smile.

He cups my cheek, tracing his thumb across my bottom lip. "Thank you, mija," he says through a sigh as he sinks low in the chair.

"No, thank you," I say to him, as I slide off my jeans and underwear. I swish some soda water around in my mouth and then grab the new box of condoms out of the grocery bag on the table. I rip open that box and wrapper with amazing speed and slide the condom on top of his still engorged penis. Andrés sits up and gives me a knowing grin before grabbing my hips and helping me ease onto him. As I straddle his waist, he thrusts into me. I'm so wet and horny by this point, I know it won't take much to make me come. Feet planted firmly on the floor, I proceed to ride my cowboy, but we've never done it in a chair before, and I forgot I'm not very tall. Bouncing up and down is kind of tricky, and I'm grinding against him instead, but then omigod!

The way his large head rubs against the back of my swollen center feels so freaking good. Andrés slides his hands up my shirt, pulls up my bra and cups my breasts, the pads of his thumbs tracing circles around my nipples. That is enough to send me over the edge, and I lose all sense of rhythm as I surrender to the orgasm. But Andrés is still bucking against me, pressing deep inside my channel, coaxing more tremors of pleasure pulsating through me.

The air whooshes from my lungs as he hauls me up and lays me on the table. I think I hear a bag of groceries fall to the floor, but I don't care. He cups my face in his hands, leans down and nibbles on my lip, and then trails kisses down my jaw and neck while pumping into me. It doesn't take long for another orgasm to build, and just as I'm about to crest again, Andrés is kissing me, driving his tongue against mine while moaning into my mouth. His head is pulsing inside me, just as that point of pleasure deep inside me shatters into a million pieces. My cry is captured by his kiss as his shallow, deep thrusts, torment my swollen sex. After several tender kisses, the rhythm of our hearts slow down to near normal, and we untangle from each other.

Andrés lifts me from the table and helps me dress before he scoops his jeans off the floor. I fall into the chair, exhausted and sore from his weight pressing me into the hard planes of the table, but damn, it was worth it.

* * *

Andrés

I take a long drink from my beer bottle and then absently stroke that little pouch in my pocket. Now doesn't seem like a good time to propose. Christina's refused even the smallest glass of wine. We've already had sex, which means any sexual tension I hoped to build tonight has been drained. Maybe after I clear the dishes, I can give her a back rub or draw her bubble bath. Heck. Maybe I'll combine the two, get her really loosened up, and then propose.

At the moment, she doesn't look like she's in the mood for anything other than food.

"Don't blink. I might inhale the whole plate." Christina twirls a giant forkful of spaghetti, and amazingly, manages to fit the entire bite into her mouth.

I wait, watching as she chews feverishly before swallowing.

"Didn't you eat today?" I ask.

She shakes her head and stabs a meatball. "I didn't have time. I've got too many jobs to work on and only two weeks left to do them."

I sigh as I dip a breadstick into the marinara. I still can't believe my girlfriend is leaving my company, although it's my own fault. Last month, after I stupidly walked out on her, she found another job working for her mom as a formal party designer. She'll be decorating weddings and quinceañeras for well-to-do clients in San Antonio and Austin. They're planning to launch Domingo Designs in January. I suppose it's for the best. I can't expect an artist with Christina's talents to airbrush cars forever.

"You don't have to finish them all," I say to her, though secretly I want her to. The new artist I hired doesn't have half Christina's talent, or her work ethic. I'll be sad to see her go.

"Yes, I do," she says after swallowing a mouthful of meatball. "I'm not leaving you guys stranded."

"How's the newbie?" I ask her, and brace myself for the answer. He's got more body piercings than should be humanly possible, and an attitude to boot, but he was the only artist with a clean record who applied. Three times this week, Christina reported he's taken extended bathroom breaks. I wonder if he's got a clean record because he's actually on the straight and narrow, or if he's smart enough not to get caught at whatever he's doing wrong.

"Talented, but a little out of touch." She wags her fork at me. "I hope you didn't hire another meth-head."

I take another swig of beer and lean back in my chair. Running five automotive businesses is much harder than I thought. I have no idea how Tio has managed twenty. But this spring my uncle plans to retire for good, leaving my cousins and me to run his empire. I still don't know if I'm the right man for the job. I hate to admit it, but leading a troop through the mountains of Afghanistan was much easier than this. Those guys, they were my brothers. I trusted them with my life. These guys here, we've got to keep the cash registers behind cages, not just because of theft from outside, but from within. It's hard when I can't trust the people working for me.

"Yeah, me, too." I groan before taking another swig of beer. "I'm fucking sick of dealing with users."

Christina yelps and practically flies out of her seat at the sound of loud banging on our front door. I jump up and reach the door in a few long strides. I groan when I see spiked pink hair on the other side of the peephole.

"Who is it?" she asks me. I look at her and laugh when I see she's armed herself with a large wooden spoon.

"It's Karri," I growl as a knot of tension coils around my shoulders.

Christina's eyes bulge, and she waves the spoon at me. "Don't let her in!"

I take a step back as Karri pounds on the door again, this time louder than the first. Then I swear when I hear the faint sound of a baby crying.

"She's got Ty!" Christina drops the spoon, pushes past me, and throws open the door.

Karri storms into our apartment like a cyclone of angst as she thrusts the baby into Christina's arms. "I think Jackson followed me. Hurry, you've got to hide us!"

I scowl as I look down at this meth-head who used to be my girlfriend's best friend. Karri's wearing an oversized blue and gold shirt with what appears to be fraternity lettering on the front. Her hair's a mess, her makeup is smeared, her jeans have more rips than should be legal, and it looks like her scuffed shoes are on the wrong feet.

What the fuck is wrong with this girl?

I look over at Christina as she tries to console the crying baby. The kid is shivering in Christina's arms.

He's not wearing a jacket, and it's freaking forty degrees outside.

Karri seems oblivious to her kid's suffering as she walks over to our kitchen table and helps herself to a breadstick. "Mmmmm, this is good. You make this, Christina?" She waves the breadstick at her.

Christina rolls her eyes and turns her back on Karri, pressing the baby against her chest and whispering soothing words into his ear.

Kari shrugs a shoulder, dips the breadstick into my plate, swirls it in the sauce, and takes another bite.

Karri is the same girl who had an affair with that *pendejo* Jackson James while he was engaged to Christina. After Karri had Jackson's baby, she said another guy was the father, and then she named Christina as the godparent. It wasn't until Ty was almost a year old that Christina learned the truth. Last we'd heard from Karri, she'd left her baby with Jackson's parents and run off with her drug dealer boyfriend.

Yeah, Karri's a selfish, using bitch, and if it wasn't for the baby, I wouldn't have let that girl through the door.

I'm so fucking pissed, I'm about ready to punch a hole through the wall. I walk up to her, snatch the bread from her hand, and throw it on the table.

"Get out," I growl.

Her eyes widen, and she shrieks as if I'm about to hit her. No doubt, she's used to that kind of treatment from her druggie boyfriend, but I was raised differently. I'm not about to hit a girl, no matter how much she annoys me.

"I knew you would come here!" A nasal voice echoes behind me. "You've got nowhere else to go."

I turn around and glare at the man my girlfriend almost married. He's wearing unbuttoned pants and no shirt beneath his half-zipped leather jacket. Karri's oversized fraternity sweat shirt is starting to make more sense. They probably met at a motel somewhere, and Karri stole the baby when Jackson's pants were down. Jackson is about an inch or two taller than me, with wide shoulders, but he's got no muscle mass at all. None. It's like the guy spends his days playing video games, or else he's just lazy. The stupid pendejo has got a lot of nerve storming into my home uninvited.

"What the fuck are you doing in my apartment?" I bellow.

Jackson's got this wild look in his eyes as he turns to me. That's when I see the faint trace of white powder stuck to his upper lip.

Fucking great.

Tyler whimpers against Christina, and Jackson spins around, glaring at my girlfriend. "Give me the fucking baby, or I swear to God, Christina, I'll…"

Christina's eyes widen as she backs up a step. Tyler whimpers louder.

I'm barely aware of my feet propelling me forward, of me grabbing Jackson's collar and pushing him up against the wall. "Or you'll what?" I snarl. Then I say to Christina over my shoulder, "Take the baby into the bedroom."

I tighten my grip on Jackson's collar and glare at him until I hear our bedroom door shut.

Jackson is cringing and averting his gaze. He's too stupid to even know how to defend himself. "That's my kid," he says through wheezy breath as some of that white powder beneath his nose falls into his mouth.

I angle my head back, not just because I don't want to inhale any of Jackson's cocaine residue, but because my girlfriend's stories are true. The guy's breath smells like a fucking dog took a shit in his mouth.

"And you're in my house uninvited," I say through clenched teeth. I still can't believe the dick has the nerve to barge into my apartment. His cocaine high must be clouding his judgment.

I hear the clank of silverware scraping a dish, and realize Karri is eating my food. I'm so fucking pissed right now, my head's about to explode.

Jackson raises both hands in a gesture of surrender, as he cowers against the wall. "Let me have my kid and I'll go."

I center my gaze on the prick with the bad breath and think I've got the perfect way to release my frustration. "I've got to take care of something first." I let go of Jackson's collar.

I hear his sigh of relief as I pull back. In the blink of an eye, I channel all my pent-up anger into the force of my fist, as I plant it square in Jackson's face.

Pain lances through my knuckles as they crash against his mouth. Damn, he's hard-headed! The release of my frustration is worth it. I don't feel bad for sucker punching the guy. He should've been prepared for it, which goes to show what an idiot he is. What the fuck had Christina ever seen in him?

Jackson covers his mouth as he slides down the wall and lands on his ass.

I lean down and speak in a low rumble. "You don't swear at my girlfriend, ever again. Got me, *hombre*?"

"That's assault," Jackson cries through his blood soaked fingers. "I'm calling the cops."

"And telling them what?" I laugh. "That you snorted coke, broke into my house, and threatened my girlfriend? Go ahead. Call the cops. Who do you think they'll arrest?"

Jackson's eyes widen and he crouches even lower, curling up in to a fetal ball on my entryway floor. Can the guy get any more pathetic?

Despite the pain searing my knuckles, I haul him up by the collar. Jackson starts to cry, and he nearly falls to the floor as his feet slide all over the tile. I swear to God, it's like I'm dealing with a fucking kid.

"Now here's what you're going to do." I growl into his ear as he flinches and flattens one side of his face against the wall. "You're going to get the fuck out of my apartment, sober up, and then you can come back tomorrow for your kid."

"I need Tyler tonight," he whimpers. "My dad will freak."

"Then call your dad and tell him to come get him."

Jackson raises a shaky, bloodied hand and points over my shoulder. "He can't know I was with her."

I don't need to look behind me to know he's talking about Karri; the stupid bitch is still chowing down on my food.

I look him dead in the eye and clutch his collar so tight, he makes gagging sounds. "You should have thought about that before you fucked her… again. I hope you wore a condom this time."

I release Jackson with a shove and point the way out the door.

Jackson stumbles over the threshold and pulls his hand from his mouth. He turns to me with a quavering lip. "I think you busted a tooth."

I ball up my hands and take a step forward. "Good. Now get out of my sight before I bust some more." I step into the foyer and watch as he sulks toward the parking lot.

I hear the sound of a fork clanking on top of an empty platter. Karri rushes the door. "Now maybe you'll go to the dentist," she calls out in a sing-song, mocking tone. "Did anyone ever tell you your breath stinks?" She turns to me with a triumphant gleam in her crazed eyes.

My shoulders stiffen as I brush past her and shut the front door. I walk into our bedroom and close the door behind me.

* * *

Christina

I'm sitting on the bed, holding Ty against my chest when Andrés walks into the bedroom. It's only when I see he's whole and unharmed I exhale a sigh of relief. Though I don't think Jackson could hurt my boyfriend, anyway. I definitely heard a scuffle outside my door, and knowing Andrés, he'd probably had enough of Jackson's shit.

"What happened?"

He looks at me with a smirk before holding up a fist. "Jackson got what was coming to him, that's what happened."

I gasp when I see my boyfriend's knuckles are bleeding. "Andrés, your hand!"

He shrugs. "It's nothing. Do you know how many times I've split my knuckles fixing cars?" He crosses his arms over his chest and winks. "Besides, you don't know how good that felt."

"I bet," I laugh. "I've been dreaming of face punching Jackson for years."

The door opens and Karri sidles in, unannounced and uninvited. Big surprise.

Karri beams down at Tyler and me. "Awww. Don't you make a good godmother?"

Tyler tightens his grip around my neck and whimpers into my shoulder at the sound of his mother's voice.

Andrés looks at my meth-head ex-BFF and scowls. He tenses up when her shoulder brushes his forearm. She smiles up at him as if they're best chums. Doesn't this girl have fucking boundaries?

Andrés takes a step away from Karri. "Do you know how to get ahold of the grandparents?" he asks me.

I point to my phone on the nightstand. "I already texted Jackson's stepmom."

I'd sent Mrs. James a message that Karri and Jackson were fighting over Tyler, and she'd better come get him ASAP. She messaged me back a few seconds later they were on their way out the door.

"What did you tell her? I don't want them taking Ty!" Karri shrieks as she lunges forward.

Andrés pushes her back with a quick thrust of his arm. "You don't have custody," he says in a menacing tone. "This is kidnapping."

Karri flaps a hand at Tyler and stomps her foot. "He's *my* baby!"

"He *was* your baby," Andrés says with a clenched jaw. "You lost your rights when you ran off with your drug dealer."

Karri gapes at him like he's grown a second head.

"He's got Celiac Disease, remember?" I ask, scooting away from Karri while clutching Tyler tighter. "Special diet? Do you even know how to feed him? Do you even have a place to live?"

"I can stay here." Karri doesn't even flinch when she says it.

Un-fucking-believable!

Before I get a chance to tell the bitch how crazy she is, Andrés says on a roar, "Hell, no!"

Karri shrieks back, looking at Andrés with wide watery eyes, and then she wails like a child.I'm so embarrassed for her.

Once again, I'm startled by pounding on the front door. Andrés swears and grabs a baseball bat out of the closet. My limbs ice over with fear when he storms out of the bedroom. I know Andrés is ten times the man Jackson is, but I also know Jackson has probably been doing drugs, most likely cocaine, his drug of choice. Who knows what revenge he's capable of while he's wired? What if he's got a bigger bat, or worse, a knife or gun? I give Ty an extra squeeze and rise on shaky legs as I peer through the crack in the bedroom door.

Relief floods through me when I see my tall, blonde, and Barbie doll perfect best friend and neighbor, Grace, and her rancher girlfriend, Violet.

I carry Tyler out to the living room, Karri lapping at my heels like a stray dog begging for crumbs. "Is everything okay?" Grace asks as she sweeps a hand through her long curls. "We heard a commotion."

Andrés looks back at Karri with a scowl. "I'm handling it."

Karri's bottom lip is hanging down in a pout. She looks terrible, her pink spiky hair a twisted mess, and her thick black eyeliner smeared down her face. She's lost a lot of weight since I've last seen her over a month ago. She once prided herself on her curves, but now she looks like an emaciated rat.

"I come back home and find out my mom is dead and my stupid brother sold our house." Karri throws up her hands. "I don't have anywhere to live! You can't just throw me out on the street!" She looks at Andrés with an accusatory glare.

Andrés squares his shoulders, his normally passionate and loving gaze turning to stone. "No meth-head is staying in my house."

"I'll take her."

I gape at Violet. She's dressed in worn denim jeans and scuffed boots, and her cropped dark hair is slicked back with gel. Grace's girlfriend has been full of surprises. When I first met her, I thought she was some rodeo groupie, but I've learned there's a lot more to this woman. She owns a successful horse breeding ranch on the outskirts of town. Grace told me Violet has taken in many wayward teens and taught them how to care for livestock and manage their thriving, organic farm.

I guess I'm not the only one shocked by Violet's offer. Slack-jawed, Grace is looking at her girlfriend, too. "W-what?" Grace asks, breathily.

Violet crosses her arms over her chest and eyes Karri like she's a piece of livestock. "She can work at the ranch."

"Ranch?" Karri stops her false tantrum long enough to cock a hand on her hip and sneer. "You mean like horses and cows and shit? It's not like one of those fucking rehab ranches, is it?"

"Sort of." Violet's face is devoid of expression. "You want a place to live or not?"

Karri props her other hand on a hip and rolls her head with an exaggerated movement. "I'm not picking up horse shit."

Violet takes a step forward, the hard angles of her face turning into a frown. "You'll do what you're told if you want room and board. I'll be waiting in my truck. You've got two minutes to decide."

Violet turns and walks out, Grace trailing behind her. I can hear Grace's high-pitched whine echoing in the corridor, and I can tell she's not happy about Violet's offer.

"Christina!" Karri waves a hand toward the front door. "You cannot make me go live with her."

Tyler is snuggling against me, and I look down to see his eyelashes are fluttering as if he's fighting sleep. His cheeks are flushed, and he feels like a little squeezable furnace. I run my fingers through his hair and feel his forehead. It's warm. Too warm. Who knows what this kid was exposed to while his parents were doing drugs today? I swear if I wasn't holding Tyler, it would be hard for me to keep from wrapping my hands around Karri's throat and throttling her.

"You're not staying here." I turn my back on her and rock the baby in my arms. I keep my gaze focused on the blank flat-screen in our oak entertainment center. It's Andrés TV, and bigger than the width of my arms. I'm pretty sure it costs more than all the furniture in our apartment.

"I can't believe you would do this to me!" Karri yells, causing Tyler to jump.

I mentally count to ten as I try to shake off the urge to give Ty to Andrés, rip the television from its stand, and smash it over Karri's head.

"Get over yourself, Karri," Andrés snickers.

I bite my lip to keep from laughing out loud.

"Fuck you and your stupid fucking boyfriend!" Karri screams before I hear her stomping out the door. I hold Ty tightly as I listen to the retreating sound of her shoes smacking against the pavement.

And just like that, Karri the tornado storms out of my apartment, and hopefully out of my life, in a whirlwind of emotion. She doesn't even bother saying goodbye to her sleeping baby. Not that she gives a shit about anyone but herself. Poor Grace. Violet doesn't know what she's gotten them into.

* * *

Jackson's stepmom shows up about fifteen minutes later with an escort built like a refrigerator, wearing dark shades, a black suit and tie, and a Bluetooth in his ear. I think he must be part statue, as I don't see so much as a muscle twitch on his face while he blocks my front door with his hands clasped in front of him.

As Mrs. James takes Ty from me, she explains Mr. James is in Paris on business.

Out of all of Jackson's family, his stepmom is the only person I've ever liked. She can be haughty at times, usually when Mr. James is around, but one-on-one, she's always been nice to me. She's only about ten years older than me and my height and dress size, a petite trophy wife, with hair so pale it practically glows.

Ty wakes up when I hand him to her, and I get choked up by his reaction.

"Mommy!" he cries before flinging his arms around Mrs. James's neck. Considering how young she is, I guess it would be odd for him to call her "grandma." Obviously, Mrs. James has assumed the role of Tyler's mother.

My heart warms at the way she snuggles Tyler and kisses his forehead. I remember Jackson telling me his dad had already had surgery that would prevent him from having any future children, making Jackson his only child. I often wondered how Jackson's stepmom felt about that, and if her husband even cared about her feelings.

Seeing her with Ty, it's plain how much this woman loves kids.

The irony is I once told Andrés I would never want a family. I didn't even consider what he wanted. I realize now how selfish I'd been.

Mrs. James lets out a shaky sigh as she whispers into Tyler's ear. "I was so worried about you."

When Mrs. James's eyes water with tears, I feel compelled to look away. At least I know she loves him. I doubt my adoptive mother ever worried this much over me.

Mrs. James walks over to a corner of the room, bouncing Ty in her arms. She's facing away from everyone, and I can tell she's trying to regain her composure. Finally, she clears her throat and turns to Andrés, a solemn expression in her darkening gaze. "I called my stepson. He told me you punched him in the face."

Andrés lifts his chin and meets her gaze with an unwavering stare. "I did."

I look from Mrs. James to Andrés and back to the big guy in the suit, hoping the shit isn't about to hit the fan. I place my hand on Andrés's forearm. If they mean to cause trouble, I'm determined to stand by my man, though I don't know how much help I'll be against that bodyguard.

Relief floods through me when Mrs. James breaks into a wide grin. "Thank you," she says to Andrés. Then she looks at me and her lower lip trembles as she speaks. "Thank you, Christina, for looking after Tyler."

"I'd do anything for Ty," I say through a tightened chest. "I've missed him."

Gawd, now I feel like crying. It suddenly hits me I haven't seen this baby in over a month, and I probably won't get the chance to see him ever again. The last time we were together, he was calling me his "Teeny." Now he acts like he hardly recognizes me.

Mrs. James walks over and lays a hand on my arm. "You know you can visit him if you like."

I shake my head. "I would, but I don't want to see Jackson."

The last time I tried to spend time with Tyler, I had to put up with Jackson's farty breath and marriage hints. As if I'd ever consider going back to that jackass. Besides, due to a misunderstanding, Andrés was so furious when I'd had dinner with Jackson and Ty, he walked out on me. We were broken up for over a week—the longest week of my life. I won't risk my future with Andrés again, no matter how much I miss Ty.

Mrs. James steals a glance at Andrés and then at me, a knowing look in her eyes. "Then maybe just us girls can take Ty out to the park or to lunch."

"I'd like that," I say on a rush of air. My chest feels ready to burst, and I practically jump out of my shoes. Andrés squeezes my hand and smiles down at me. His approval makes me feel even more elated.

"Teeny!" Tyler squeals and then flaps his hands.

I lean over and plant a kiss on Tyler's cheek, his very warm cheek, and realize this baby is probably coming down with a fever.

Mrs. James must see the concern in my eyes. She places a palm on Ty's forehead and then gasps. "I need to get him home," she says as she rushes toward the door. "I'll call you," she says over her shoulder.

I don't get to say goodbye to Ty, but I know his health comes first. He's already had a major health scare before he was diagnosed with Celiac Disease. I'd hate knowing he may be getting sick. Still, I cling to the hope that once he's better, I can see him again.

"You ready to finish dinner, mija?" There's a softness in Andrés's gaze, and I realize he senses my distress over Ty leaving.

I take his outstretched hand and let him lead me to the kitchen. That's when I notice it appears a bomb went off on our table. Breadsticks are scattered everywhere. A bowl is tipped over, and spaghetti sauce is running down a chair leg. Andrés's plate looks like it was ravaged by wild dogs.

"What happened to your food?" I gasp.

"Karri happened to my food," Andrés says through clenched teeth.

Holy crap! Now I feel terrible. Though I no longer consider Karri my friend, I still feel partly responsible for her showing up at my door.

"Sit down." I lead him to my chair, as his chair is covered in sauce. "Eat my food. I'll get another plate and an ice pack for your hand."

Just as he eases into the seat, he jumps up. "Shit!"

"What?"

Andrés turns to me with his hands in his pockets and a wild-eyed expression. "It's gone!"

"What's gone?"

"N-nothing." He averts his gaze and shakes his head.

Then he lurches to the front door. I'm pretty sure my heart stops beating. I see it there on the floor—the black pouch that looks suspiciously similar to the one that holds the engagement ring he'd almost given me last month. He hastily slips it in his pocket and turns to me with a sheepish grin.

"It must have fallen out when I punched Jackson." He shoves both hands in his pockets and rocks on his feet, looking at something beyond my left shoulder. I cast a glance behind me. The microwave? Is that what's got his attention, or is he just having trouble looking me in the eye?

How long does Andrés plan on carrying that ring around in his pocket? I tell myself I should be happy he's still carrying the ring, but then I wonder why he doesn't give me the damn thing. The sting of his indecision feels an awful lot like rejection.

"Maybe you should keep it in a safe, so you don't lose it again," I say, unable to mask the hurt in my voice. I can't look at him a moment longer, so I turn my gaze to the floor. Oh, great, breadcrumbs and spaghetti sauce on the tile. Karri leaves a trail of destruction wherever she goes. I angle my toe and squish a crumb beneath my shoe, imagining that crumb is my heart being crushed under the weight of that little black pouch.

Andrés bridges the short distance between us, and before I can stop him, he takes my hand in his. "I'm sorry." His voice is barely a whisper, but when he cups my chin and turns my gaze to his, I'm struck by the intensity in his dark eyes.

And then my legs weaken when he falls to one knee and pulls that pouch back out of his pocket. He drops the ring into his palm and holds it up to the light. It's just as I remember, a beautiful circle of emeralds with a large, luminescent diamond in the center.

"I love you, mija." His deep baritone has a nervous edge to it, and though I can see he's trying to keep his composure, his hand trembles slightly. "Marry me? Be mine forever?"

"Yes!" I fall to my knees and throw my arms around him. "Yes, I'll marry you."

I'm barely aware of Andrés removing my arm from his neck and slipping the ring on my finger. But I'm very aware of him pressing into me, of his lips on mine. I grab his hair by the roots, clinging to him. We share a kiss that is so explosive, tremors take hold of me, rocking me to my core. And then he sweeps me into his arms and carries me into the bedroom.

Chapter Two

Christina

Damn! What the hell is wrong with me? What the hell is wrong with us? Andrés had to have known, too. I look over at my sleeping fiancé. It wasn't until after we'd shared mind-blowing sex and polished off a huge pot of spaghetti that I realized we'd forgotten to use a condom. I'm getting really careless. Really careless. I didn't intentionally mean to forget the condom this time. Did I? I drape my arm over my head and groan. This damn sinus infection makes my head feel like it weighs a hundred pounds. That's why it's so hard to remember to be responsible.

I think about that pregnancy test stored under my bathroom counter. I know it's too early to tell if I conceived last night. I think the directions on the box said I have to wait a week. Even if I didn't get pregnant last time I was careless, I know I could be now.

I hold my hand up and squint at the shiny emeralds and diamond as they gleam in the morning sun. It is the most exquisite ring I've ever seen. I can't believe the gems belonged to his grandma, and Andrés tore apart her ring to make this for me. I clutch my hand to my chest and sigh. This ring is a treasure, not just because of the expensive stones, but because of the meaning behind them.   Considering how close he is to his family, I know the significance of this ring. When he asked me to be his forever, he meant it.

And when I told him "yes," I'd meant it, too. Though I know the girl isn't supposed to give the guy an engagement ring, I wish I had something as special to give Andrés in return.

My hand falls to my stomach as I think I may already be carrying his child. Knowing how much Andrés wants children, I'm sure that would make him happy, but would it make me happy? I'm about to start a new career. I'm only twenty-one. Am I ready for children? Andrés is five years older than me. He's been to war twice and now he's running successful businesses. I know he wants to start a family. I just hope we can wait a few more years, if it isn't already too late.

I roll over and clutch my stomach as it makes this loud rumbling noise. It feels like a hollow drum, and I swear my insides must be gnawing on each other, that's how hungry I am all of a sudden. Weird because I've kind of felt off these past few mornings. I can't put my finger on it, but it's taking me longer to get out of bed, and I've been lightheaded. It could just be my sinus infection or it could be that I'm pregnant.

Goddamn, I'm taking that test!

I throw the covers off me and rush to the bathroom. I've got to pee anyway. Might as well kill two birds with one stone.

* * *

Two lines. Two fucking lines.

I check the words on the box for at least the tenth time and make sure I've read the directions carefully. Two lines means positive, and positive means pregnant.

Fuck! Fuck! Fuck!

I fling that stupid stick across the floor and slide off the toilet in a sobbing heap. This cannot be happening.

"What's wrong, mija?"

Andrés is poking his head through the door, looking down at me with a crease marring his brow. I don't know what to say, and honestly, I'm too choked up to speak, but then his gaze settles on the empty pregnancy kit box and he steps inside the bathroom and picks it up. He looks from the box and back to me with wide eyes.

I still can't speak, so I answer him with a nod.

"*Aye Dios Mio*," he breathes as he sits on the floor beside me. He pulls me into his lap, kissing my forehead and stroking my back.

That's when I really lose it and start bawling like a baby. He holds me like this for a long while. I still haven't regained my composure, but then a shiver steals up my spine, and I shudder in his arms. There's a draft on the floor, and I'm not wearing a stitch of clothing. Without saying a word, Andrés carries me to bed and we snuggle beneath the comforter. He leans over me and rubs warmth into my arms while kissing my temple.

That feels kind of good, and damn my stupid hormones, I'm turned on. What's wrong with my body? I thought I wasn't supposed to get horny after getting knocked up. But now's not the time for sex. My fiancé and I have some talking to do.

I can feel Andrés's gaze on me, but I can't face him, so I turn on my back and stare at a crack in our ceiling. "The night we made up, I forgot my pills at my mom's house. I didn't even realize it until the next morning. I'm sorry."

He's leaning over me, tracing his fingers up and down my arm. "It's okay." There's not even a hint of panic in his voice. This should comfort me, but it doesn't. An uneasy feeling settles over me when I realize it's because Andrés wants this. He wants to settle down and have babies.

"No, it's not," I groan. "I'm not ready."

Ugh. I drape my arm over my eyes as a wave of nausea hits me. Thinking about all my new responsibilities is making me queasy.

"We'll get through it," he says. "We can do this."

What is he, my coach? Is this some kind of unplanned pregnancy pep talk?

It's like he's not seeing the bigger picture. We're not just going to be responsible for feeding and clothing a child: we've got to be role models. My parents never taught me values. The only thing they taught me was to fend for myself, and I don't even do that well half the time. If it wasn't for Andrés keeping me sane, I don't know where I'd be. And though he's been my rock these past six months, this situation is totally different, because it doesn't just involve me and him. It involves our child, too.

"We're going to get married, anyway," he's saying, "plus we've both got good jobs."

"I haven't even started my new job." Another wave of dizziness washes over me, and I close my eyes because the room tilts to one side.

"You think your mom is going to fire you?" Andrés asks with laughter in his voice.

So glad someone thinks this is funny. "How can I be a wedding designer and raise a baby?"

It all seems too daunting. My mom and I haven't even gotten this design company off the ground yet, and I'm pregnant. I remember Karri's pregnancy. She was always rushing to the OB for stomach cramping. She threw up about every meal, even through the last trimester. More than once, we thought she was going to miscarry. I'm already starting to feel sick, really sick. What if I'm too sick to work?

"Your mom is raising two kids," he says, lacing his fingers through mine, squeezing my hand. "And designing furniture, and managing galleries."

"Yeah," I argue, "but my mom is almost forty, and she's had years of practice being a responsible adult."

Andrés leans closer to me, so close I can feel his breath on the nape of my neck. I don't dare open my eyes because I'm afraid this queasy feeling will return. He strokes my face with the tips of his fingers. "It's my baby, too. You think I won't help you? Your mom will help us, and my cousins, and don't forget Tio and Tia. We'll be lucky if Tia lets us see our baby at all."

I resist the urge to melt beneath his touch. I love it when Andrés caresses me.

"I love you, mija." He feathers soft kisses on my earlobe and down my neck. "It will all work out. I promise."

A soft moan escapes my lips. Andrés's touch is exquisite, and so enticing. If I didn't know any better, I'd say Andrés was trying to distract me from the ugly reality that I'm going to be a parent and I'm not ready.

I jerk, and my eyes fly open at the sound of the rumble coming from my mid-section.

"Was that your stomach?" Andrés asks.

"I'm hungry." I shrug apologetically. I had a huge dinner last night, but I'm famished. I realize this is probably one of those wonderful side-effects of being pregnant. I wish Andrés would take me out to eat. Though I normally crave chorizo and egg tacos, I can't get my mind off a heaping plate of pancakes with blueberries and whipped cream. Plus, crispy bacon, fluffy scrambled eggs and a big cup of coffee would be nice. I'm eating for two, but I'll probably gain enough weight for three.

"Do you want to go to IHOP?" he asks.

Andrés is either a mind reader or an angel from heaven.

I struggle to sit up and will the dizziness to subside. Worrying over my pregnancy isn't going to solve my hunger issue. We'll go discuss our doomed future over pancakes.

* * *

I normally don't like sweets for breakfast, but after I practically inhale blueberry pancakes loaded with extra whipped cream, scrambled eggs and two sides of bacon, I sit back and sip my coffee while dabbing the sides of my mouth with a napkin. Andrés is in the booth across from me, smirking at my empty plate.

"You sure you got enough, mija? Should I ask them to bring out the whole pig?"

"You're funny," I say, snatching a leftover wedge of toast from his tray. "I haven't had an appetite all week with this sinus infection. I'm just making up for lost time." I sniffle loudly, as if to prove my point, although I'm feeling a lot better today. The antibiotics must finally be working.

I slather the toast with strawberry spread and take a bite. Mmmmm. I can't believe I'm still hungry.

Andrés's smile widens as he nods at my pilfered toast. "Who said I was finished?"

I give him a sharp look: after all, he's partially responsible for my appetite. "I did, that's who." He pushes aside our plates and pulls out his iPad. "We need to set a date." He opens a calendar on his screen.

I frown when I notice how much work shit is on his calendar. I can't believe he's got time left over for me.

"I wanted a spring wedding." I lean back and groan as I settle a hand on my full belly, "but I'll be as big as a house by then. Maybe we should wait until after the baby."

Andrés's shoulders tense and panic flashes in his wide eyes. "You know my family's old-fashioned, mija."

"So you want to get married soon? Do you know how long weddings take to plan?" When he asked me to marry him, I thought we could still have a lengthy engagement, time enough for me to figure out what kind of wedding I want and plan our honeymoon.

Andrés shrugs, scrolling through the dates on his calendar. "You don't have to plan it. We can get married at Tio's ranch. My family will take care of it."

I lean forward, eyeing him intently. Does Andrés think our wedding is going to be another backyard barbeque? "Are you serious?"

I've got to pick out a dress, arrange a caterer, and since I'm supposed to be a wedding designer, I've got to decide on a theme.

"Yeah," he says casually, as if planning a wedding is no big deal. "My cousin Rosario got married at Tio's house a few years ago. We had a Tejano band. My family made all the food. Uncle Arturo made the cake and tamales."

I perk up like a dog with a new bone. "Tamales?"

His smile widens. "Of course."

Andrés found my weak spot. He knows how much I love tamales. But tamales at a wedding? I haven't been to many weddings, other than the few my parents brought me to at the country club, and I'm fairly certain tamales weren't on the menu. But this isn't going to be a country club wedding. Those rich snobs are part of my old life. Andrés is my life now, and so is tasty Mexican food. I take another sip of coffee while I think long and hard about what I want my wedding— our wedding—to be about, and the more I think about it, the more I like the idea of saying our vows at Andrés's uncle's ranch. We'd be surrounded by people who love us, with the awesome Texas Hill Country as a backdrop. Plus, we'd get to eat great food. What's not to love?

"Your Uncle Arturo is the baker, right?"

"Yeah. He owns restaurants and a bakery in San Antonio." He nods as his eyes light up. "He makes the cakes for all our parties."

I smile. I remember his uncle's cakes. He made this amazing chocolate layer cake for Tio's sixtieth birthday party. It had whipped, creamy frosting and a gooey, fudgy center.

"I love his cakes." I rub my hands together and lick my lips. "What about that triple chocolate thing?"

He leans forward, and there's this intense look in his gaze, like he's about to reveal something top secret. "You should try his red velvet."

My mouth falls open, and I gape at him for a long moment. Red velvet is my most favorite cake of all time. Just the thought of it and my mouth waters.

"You really *are* my soul mate," I squeal, reaching for his hands.

He smiles and squeezes back. "We still need to set a date." Then he taps on his iPad and shows me the calendar. He's got January fourth open. January fourth!

I gasp and pull back. "That's two weeks to find a dress and come up with a theme. Are you crazy?"

He flashes a sideways grin. "That way you don't have time to change your mind."

"You're funny." I laugh and roll my eyes. As if I'd want to change my mind. "Let's tell our families first, and then we'll come up with a date."

"Who first?"

"My mom's expecting us. We can tell her tonight and your family tomorrow."

I should feel a sense of relief when Andrés nods in agreement. We're actually going to get married. We're planning the celebration and setting the date. But as a strange unease settles in the pit of my stomach, I feel anything but relieved. I already know Andrés's family will be overjoyed when they find out we're getting married. They've been bugging us to settle down and have kids, anyway.

But what about my mom? Weird, because even though I met my birth mom a few weeks ago, I feel as if I've known her a lifetime. Despite the fact that she was forced to give me up for adoption when she was a teen, we've grown close over the past few weeks. I wonder what she'll say about Andrés and me getting married so quickly. She'll probably think we're only doing it because I'm pregnant, especially when she finds out Andrés wants to marry in two weeks. My mom's opinion means so much to me. I only hope she approves.

Chapter Three

Christina

Andrés swears he's driving safely, that he isn't going too fast around the turns, but the two hour trip to my mom's house feels like I'm stuck on Dante's roller coaster ride into hell. It takes all my willpower not to vomit all over the leather seats in Andrés's truck. I even make him stop twice because I feel like I'm unable to hold my breakfast a minute longer. Some fresh air and a few burps later, we're back on the road, and I'm sick all over again.

So this is what morning sickness feels like.

It fucking sucks.

My head is swimming by the time we pull into my mom's drive. I don't even have the strength to get out of the car. I rest my cheek on Andrés's shoulder as he carries me inside. My head is throbbing, and to make matters worse, my mom is fussing at me from behind Andrés's shoulder. He carries me to our upstairs bedroom and lays me on the bed. I curl up in a fetal ball, close my eyes and groan as a wave of nausea overpowers me. I mumble something about the annoying glare from the overhead lights, but I don't think they hear me. I groan louder and try to open just one eye, but it's like I'm stuck on a merry-go-round. I just want to the room to stop spinning. Is that too much to ask?

Mom is sitting beside me, stroking my hair, which kind of feels nice, but the misery I'm feeling trumps everything. I lean over and start to gag as bile projects into my throat. I'm vaguely aware of Andrés holding a waste-basket beneath my chin and of my mom holding my hair before I lose my breakfast.

And boy do I lose it, all of it: pancakes, eggs, a double order of bacon, and a stolen toast wedge plus two cups of coffee come racing back up, burning my throat and singeing my nostrils on the way out. I heave and heave until there's nothing left but bile, and then I heave some more.

When I'm finally finished, I lay back on the pillow and lick my parched lips. Despite the burning in my nasal passages, I can still smell the rancid stench of my own breath, a mixture of rotten blueberries and curdled cream.

I'm never eating blueberry pancakes again.

Never.

I don't know who lifts my head up and forces me to drink water, but the beverage is a welcome relief to the burning in the back of my throat. I take several sips before I lie back down. The world doesn't swim so much when my eyes are closed, so I think maybe I'll keep them closed for a little while. Maybe I'll even take a nap. For some reason, I'm exhausted.

* * *

Andrés

"Is my daughter pregnant?"

How did I know this question was coming? I'm sitting awkwardly on the living room sofa, drinking sweet tea (but I could sure use a beer) while Christina's mom, Jenny, gives me the death stare. Not that I blame her. If Christina were my daughter, I'd probably beat the shit out of me.

Even though the woman is petite like Christina, she appears to be much bigger when she puffs up her chest and clenches her fists, glaring at me like she wants to stick my dick in a wood chipper. I size her up while I think of my best possible answer.

I'm usually good at sweet talking my way out of sticky situations, but there's no talking myself out of this one.

"Yes, ma'am," I say through a shaky breath as I set my tea on the coffee table.

If Jenny's eyes were guns, I'd be full of holes by now. She snatches my tea glass off her coffee table and slides a wooden coaster beneath it.

My shoulders slump when I realize I'm not exactly earning any browning points with this lady. I get the feeling she's wondering how much she can get for my body on the black market if she chops me to bits and sells the parts.

"Is that why she has that ring on her finger?"

"No." I shake my head. "I asked her before we found out."

At least nobody can accuse us of getting married because I knocked her up. Baby or no baby, I'm still intent on making Christina my bride.

Jenny sets her tea glass on a coaster and taps her chin with her finger. "When are you planning on getting married?"

"Soon, I hope. " I swallow back a bit of nervous tension when I realize I sound a bit too eager.

Jenny arches a brow, eyeing me intently. "You walked out on her three weeks ago. How can she depend on you to stay with her now?"

Damn. The thing is, I don't blame Jenny for not trusting me, not after I acted like a jealous pendejo when I'd walked out on Christina because she went to dinner with Tyler and Jackson. I knew Jackson was using the baby to get to Christina, and I was right, but it was still not a good enough reason to break up. Christina cares for that baby. I had no right to tell her she couldn't see him anymore.

My mouth goes dry, and I'm tempted to grab that tea off the table and chug the whole glass, but something about the way Jenny is glaring at me makes me afraid to move a muscle. I lick my parched lips and cough to clear my throat. "I love Christina. I'm not going anywhere."

Her brow furrows and she rolls her eyes. "Raising a baby isn't easy."

Now I know who Christina gets her eye rolling from. If we were in a different situation, I might laugh at how identical those two look.

"I know that." I make a sign of the cross, and then lean forward, hoping she can read the sincerity in my gaze. "But I swear I'm not walking out on my family."

Jenny leans forward, too, which is awkward, because we're only a few breaths apart now, good face-slapping distance. She jabs a finger in my chest, twin firestorms brewing beneath her emerald gaze. "Good, because if you break her heart again, I will make your life a living hell."

I swallow a lump in my throat and nod that I understand. I release a shaky breath when she backs up and picks up her glass. My cue to do the same. I grab my glass and quickly scoot back in my chair, putting as much distance between us as possible. Two tours in Afghanistan and this tiny little woman has got me ducking for cover. I down the tea in a matter of seconds, and then eye Jenny warily while I set it on the table.

She's got every right to be angry, I keep telling myself. *You walked out on her daughter and then knocked her up. You deserve this.*

Just when I prepare for another tongue lashing, she whips out her phone and taps the screen. "I guess I need to start making wedding plans. You'll probably want to do this in Austin, right?"

I nod in agreement, maybe a little too hard. Damn. I'm not a bobble-head doll.

"I'll need to start looking up venues and caterers and working out a date."

I nod again. It seems to be the only thing I know to do at the moment. She's probably wondering how her beautiful, talented, smart daughter ended up with an idiot like me.

Luckily, she seems to have tuned me out, because she's already calling a caterer in Austin and asking if they have any openings.

Shit. That was fast. Weird, because Christina is still sleeping. Shouldn't Jenny consult with Christina first? Or how about me? And who said we were having the wedding catered? Christina and I already decided my family would make the food. I should probably say something to Jenny.

Two tours in Afghanistan, I remind myself. *Two freaking tours.*

I clear my throat and lean forward.

Jenny waves me away before rising from her seat and walking toward the window.

Well, fuck!

* * *

Christina

I wake up with a splitting headache and a throat that feels like sandpaper. I struggle to sit up against the headboard, heaving a sigh of relief when I open my eyes and the room is no longer spinning. It's at an odd tilt, though, and I get the feeling I'm in one of those crazy fun houses with floors at awkward angles. I know one side of my mom's home didn't sink into the ground while I was asleep. Oh, well. A tilted room is better than a spinning room.

I grab a glass of water off the nightstand, swearing as I slosh about half of it all over the bed. I spill more down my neck as I miss my mouth on the first few tries.

Damn. Losing my equilibrium sucks.

I finally manage to down what's left in the glass. The cool water is amazingly refreshing, soothing the burn in the back of my throat.

Vomiting blueberry pancakes sucks, too.

My arm feels like a runaway crane as I wave the empty glass awkwardly toward the table. I swear when the glass misses and falls to the floor with a thud. Luckily, I don't hear it break.

I close my eyes and lean back into my pillow. I groan at the pain in my head, as if a monster earthquake has cracked a chasm in my skull.

Could this really be morning sickness? Really? I don't remember it being this bad with Karri. Then again, she'd probably been too hopped up on drugs to notice.

A few seconds later, I hear a gentle tapping on the door.

"Feeling better?"

I open one eye and then the other. Mom is picking the empty glass up off the carpet. She's still in her pajamas, so I figure it must be morning. Her auburn hair is pulled back in a messy bun, and her eyeliner is slightly smudged. Doesn't matter, though. She's still beautiful. Her cheeks have that youthful flush and her green eyes are big and gorgeous with or without makeup. I hope I look this good when I'm thirty-nine.

I flash a weak smile. "The room's not spinning so much."

"I remember morning sickness." Mom leans down and pats my hand. "It wasn't so bad with you, but with the boys it was terrible."

I gape at her for a long moment. Shit. She already knows I'm pregnant. Then again, how could she not know when I'm a barfing mess? I was hoping I could break it to her some other way.

"You forgot your pills at my house, remember?" Mom says as if answering my thoughts. "You show up three weeks later sick with a sulking fiancé."

"Sulking?" I struggle to sit up on my elbows. "He's sulking? Where is he? "

Mom pulls up a chair and sits down beside me. "Downstairs with Doc."

Oh, great. I wonder how Andrés has been dealing with my mom and stepdad. Doc is a sweet guy, but I can imagine him and my mom giving Andrés a lecture. I wonder if they are the reason Andrés was sulking, or maybe the reality of me being pregnant has finally sunk in. I've had three weeks to stress over this. He just found out this morning.

"Is he still sulking?" I ask, almost afraid to know the answer.

Mom heaves a sigh, and then eyes me pointedly. "If either of you are having second thoughts, I need to know before I start planning this wedding."

"I'm not having second thoughts." I sit up straighter and, luckily, the room looks less tilted. "I love him, and I think we've got the wedding mostly planned." I hope my mom doesn't think I expect her to plan this wedding, especially not when Andrés wants to get married in a few weeks. "We're doing it at his Tio's ranch. His aunts are going to make tamales and cake."

Her eyes widen, and she's got this expression that looks a mixture between amusement and horror. "Christina, don't you want a *real* wedding?"

"This would be a *real* wedding." I can't pretend I'm not offended by her comment. I know what she's talking about. I was raised by socialite parents, after all. My adoptive mother would have wanted me to have a grand wedding at the country club, or maybe someplace posh like Paris. She would have had a heart attack at a backyard wedding with tamales and Tejano music. But I guess I had hoped my birth mom would be different.

"No, no," she says, laughing, which makes me feel even worse. "Like a formal reception at a five star hotel with a caterer and little mints on the tables."

"Little mints?" I ask. I know the mints are small, but they are the start of something big. And big weddings take time, and money, something neither Andrés nor I have at the moment.

"And fondue and shrimp puffs," she says in the same tone Grace uses to scold her evil Chihuahua when she catches him chewing her shoes.

Ew. Fondue and shrimp puffs, something The Cobra, aka my evil adoptive mother, would want for my wedding. Fondue is okay, I guess, but I don't like shrimp unless it's in Spanish rice. I rest a hand on my stomach and groan. Just the thought of shrimp puffs makes me queasy.

"I like Mexican food," I say, but this wave of dizziness makes me say it with less conviction than I'd intended.

"It's a special occasion food," Mom says matter-of-factly, as if it's a perfectly natural thing to serve vomit -hors d'oeuvres at my wedding.

I close my eyes and try to imagine Andrés eating shrimp puffs and little mints. I try to imagine him sipping champagne and dipping strawberries in a chocolate fountain. But the only image that comes to mind is Andrés drinking a Corona with a lime wedge. I can see him eating brisket or fajitas, but finger foods? He'd probably pile all the shrimp on to his plate and smother it in hot sauce.

"Shouldn't our special occasion be filled with food we like?" That wave of dizziness turns into a hammer, pounding a nail right in the center of my forehead. Ugh. I lay back and look at my mom with eyes half-open. Can't she see I'm in no mood to discuss seafood pastries? Whoever thought it would be a good idea to combine the two, anyway? What's next, the anchovy doughnut?

"What would you rather serve your guests, a tamale or a shrimp puff?" she asks me haughtily, which is not a good thing. I'm having Spitting Cobra *déjà vu.*

"My guests?" I ask through a groan. "It's mostly going to be Andrés's family and you guys, Grace and Violet, and a few sorority sisters. I'm pretty sure they all like tamales."

Mom leans in and clasps my hands. She stares at me with watery eyes. Great. I hate watching people cry, especially her.

"Christina," she says with a shaky voice, "you're my only daughter. My only. All these years we spent apart, all the milestones I missed. Let me make it up to you. Let me throw you a lavish wedding."

"Mom, I—"

She holds up a silencing palm. "I want to do this for you. I'll pay for everything. We'll fly to New York and have your dress made. I know some of the top designers." She smiles at that, as if I'd be happy to travel anywhere other than to the bathroom and back.

I sink back into my pillow as that nail in my forehead twists and turns. The sharp ache is so severe, it sends another wave of nausea straight to my empty gut. I hate being pregnant. Why did I even bother waking up? I wish there was some way I could sleep through the next eight months.

I'm not in the mood to argue, so I nod my assent and close my eyes. She can serve the shrimp puffs. I'll probably be too sick to eat anything, anyway.

* * *

I'm resigned to lying in bed the rest of the day, doctor's (aka, my stepdad's) orders. Luckily, my stepdad was an ER doctor for several years before he became a pediatrician, and he's had experience dealing with severe morning sickness. He made me ginger tea and gave me motion sickness bracelets, which seem to be working, because the room has only a slight tilt now. It sucks not being able to do anything, but Andrés and I pass the time playing poker. Too bad strip poker is out of the question, but I'm too queasy to think about anything sexual right now.

I stare down at my hand, hoping a pair of sevens beats whatever Andrés is holding. I peer at him over my cards, and the guy's face is totally unreadable. I'm usually pretty good at gauging his moods, but not when it comes to cards.

Oh, well. What's a few more chips added to Andrés's growing pile? "My mom wants us to have a different kind of wedding." I almost quote her by saying, "real wedding" but I know Andrés would be insulted. Truthfully, I was offended when my mom said it, but I don't think she meant to come off that way.

"Is that what you want?" he asks, keeping his eyes on his cards.

I heave a sigh. "I don't know. I was kind of looking forward to tamales."

"Tell her."

"I can't. She says she's been dreaming of this day."

Andrés looks up, and I think I see a flash of anger beneath the surface of his dark gaze. "This is *your* day."

My day? Why does that bother me? Doesn't he feel like part of this wedding? "This is *our* day, Andrés." And then I recall my mom telling me Andrés had been sulking earlier. Is he feeling rushed? Does he feel obligated to marry me now that I'm pregnant? I know he said he wanted kids, but is this baby too soon for him? I lean forward and grasp his forearm. "Are you sure you still want to do this?"

Andrés sets down his cards and cups my face in his hand. "I've never been more sure of anything in all my life."

As tempted as I am to get lost in his seductive smile and those large, Spanish eyes, I can't seem to turn off that nagging voice in the back of my head.

"No second thoughts?"

Andrés drops his hand. "None. You?" His face is a mask of stone again, except for the expression in his eyes, so intense, I feel compelled to look away.

My throat suddenly feels tight. "No." I shake my head. "I love you."

"I love you, too, mija." His mouth hitches up in that devastatingly sexy half smile that usually lands him in trouble. If only I wasn't so sick. "So you going to tell her, or do I have to?"

"No, not you." I shake my head and instantly regret it, as I'm overcome with dizziness.

"Good." He laughs. "I'm already on her shit list."

I moan as I lean back against the cushioned headboard. "She wants to meet with a wedding planner Monday. The least I can do is hear them out, and then if I don't like their ideas, I'll say something."

Chapter Four

Andrés

The nightmare is back. I'm navigating the Hummer down the windy incline. James is sitting beside me. Two fresh-faced soldiers, brand new to the unit, and to the Army, are in the back. I swerve when I see the pothole, and the force of the blast knocks the vehicle on its side. It skids down the incline for several yards, and when it finally comes to a halt, James, or what is left of James, is lying on top of me.

I can't do anything, I'm so numbed from shock. The blast knocks out my hearing, and I drift in and out of consciousness several times. I have no idea how long I lay there with my best friend's body on me. Minutes? Hours? Of one thing I am certain: after the dust from the blast has settled, I hear not a sound from the other guys in the truck. Not a sound. But I smell their blood in the air.

While I lay there in agony, waiting for help to arrive, I hear it, the faint sound of a baby crying.

A baby?

Where the hell did a baby come from? Is it injured? Does it need my help? I'm struggling to get up, but James's corpse is holding me down. I push James, but it's like fighting a brick wall. The baby's cries intensify, and I'm panicking now. I cry out for someone, anyone, to come help us.

"What do you think you're doing, Andrés?"

I holler as I look up. James is gone, and my tio is in his place. One side of his face looks like it was bashed to a bloody pulp. The right half of his bottom lip has been detached from his face and his right eye socket is a hollow mess of ooze. He's pressing down on my chest with a tire iron.

"Get back to work, mijo," he scolds. "You're wasting daylight."

* * *

Christina

"Andrés, wake up. Please."

I'm barely aware of the tears streaming down my face as I try to wake my screaming fiancé. He's thrashing about in bed so violently, I don't have enough time to get out of the way as his hand crashes down on my ribcage.

"Ouch!" I scream, cradling my side. I kick off the covers and scoot out of bed just before his fist comes crashing down again.

"What's going on in here?"

I turn to see Doc standing in my doorway. He's wearing nothing but white cotton undies and holding a baseball bat above his head like he's a caveman preparing to club his next meal. With his slight paunch, greying beard, little round spectacles and jovial smile, my stepdad reminds me of Santa Claus. I've never seen him angry or upset. To say his barging in here like this, wielding a baseball bat is unexpected, is an understatement.

"Andrés is having a bad dream," I cry.

Doc flips on the lights, sets down the bat and walks to the other side of the bed. I avert my gaze, not because I don't want to see my stepdad in his underwear, but because he's wearing them backwards.

My mom rushes in. She's fastening her robe and I can clearly see she's naked underneath.

If my fiancé wasn't thrashing around in bed like he's possessed by a demon, I might be a tad embarrassed for them right now, but I'm too overwhelmed to feel anything.

"What's happening?" Mom asks me.

"I don't know," I say with a quavering voice. "I thought his Army dreams were over."

Mom pulls me to her and I lean my head on her shoulder while watching my fiancé.

"Andrés, wake up." My stepdad shakes him hard on the shoulder.

Andrés swats at him. "What about the baby?" he mumbles.

"Andrés, you're dreaming," my stepdad tells him as he shakes him harder.

Much to my relief, Andrés mumbles a few more times before opening his eyes. He lies there for a moment, looking wide-eyed at Doc before he sits up and stares at my mom and me.

"What happened?" he asks as he rubs the sleep from his eyes.

"You were dreaming," I tell him as I wipe a stray tear from my cheek. I thought Andrés had conquered these dreams and now they're back. Why? And what had he mumbled about the baby? Though somewhere in the back of my mind I suspect the answer, I want so much to deny the obvious truth. He's not ready to be a father. He's not. And this dream confirms it. Why else would the nightmares come back?

"Christina," Doc says as he points at me. "What happened to you?"

It's only when I look down and see I'm clutching my side do I register the bruising pain. I guess I was too stunned to notice earlier, but my side aches.

"I-I don't know," I mumble, though I remember exactly what happened.

Mom spins me around and lifts my T-shirt. She gasps at the big red bulls-eye that is already starting to bruise.

Instinctively, I pull my shirt down and pull up on the drawstring of my pajama pants.

"Mija." Andrés's eyes widen. "Did I do that to you?"

My eyes well up with tears at the horrified expression on his face. As if the guilt from his best-friend's death in Afghanistan isn't enough of a burden, now he's got to live with this?

My throat constricts as I slowly nod. "You didn't mean to."

Andrés covers his face with his hands and sags against the headboard. "What have I done?"

"It was an accident, baby. It's not your fault." I climb back into bed and try to pry his hands from his face, but he jerks away.

"I'm a danger to you."

The dark, hollow sound of his voice frightens me. "No, you're not," I cry. "You love me and I love you. We'll get through this."

But Andrés doesn't say a word as he turns back to Doc. "Did I hurt the baby?"

"Let me take a look at it." Doc walks over to my side of the bed.

"We're fine," I snap.

I let out an exasperated breath at the shock in his eyes. I didn't mean to snap at my stepdad, but this is all too much. I don't want my parents making a big deal out of this. Andrés feels bad enough already.

I wince when Doc lifts my shirt and feels my ribcage.

"These are your ribs," Doc says as he runs a hand across my sore spot. "The baby is all the way down there." He points to my stomach and then looks at Andrés with a reassuring smile.

Damn, it hurts. It takes all of my willpower not to slap Doc's hand away.

"So the baby is fine?" I ask Doc.

He nods, and I yelp as he presses against my ribs again.

"Bruised but not broken," he says.

I turn away at the look of pity in his gaze. I want to tell him he's wrong. Very wrong. Because my fiancé is not well, and my heart feels like it's shattered into a million pieces.

Chapter Five

Christina

I head downstairs as soon as I wake up. Luckily, the room isn't tilted anymore. In fact, I'm feeling a lot stronger, other than the growing hunger in my gut and the aching pain in my side. I hurry to the kitchen and pour a cup of coffee, not for me, but for Andrés. That's when I notice the decorations. They're everywhere. Ornaments and pinecones, wreaths and mistletoe. It looks like Hobby Lobby exploded all over my mom's kitchen. A tiny stereo sits by the kitchen sink, blaring Trans-Siberian Orchestra music. It's kind of an odd feeling being in such a festive home, and I realize this is what my holidays would have been like had I been raised by my real mom. If only.

Andrés and I have one tiny tree on an end-table in the living room. A shame, really, considering I'm supposed to be going into the party decorating business. The Cobra never decorated our house for the holidays, except for a solitary white tree, empty cartons of eggnog, and bottles of Southern Comfort. And she certainly didn't listen to Christmas music.

I carry Andrés's coffee into the living room. The rest of the house is decorated with wreaths and ornaments, too, and at the far end of the living room is a tree so tall, I wonder how my parents fit it through the front door. Even from across the room, I can smell the fresh scent of pine. The tree's all aglow in whites, golds, and reds, and something about it warms my heart. It reminds me of Christmases at Karri's house, though on a much grander scale.

Then warm fuzzies in my heart shrivel up at the sight of Andrés lying across the sofa at an awkward angle. His legs are too long, so his feet are propped up on the armrest and his head is scrunched at the other end.

He shifts around, so I sit next to him and set the steaming mug on the coffee table. "Good morning, baby." I hope he doesn't notice my smile is forced. I hope he can't tell I spent half the night crying over him. After my parents left our room, Andrés took his pillow and a spare blanket, mumbling something about not wanting to hurt me again, and he left me. In the seven months we've been dating, I haven't slept without him, other than last month when we'd broken up for a week. I missed him last night. I missed snuggling into his warm body. I missed the way he kisses my neck and tells me "good morning." I hate that he felt we needed to sleep apart.

Andrés looks up at me and flashes a smile that doesn't quite reach his eyes. "Good morning, mija."

I motion to his bare feet hanging over the couch. "You don't look comfortable."

"I'm fine." He kicks the blanket to the floor and sits up. He narrows his eyes before reaching for the hem of my nightshirt. "Let me see your side."

"Andrés, stop." I try to swat him away, but he's too fast. He lifts my shirt before I can stop him.

He gapes at the angry purple and red bull's-eye. "Fuck!"

I turn up my chin and put on my best big girl smile. "It doesn't even hurt."

Actually, that's a lie. It hurts like hell, but the pain is bearable as long as I don't breathe too much. All night I had to envision myself breathing through a straw just to manage the pain. I'd thought about asking Doc for a painkiller, but I'm not risking my baby's health with drugs.

"Liar." He courses his fingers through his thick hair, clenching the roots. "I'm sleeping on the sofa from now on."

I suck in a sharp breath. "Andrés, no!"

"Yes. What if next time it's not your ribcage?" Andrés squeezes my shoulders, and the pain reflected in his eyes breaks my heart. "What if it's your stomach? What if I hurt the baby?"

"For how long?" I ask, though my throat is constricted with emotion. Tears well in the backs of my eyes, and it takes all of my willpower to hold them at bay.

Andrés fixes me with a determined expression. "Until these dreams stop."

"You need to go back to that doctor." I hate the whine that slips into my voice. I know Andrés needs me to be strong right now. I do my best to put on a straight face, but my emotions are like a ping pong ball pinging all over the place, and I don't know if I want to scream, swear, or fall to pieces.

"I plan on it."

Andrés wipes a tear off my cheek. Damn tear. I didn't mean for it to fall.

"Is there anything I can do to help?"

"Stay with me."

The hard angles of his face soften, then sadden.

I cup his face in my hands, imploring him to read the sincerity in my gaze. I hate seeing him like this—vulnerable, scared, broken.

"Forever," I manage to choke out before more traitorous tears spill over my eyelids. "I love you."

* * *

After browsing the sites of several bridal shops in Austin, I've convinced my mom we don't need to fly to New York for my dress. Considering how sick I was yesterday, I don't think I could tolerate the flight, anyway. We're looking through a site and I'm floored by all the pretty dresses. Now comes the hard part, finding one to fit a petite woman who's five foot three, basically a child.

When we'd started searching for bridal gowns, Andrés made a few jokes about first communion dresses before my mom talked him and Doc into taking my brothers outside for a game of tag. Sadly, Andrés wasn't far off the mark. Some of the flower girl dresses looked like they'd fit me.

I've found several styles I like, but I wonder how long a dress would take to hem.

"Can they have the dress ready in two weeks?" I ask my mom.

She pulls away from her laptop monitor and gapes at me. "Two weeks? That's not enough time to plan a wedding. Now, if we waited until the spring…."

"I'll be as big as a house." I laugh. "Andrés and all of his cousins were big babies. He was ten pounds!"

Mom taps her chin with the end of a pencil as she pulls up a calendar on her monitor. "What about February first? That gives me six weeks to plan, and you'll only be nine weeks pregnant."

I know Andrés wanted to get married sooner, but my mom is right. Two weeks isn't much time to plan a wedding.

I look down at my stomach, which is flat at the moment, despite the fact that I ate four wedges of toast and two servings of scrambled eggs. I wanted bacon, but Doc said I shouldn't eat anything greasy. Andrés had the nerve to agree with him.

I smooth a hand over my abdomen. "I shouldn't be showing at nine weeks, right?"

"Not too much. You won't be able to wear a form fitting dress." Mom clicks on the mouse and exits out of all the screens with the hip hugging dresses I've selected. "I've always preferred the traditional gowns, anyway."

She pulls up this big, puffy thing with sequins that looks like a cotton ball on steroids.

My head starts to spin, and I'm afraid it has nothing to do with morning sickness. There is no way I'm wearing that monstrosity to my wedding.

My mom is apparently oblivious to my horrified expression as she adds the page with the puffy gown to her favorites. "This might work if I hire the right wedding planner."

I still don't see why my mom needs a planner. They are expensive, and they take care of things that we could do ourselves, like hiring the caterer and venue. If we had the wedding at Tio's ranch, we wouldn't need a wedding planner.

I open my mouth to say something, but nothing comes out. Why don't I speak up for myself? What's wrong with me?

And though I want to deny the truth, I already know the answer. I've only known my birth mother for three weeks. She's missed so many of my milestones already. If I take away my wedding from her, I know she'd be disappointed. Maybe she'll think I'm ungrateful. Considering the hellish upbringing I went through with my adoptive mother, I'm not willing to risk anything that would jeopardize my relationship with my new mom.

I look over at her. She looks blissfully happy as she hums to herself while doing a search on wedding planners.

I slouch in my seat as I get this sinking feeling in my gut, like our wedding is turning into a runaway train with my mom at the helm, and I'm an unwilling passenger.

Chapter Six

Christina

"Are you better, Sissy?"

"For the most part." I look down at my brother, Gio, as he tugs on my shirt sleeve. Gio's shadow, my youngest brother, Manny, is right behind him. They are only three and four years old, and I'm not being biased when I say they are the cutest brothers ever.

They have golden brown skin, thick dark hair, and chubby cheeks like my stepfather and my mom's bright green eyes and wide smile—my eyes and smile.

I'm not quite sure who they inherited their naughtiness from. I was always an obedient child. Although it was mostly because I was raised under my adoptive mother's cloud of manipulation and degradation. My real mom, Jenny, was just a teen when she gave birth to me and was forced to give me up. I'm thankful we found each other, and that I found my new brothers. In the few short weeks I've known them, I honestly don't know how I could live without them.

Gio bats thick lashes and give me his best pleading gaze. "Because you promised you'd play tag with us."

I groan as I look across the sofa at Andrés. Shit. I was hoping my brother would have forgotten about tag. Though I would ordinarily love to play with them, my body is so sore, it feels like I ran a marathon. Andrés and I have been relaxing together for the past half hour. Actually, I've been enjoying a nice foot rub and a good book while he answers work emails and texts with his free hand.

"I know," I say as I set it down and rest my hand against my temple. I heave an exaggerated sigh. "I'm still a little dizzy."

I feel a pang of guilt at the look of disappointment in my brother's eyes.

Gio scrunches his face and plants both fists on his hips. "But Doc said you had morning sickness, and we've already had lunch."

"Yeah." Manny wags a finger at me. "Peanut butter and jelly and celery sticks."

Gio looks over at Manny and makes a face. "I hate celery."

I laugh when I see the bulge protruding from Gio's pocket. "Is that what I saw you stuffing down your pants?"

His eyes go wide and he shakes his head a little too hard. "No."

"Don't lie to me." I point as the head of the stalk. "You've got one hanging out of your pants."

Gio gapes at the celery and shoves it back down. "I was saving it for later," he says as he averts his gaze.

I roll my eyes as I hold out my hand. "Give me the celery."

Gio pulls the stalk out of his pocket, and that's when I notice a bulge in the front of his pants. I impatiently wag my fingers. "All of them."

If his lip hung any lower, it would hit the floor. "Do I have to eat them?" He pulls out three more celery sticks and places them in my hand.

"No." I laugh. "I'm not going to make you eat underwear food. Go throw them in the garbage and wash your hands."

Gio marches toward the downstairs bathroom, his feet stomping loudly across the wood floor.

I arch a brow at my suspiciously quiet youngest brother. "You, too, Manny."

He shields his butt with his hands and takes a step back. "I don't have no celery."

I pull my feet out of Andrés's grip and stand up. Andrés doesn't say a word. He's been too preoccupied with work to pay any attention to us.

I take a step toward my brother, who takes another step back, but not before I get a good look at the bulge extending from his butt. "So are you growing a tail, then?"

He flashes the most adorable, sheepish grin, and my heart sighs. These boys really know how to work me over.

I point a finger at him and do my best to keep a straight face. "Just because your brother does something naughty, doesn't mean you need to do it, too."

Manny solemnly nods before hobbling toward the bathroom like his shoes are ten sizes too big. I look over at Andrés, who has finally set down his phone. "That celery must be wedged up there pretty high." I laugh.

He folds his arm behind his head, smirking. "Welcome to parenthood, mija."

I arch my neck back, looking at him through slitted eyes. "Our kid's not going to be like that."

Andrés's smirk turns into all-out laughter. "You think underwear celery is bad, you haven't seen nothing." He lifts the front of his thick, wavy hair and points to a small scar at the base of his temple. Then he holds out his right hand and taps the scar running down his thumb. Finally, he cranes his neck, showing me the little nick on his beautiful bronze skin.

"These are from my cousins," he says with a knowing look in his dark eyes. "Rusty screwdriver, sharp pencil, and broken glass."

My hands fly to my mouth. "Shit, Andrés!" Why would kids do that to each other?"

"Don't worry." He flashes a mischievous grin. "They've got bigger scars."

I slowly sit back down on the sofa as I gape at the scar on his hand. It's the worst of the three, raised and jagged. I wonder if it was caused by the screwdriver, pencil, or glass. Either way, it had to have hurt. I don't know why I'd never asked him. I assumed he'd gotten his scars during his tours in Afghanistan.

A sinking feeling twists a knot in my stomach. After this baby, Andrés will probably want more. In fact, I know he will. He's always said he wanted a big family. I hope our kids don't turn out like Andrés and his cousins. I don't think I could handle them.

"I hope we have a girl," I say through a shaky breath.

Andrés snickers while turning over his hand. "My cousin Marie gave me this one."

My stomach sours, and my chest tightens, and I try my best to keep my expression impassive. I don't want Andrés to see me on the verge of a meltdown, because I'm not ready to have a baby.

* * *

After playing all day with my brothers, I'm exhausted by the time we get home that night, although I shouldn't be, considering I slept most of the way. We were supposed to drive to his aunt and uncle's house tonight and tell them about the wedding, but we've decided to hold off until Christmas Eve in two more days. I can tell Andrés is tired by the slump of his shoulders, and I wonder how well he slept on that couch. Andrés helps me out of the car and refuses to let go of my elbow until I'm lying on the sofa.

Even though my head feels fuzzy, it's not nearly as bad as it was this morning. When I see Andrés come inside with our bags, I rise on shaky legs. I need to help him unpack.

He comes over to the sofa and puts a hand on my shoulder. "Relax , mija. Those bags can wait until tomorrow. I'll make you a virgin sangria."

I reach for him before he can turn away. "I don't want anything to drink. I want you." I nuzzle his hand, kissing his palms and the tips of his fingers.

Andrés responds with a groan and then he sits on the sofa, pulling me into his lap.

I sigh into his warm embrace. "I love it when you hold me."

His lips linger on my forehead. "I love holding you."

I run my fingers through his thick hair. I pull his head down to mine until our mouths are nearly touching. "Then sleep with me tonight."

Andrés pushes me back with a hand on my collarbone. The softness in his gaze is gone, replaced by a look as hard as granite. "I'm not arguing with you on this. I'm not hurting you again."

I don't know why, but my throat constricts, and my eyes water. I swear my hormones turn me into a crying baby for the stupidest reasons. I'm not normally so weepy, and I can't stand myself for it, which, unfortunately, makes me even sadder.

"Don't cry, mija." Andrés strokes the side of my face with the tips of his fingers. "Please don't do this."

I want to tell him I can't help it, that my body is changing, and I have no control over these unruly pregnancy outbursts. But at the feeling of his heated skin on mine, desire shifts my body in the opposite direction, and I feel like a ship being tossed about in a hormonal storm.

Damn. I'm turned on, and there's nothing I can do about it now. I come up on my knees and lower myself onto him, straddling his waist as he wraps his hands around my hips. I reach between us, stroking my hand up the length of his erection. Just the feel of his desire causes the moisture to pool between my legs.

Licking my lips, I look into his smoky gaze. "Will you still make love to me?"

He responds by grabbing my hair by the roots and pulling my lips down on his. I sigh into him as his tongue delves deep into my mouth, thrusting, teasing, torturing.

His hands are underneath my shirt and then beneath my bra. He squeezes my breasts and pinches my nipples so hard they burn. I don't know whether I should push him away or beg him for more.

Chests heaving, we pull away from each other. One look in his smoldering eyes, and I know he's as aroused as I am. The currents of desire that shoot through me are more powerful than anything I've ever felt before. I briefly wonder if my lust is another side effect of pregnancy, but I'm too damn horny to care.

We can't get each other naked fast enough. I'm pulling down his jeans and he's ripping off my shirt like our clothes are on fire. I kick the rest of our discarded clothes to the floor and wrap my hand around his magnificent erection as it springs from his underwear. Then his mouth is on my bare breasts, suckling one nipple, then swirling his tongue around the other. I clench his hair while he continues to trace kisses downward. His mouth lingers on my abdomen, and he strokes and kisses it with such tenderness, I nearly weep all over again.

Whatever fear I have about him not wanting this baby melts away as he pulls me into his embrace and carries me to the bedroom.

He lies down on the bed and I straddle his face. He drives his tongue into me until I think I may explode in his mouth. My juncture is dripping wet and thrumming with need, the need to feel Andrés inside of me. I pull away from his torturous tongue and climb down his body, wasting no time sliding onto him.

I ride up and down his slick erection while panting into his mouth. I'm not slow. I'm not gentle. I know I'll be sore tomorrow, but I don't care. He begs me to stop, but I fear I may die if I don't continue. He cries out, and then his shaft pulses inside me like a heartbeat, unraveling my remaining threads of resistance. I give into the euphoric waves and fall limp against his chest as the orgasm consumes me, sending vibrations arcing from my core all the way to the tips of my toes.

I let out a startled cry as Andrés flips me over and latches onto my neck with his teeth. He drives into me, hard, ramming against my swollen center. A bead of sweat rolls off his forehead and onto my cheek as he lifts my leg over his shoulder. I lift the other leg and cry out as he buries his entire length inside me. The pressure from his thick head pounding against my aching channel is enough to make me come undone again, and again.

We make love with abandon well into the night. His kisses burn, his touch ignites, and his long, hard cock driving into me enflames. I never knew playing with fire could feel so good.

I'm vaguely aware of Andrés washing between my legs before fatigue overwhelms me. I want badly to beg him to sleep with me tonight, but I'm so tired, keeping my eyes open is too much of a struggle, and I can't even form the words to speak.

He whispers goodnight into my ear, and his lips brush my temple. My heart aches when I feel his weight lift from the bed. I know he wants to keep me safe, but my last coherent thought before I surrender to fatigue is that sleeping in separate rooms is no way to start off a marriage.

Chapter Seven

Christina

I wake up to the smell of frying bacon. At least I think it's bacon. Whatever it is, it's got a pungent undertone. I hope the bacon isn't rotten. That's the last thing I need to eat right now. I sit up and instantly regret it. I might have moved too fast because the room tilts to one side.

Shit. Not this again.

I close my eyes and wait for the dizziness to subside. Luckily, the room is back to normal when I open my eyes, but I still feel kind of queasy. I heave myself out of bed and groan as pain lances up my side.

Damn bruise. When is it going to stop hurting?

A thick fog settles over my brain, and it takes a few moments for me to remember I have to get ready for work. Ugh. Work. I've got three motorcycles and a flower delivery truck waiting on me at the shop. I wish I could turn them over to the new artist, but these customers specifically requested me. Honestly, the way I'm feeling right now, all I want to do is crawl back into bed and sleep the rest of the day.

My senses perk up at the smell of freshly brewed coffee, so I take a quick shower, slip on my work jeans and T-shirt and trudge toward the kitchen.

Andrés is laying out food on the table, so I come up behind him, snake my arms around his waist, lean up and kiss him on the back of the neck. I soak up his warmth and savor the feel of him. My bed was cold and lonely without him. I wish he didn't have to sleep on the sofa. I'm almost afraid to ask him if he had another nightmare last night, but I need to know. I thought about little else while I was getting ready. The thought of Andrés suffering through this weighs heavily on me.

"Did you have any bad dreams last night?" The question comes out on a strained breath.

Andrés turns around and shakes his head. "No."

Relief washes over me. I know it's probably too soon to insist he come back to bed, but at least this is a good sign. Maybe the dream was just a result of the shock of finding out he's going to be a father. Maybe now that the shock has worn off, he won't have any more nightmares. Hopefully.

He clasps my hands in his, looking down at me with a scowl. "Where do you think you're going?"

I force a smile. "I'm better, Andrés." It's not a total lie. Even though I still have slight morning sickness.

He arches a brow, eyeing me with a smirk. "Do you think I'm going to let you work around paint fumes?"

"I'll stop if I feel sick." I walk to the counter, so he doesn't see I don't feel well right now. I belch into my fist. Yuk. It tastes like vomit. I grab my cup of coffee off the counter and take a sip. Mmmm. Hazelnut. The warm, sweet liquid masks the nasty taste in my mouth and soothes my parched throat.

"And what about the baby? Those fumes aren't good for our child."

I turn on my heel, nearly spilling coffee down my shirt in the process. The room tilts, and I lean one hand against the counter for support and then close my eyes. Okay, note to self: no sudden movements while pregnant.

"Mija, you can't paint cars anymore."

My eyes fly open. "But you need me." Even as I'm mentally berating myself for the emotion that slips into my voice, I realize he's right. Shit. The paint fumes. I had forgotten all about that. I recall all of the warning labels on the paint cans, something about "do not inhale" and "toxic to the developing fetus."

Hopelessness washes over me as I slouch against the counter. I feel so bad letting him down. I know the new artists aren't dependable.

My eyes water, and I can't help the tears that spill over.

What the fuck, hormones? Leave me alone already!

Andrés comes up to me and wipes my tears with the pad of his thumb. I read the pity in his soft gaze.

This sucks.

"What am I supposed to do all day?" I ask through a sniffle.

"You've got a lot to do, mija. Start with calling your doctor."

I check the microwave clock. It's already seven-thirty. Her office should be taking appointments in a half hour. Doctor Brewer has been my GYN for the past three years. She's the only doctor I trust. Unfortunately, she's also in high demand. I'll be lucky if I can see her this week.

Andrés motions to the spread on the kitchen table. "I made you breakfast."

He leads me by the elbow to the table and pulls out a seat. After I sit down, he puts my coffee and plate in front of me.

I narrow my gaze at the meat strips that look more like processed cardboard than bacon. It doesn't smell like bacon, either. I fan my nose and push the plate away. Whatever this crap is, I think it's gone sour.

"What is that?"

"Turkey bacon. This is a healthy breakfast." Andrés picks up a strip and takes a bite. "Mmmm." He frowns, and I can tell he wants to spit it out, but then he chases it down with a large swallow of coffee. He's so not fooling me.

I scowl down at the little plastic cup of pink goo by my napkin. Yogurt. Ugh. What happened to eggs and pico de gallo? Surely chicken protein and vegetables isn't unhealthy. "I don't like yogurt," I say as I push the cup toward Andrés.

He picks it up and sets it back down in front of me. Then he sprinkles some brown crap that looks like granola on top of it.

"It's got calcium, mija. Our baby needs it." He bats his thick lashes and looks at me with sad, dark eyes.

Damn. I know I can't refuse him.

I sigh as I pick up a spoon. I wonder if Andrés realizes how much sugar is in this crap. I try not to concentrate on the taste of strawberry and cinnamon overload as I swallow a spoonful and wash it back with a gulp of coffee.

"Easy on the coffee," he says. "You only get one cup a day."

I clench the handle while eyeing him over the rim of the cup. Sadly, it doesn't look like he's kidding.

One cup! How will I have enough energy to get through the day? I'll be napping by noon.

Oh, well. I heave a sigh as I sink into my chair. I don't have a job at the moment, so I guess I'm free to take a nap. I stifle a yawn as this feeling of fatigue washes over me. Why did I even bother getting out of bed?

Andrés is already tapping on his phone. His workday has officially begun. He'll be texting and emailing his assistant managers the rest of the day and even during dinner.

I mentally make a list of things I can do. I don't have any wedding planning until I hear back from my mom. I guess maybe I can paint at home. I've got a few blank canvases, and I've been dying to paint portraits of my brothers.

I groan when I think about what's in those paints. Unless I get the cheap, kiddy finger crap, I doubt I'll be doing any painting for a while.

I sink even lower in my seat as I absently swallow a spoonful of the yogurt granola crap.

That's when it hits me. My life isn't mine anymore.

* * *

Looks like I don't have time for that nap after all. After calling my doctor's office and finding out she can't see me for another two weeks, I was contemplating going back to bed. I was feeling so exhausted after only one cup of coffee, I had to drag myself out of the house when my mom called. She's already hired a wedding planner, and we're meeting at a posh lakefront restaurant.

I search for a decent country song on the radio, stuck in bumper to bumper traffic, hoping I'm not late. I can't see what's causing the delay because there's a garbage truck ahead of me. I've got the heater turned off and the windows rolled up, but it still doesn't help to mask the smell which permeates the car. It's so strong, I'm fighting the urge to open my door and vomit all over the freeway.

This truck is a metaphor for my life: I'm just trying to get ahead, but there's always this big pile of shit blocking my path.

I pop a stick of gum in my mouth, hoping the smell of spearmint will overpower the truck's fumes. I tap out an erratic staccato on my steering wheel, before fidgeting with the buttons on my shirt and then checking my reflection in the mirror. My nose isn't so big and red, anymore. My sinus infection is finally clearing up. Remarkably, I actually look pretty today. Though my pregnancy hormones are sabotaging my psyche, they're doing wonders for my skin. My cheeks have a natural glow and my eyes are greener than ever. Even my hair has a healthy sheen, and I didn't use any product.

I only wish I felt as confident as I look. I have to admit I'm kind of nervous about meeting this planner. My mom has been a steamroller, crushing all my wedding ideas. I can only imagine what two of them will do to my wedding. All I want is a small reception at Tio's ranch, where we eat tamales and cake and dance to a Tejano/country band. Instead, I'll be wearing some cotton candy fluff-ball, eating shrimp pastries and sipping champagne. No, not champagne. Damn. Ginger ale.

I get the feeling my wedding won't be fun at all, which sucks because Andrés is right. This is my special day, not my mom's. Even though I don't want to disappoint her, I come to a decision while I breathe in garbage fumes. I love her, but there is no way I'm letting her take my wedding from me. I'll listen to what my mom and this planner have to say, and then if I disagree, I'll let them know I want my wedding done *my* way. End of discussion.

I've been brow-beaten my whole life, first by my emotionally abusive adoptive mother and then by my ex-fiancé. I refuse to be bossed around on the most special day of my life. I just hope my mom can forgive me.

* * *

I cringe at the sound of 80s Christmas music filtering in from speakers overhead. My mom and the wedding planner are drinking red wine, chatting like old friends in the back of the restaurant. Behind them, an expansive window offers a beautiful view of Lake Travis and its multi-million dollar homes. But I don't give a damn about the lake right now. As I look into the wedding planner's familiar thin veneer of a fake smile, all I care about is getting the fuck out of this restaurant, after I expose the witch to my mom.

Mom stands when I approach. She's practically beaming ear to ear when she motions to the jackal sitting across from her. "Christina, this is Nora Richards, our new planner."

Nora abruptly stands up, nearly knocking over her chair in the process. Uh, oh. Someone's been hitting the red wine early today. No surprise there. Nora was always a lush.

"Hello, Christina, darling, it's so nice to see you again." She runs a hand through her dyed brassy red up-do and then spreads her arms wide, as if she's expecting me to hug her.

As if.

Un-fucking-believable.

I take a step back and scowl. Nora's face is so tight from excessive plastic surgery, it's hard to gage her reaction, but I think I see her lips twitch in annoyance. Either that, or her collagen air bags have sprung a leak.

I look at my mom, trying my best to keep my tone even. "Nora is my adoptive mother's best friend."

Mom gasps and splays a hand across her chest. "What?"

I cock my hand on my hip and shoot Nora another glare before turning back to my mom. "Can we go now?"

I don't want to spend another second in this woman's company. When I was a kid and my dad had to go out of town on business, Nora would come over and get shit-faced with my adoptive mom. On those nights, she would order me a pizza and force me to stay in my room. I didn't squawk. It was better than watching them pop pills and badmouth their husbands.

I'd usually find them sprawled on the living room floor, along with a few empty wine bottles. The DVD player would still be showing some porno with several guys with big dicks banging one chick. One time, I even found a vibrator in the bathroom sink. It was still buzzing around and rattling the drain. I never used that bathroom again. When I got older, I'd spend the night at Karri's house when Nora came over. I'd come home to find condom wrappers in the garbage. This was after my dad raped me, so I didn't tell the asshole. He probably knew about it, anyway.

"Nora." Mom looks at the planner with horror in her eyes. "You're Vivian Duval's best friend."

Surprisingly, Nora's still keeping a straight face. It must be hard for her to maintain the illusion that she's not a total bitch for this long. Either that or her surgeon's done a heck of a job tightening up her skin so she can't move her facial muscles. I swear I could bounce a quarter off her cheek.

When Nora reaches for her wine glass, I take another step back and brace myself. I also shoot my mom a warning look. Last time Nora had a glass of red wine in her hand, The Cobra took it from her and threw it in my face.

Nora tosses the liquid down her throat before setting the glass back on the table. She picks up a cloth napkin and daintily dabs her lips. She clears her throat and then looks my mom and me in the eyes. "Former best friend. After seven years of blackmailing me, I can finally say I'm free of that awful woman." Nora makes a face that so horrifying it's comical. If she screws up her mouth any tighter, she's sure to pop a stitch. "It cost me my twenty-three year marriage, but Christina,

I don't blame you for your hesitation." She clasps my shoulder. "I wouldn't want to be friends with anyone who associates with that snake in the grass, either."

I look down at her hand on me, at those long, gaudy hot pink fingernails with rhinestone flowers on every tip. I imagine those little flowers are poisonous, and she's burning my flesh.

When I jerk out of her grip, I think I see a flash of venom in her gaze, but it's quickly gone. Even though she's smiling at me, her eyes are eerily empty. Maybe she's not The Cobra's friend anymore, but I still don't trust her. After all, what kind of a woman would be friends with that snake in the first place?

"Nora, do you mind if I speak to my daughter alone?"

Nora smiles at my mom as she smooths a hand over her hair helmet. "Of course not. I need to use the powder room, anyway." She sweeps out of the room with her exaggerated swagger, her "I'm not really drunk, but a washed up runway model" walk.

I scowl as she leaves.

I turn to my mom with a pleading gaze. "Mom, don't trust her. She's just like The Cobra. Just like her."

Mom's got this sheepish look as she flashes a half-hearted smile. "I've already given her a deposit."

"You what?"

Mom heaves a sigh and then falls into her chair. "Christina, Nora Richards is the premiere wedding planner in all of south Texas. Her reach extends from San Antonio to Houston. Every socialite knows her—and uses her. Just think what she can do for our business."

I pull up a chair and search her gaze, looking for any sign of hope. My heart sinks when she looks away. I am *not* using Nora Richards as my wedding planner. Hell, no!

"She's a two-faced whore." I try my best to keep my tone even. I don't want to upset her.

Mom's face falls, before she casts her gaze down and toys with the edge of her napkin. "She's already booked Domingo Designs for three weddings in February and four in March."

I clench my hands. "Shit."

Mom leans toward me and grabs my arm. "Christina, you heard her say they're not friends anymore. Your adoptive mother must have ruined this woman's marriage. I don't know all of the details, but she said her husband filed for divorce after she admitted to an affair that happened twenty years ago."

I roll my eyes. "I don't buy her story. She's probably had more affairs than that."

"Well, whatever happened, I bet Vivian knew and was blackmailing her."

"So Nora finally came clean," I say dryly.

Mom nods. "Who knows what Nora's had to do to keep that snake quiet?"

Knowing my sick and twisted adoptive mother, Nora was paying her off, and she was probably tired of financing The Cobra's collagen injections. I almost want to feel sorry for Nora, but how can I trust someone who was friends with The Cobra? Then I remember up until a few months ago, Karri was supposedly my best friend. I wonder if people have judged me because of my association with Karri? If only I could turn off that little voice in my head screaming "Don't do it!" when I think about handing over the most important day of my life to Nora Richards.

I square my shoulders as I sharpen my gaze. "I still don't trust her with my wedding."

"Sweetheart." Mom pats my hand and drops her voice to a soft whisper like she's trying to soothe a crying child. "Do you think Nora would risk her company's reputation and sabotage your wedding? Do you think she'd risk the lawsuit? Because believe me, I'd sue that woman into oblivion if she ruined my little girl's special day."

My mom smiles at me with the sweetest, most angelic expression, and damn me, but the wider her smile, the more my heart softens.

As much as I hate to admit it, I know she's right that we could use Nora as a connection to boost our new business. Nora's got an in to all of the richest clients in south Texas. The more I mull this over, the more my heart sinks and my stomach sours. Yeah, we probably need to play nice with Nora. I just wish we didn't have to use her for my wedding.

Chapter Eight

Christina

I'm feeling a little better after our lunch together. Nora thinks she can book the wedding at a San Antonio hotel on The Riverwalk. Andrés and I took our first vacation together there, so the beautiful landmark holds a special place in my heart. The more I think about having my wedding on the river, the more I think it will be absolutely perfect.

Nora was surprisingly polite during lunch, even apologizing several times for the way my adoptive mother treated me at our chance encounter last month. Nora had been there to watch The Cobra throw wine on me and then get kicked out of the country club. Nora even told me that was her turning point. After watching me stand up to that snake, Nora finally summoned the courage to end their so-called friendship and tell her husband about the affair before my adoptive mother beat her to it.

Nora makes eye contact with me several times while relaying this story. I want so badly to believe her. So why is it that, as my mom and I leave the restaurant and shake hands with Nora one last time, I still have this queasy feeling? I keep telling myself it's the pregnancy hormones.

At least I hope it is.

Mom and I drive straight to a bridal boutique we found on the internet. I huddle inside my jacket as we make our way through the parking lot. Yesterday, it was in the low seventies and today it's in the mid-forties. I've lived in Texas my whole life, and I still can't understand the weather.

When we walk in the door, I sigh in relief when I feel the warmth from the heater, but then my senses are hit with a blast of nauseating oldies Christmas music. Bleh. Even though I'm excited about Christmas in two more days, the holiday music is starting to wear on me. Still, I do my best to shrug it off. I'm looking forward to spending the holiday with my new family, and I can't wait to see my brothers' faces when they open the remote control helicopters Andrés and I bought them.

The salesladies are helping a bride who appears to be having a breakdown. The poor woman is surrounded by a cluster of bridesmaids in hideous foam green dresses. She looks like she's about to be swallowed up by a taffeta tsunami.

I know it's none of my business, but I can't help but wonder what's causing this woman's breakdown. Mom and I exchange questioning looks before we hear the woman blurt out, "I can't go through with it. I can't!" Then she cries into the fabric of her white gown. The saleswomen are panicking, begging the bride to take off the dress before she ruins it. The bridesmaids are telling her everything will all work out. Two matronly women, I suspect to be the mother and mother-in-law, are off to the side, bickering. I even hear one woman call the other a "meddlesome bitch."

Wow.

My heart clenches when I hear the bride sobbing even harder. This is no way to start off the happiest time of her life.

"Oh, Christina." Mom leans over and whispers in my ear. "Look at that dress."

I turn at the gown she's pointing to, a big frilly number that looks like a cross between a ballet dress and a vat of cotton candy. Ew. Not wanting to hurt her feelings, I force a smile as I follow her toward the monstrosity. I don't know how my petite mother manages, but she actually pulls the dress down without being crushed under an avalanche of fluff.

It's when my mom removes the big eyesore from the rack that I see the other dress.

My dress.

It's perfect. A strapless silk beauty with a modest rhinestone pattern across the bust and a simple satin gown that is dissected at the waist by a pink sash and hugs the hips before cascading straight to the floor. Though the dress doesn't have any puffy hoops, the train that connects to the back gives it a fuller look.

"Omigod!" I squeal as I pull the dress down. "It's perfect!"

Mom frowns as she squeezes the big ball of fluff to her chest. It crackles and pops beneath her grip as if it's made of bubble wrap. "Christina." She seems to deflate. "It's so plain."

"I know." I nod as I run my hand down the smooth fabric. "A blank canvas."

Recognition flashes in her eyes. "You're going to decorate this dress yourself, aren't you?"

"I'm an artist, remember?" I look at her with breath hitched. I really hope she approves, because what I have in mind for this gown will completely transform it, and if it doesn't turn out, there goes any chance of a refund. Even though the fabric paint I plan to use is non-toxic, it's permanent. Once the color sets, it's there for good.

"Why didn't I see that coming?" She laughs as she heaves that other dress back onto the rack. Then she locks elbows with me and leads me to the dressing room. "Let's go try it on."

* * *

Not only is this the perfect dress, it's the perfect fit. I only wish it was the perfect price. Nearly two thousand dollars for a simple silk gown! Luckily, it comes with an elegant veil made of silk and lace with a pink headband that matches the sash. My mom doesn't bat an eyelash as she swipes her credit card and the clerk hands us the dress. I'm so excited, I practically float toward the door as we leave.

But then I falter, nearly tripping over my gown as I spy the crying bride over my shoulder. Her mascara is running down her bright pink cheeks in heavy globs and there are makeup stains all over the gown. Both mothers are arguing with a saleslady, who's demanding they pay for the dry cleaning. I feel frozen in place as the bride gives me a knowing look right before she takes a drag from a cigarette. She doesn't even flinch as angry red embers land on her gown.

She points her cigarette at me before taking another hit. When she looks at me, it feels as if a thousand tiny spiders are burrowing into my skin. I know the meaning behind her gaze.

You're next.

The saleswoman screeches and knocks the cigarette from the bride's hand. My mom grabs me by the elbow and hurries me out the door. "We don't want to get caught up in that," she says in a strained whisper.

"No, we don't," I say. *No, we don't.*

* * *

Andrés

"Hey, doc. Thanks for seeing me on such short notice." I clasp his hand, cringing when he quickly pulls away. Must be my sweat-drenched palm. Why do my hands always go clammy when I visit this shrink?

"Of course," Doctor Barnes says as he takes a seat in the upholstered leather chair across from me. "Luckily, I had a cancellation today."

I follow his lead and sit down. As I struggle to get comfortable in the oversized chair, I adjust my stiff shirt collar and breathe a sigh of relief when I loosen my belt. My jeans have been feeling tighter. Must be all the Mexican take-out and sitting I've been doing lately, lots and lots of sitting, as I learn to crunch numbers for my soon-to-be new businesses.

"So how are you doing?" Dr. Barnes asks me as he picks up his note pad and pen.

I hate that notepad. I don't want him to scribble down my faults. I want him to look at me and listen. That's it. I think about telling him to put the paper down, but I know he's following protocol, and if four years in the Army has taught me anything, it's to follow protocol.

"Not good." I drum my fingers on the armrest, gaze averted. If he's going to keep scribbling in that fucking pad, I shouldn't have to watch. "The dreams are back."

"What's going on?"

I briefly make eye contact with the doctor before looking away. "I had another dream when we were visiting my fiancé's parents." I stop and bite on my lip. Doctor Barnes doesn't need to hear the rest of the story, how I left a big angry bruise on Christina's ribcage. How close I came to punching her in the gut and hurting our unborn child. Anger and shame wash over me when I recall the image of her rolling out of bed, wincing and clutching her side.

"Fiancé? So I take it she said yes." I look at the doctor. Thankfully, he's set down that pen and paper, and the lines around his eyes crinkle as he smiles.

"Yeah. We set the date for February first."

"Congratulations," he says. "That's right around the corner."

Doc picks up his pen and starts scribbling again. I fight the urge to lean forward and read what he's writing. Probably something about how we're rushing into this. How we only just broke up and now we're jumping into marriage.

"We just found out she's pregnant," I blurt.

I don't know why I feel the need to tell him about the baby. Maybe I'm trying to justify why we're getting hitched so soon, and then I wonder why I'm doing that. Christina and I love each other. That's why we're getting married. The baby pushes up the date, but that doesn't change the fact I want her to be my bride. Now I'm bothered because I'm sitting here silently making excuses for us. What the hell is wrong with me?

"You've got a lot on your plate," Doctor Barnes says in a flat voice. A voice that doesn't pass judgment. It's bullshit. "So tell me about this dream," he asks as he taps the pad with the point of his pen.

I exhale a shaky breath as I mentally try to switch gears. I remind myself I'm not here to be judged. I'm here to get help. I close my eyes and bring back memories I've been trying to bury. My dreams are so vivid, I feel as if I'm living inside these nightmares. It doesn't take long for me to summon the images of my dying friends, taste copper on my tongue, and see my uncle's mutilated body lying on top of me. "We're back in the Hummer, only this time there's a baby in the back seat. I'm trying to get to him, but I can't. My uncle's on top of me."

He arches a brow. "Your uncle?"

"Yeah." My eyes shoot open and then a shudder steals up my spine. "He's telling me to get back to work."

I think I see a flash of recognition beneath the reflective glare of Dr. Barnes's glasses, but then he plasters on an impassive expression. "You're taking over his businesses, right?"

"Five of them." I groan when I think of all the work piled on my desk waiting for me. This doctor's appointment is going to put me behind, which means I'll be working late tonight.

"How's that going?"

"Rough." I course my fingers through my hair, squeezing at the roots and doing my best to release the pent up tension that's winding a noose around my neck. "Christina was my best artist. I lost her when we found out she was pregnant. I've got to go in and fire a mechanic today. We think he's been stealing parts."

"Do you like your job, Andrés?"

I can feel the current of doubt resonate beneath the doctor's question. He knows I don't like my job. I know why he's asking. I know what he's doing. Little does he understand I can't quit. I'm stuck running Cruz Automotive Body and Repair shops. Chained to this future by a strong sense of family responsibility. I can't walk away from my duty. Besides, even if I was willing to shame my uncle, what about Christina and our baby? I have an obligation to take care of them, too.

"I like the pay," I tell him. I know I'm evading the question, but it's true. I do like the money. My wife and child will be provided for as long as I've got this job.

He eyes me with a knowing expression. "Besides the pay, do you like your job?"

I exhale a frustrated breath and shake my head. Though the truth hurts, I've got to admit it to someone. I think holding it all inside is what's causing a lot of my stress. "No. When I was in the army, those soldiers were my brothers. I could count on them to watch my back. Here, it's every man for himself."

The doctor eyes me thoughtfully. "Why do you think that is?"

"I don't know." I shrug. "It's just different. I'm not their brother, you know? I'm their boss. I don't even get to work on cars, I'm so busy doing paperwork."

"Do you miss dodging bullets and landmines?"

"No." I can't keep the edge of bitterness from my voice. Why the hell would he think I miss dodging landmines? "I miss doing something other than sitting on my ass looking at numbers."

Doctor Barnes sets down his notepad, steeples his fingers together in front of his drawn mouth and regards me for a long moment. "Have you told your uncle this?"

My heart stops at the thought. "I can't."

"Why?" I don't like the incredulous tone in his voice. As if he thinks it would be so easy for me to crush my uncle's dreams.

"I don't want him to think I'm ungrateful," I answer with a groan. "He's giving my family financial security. He's giving my child a future."

The doctor leans forward, eyeing me intently. "What about *your* future? Where do you see yourself in ten years?"

"Tired, stressed, stuck in a job I hate."

As Dr. Barnes assesses me, he doesn't have to say a word. I know what he's thinking. *If that was my future outlook, I'd be having nightmares, too.*

Chapter Nine

Christina

Andrés doesn't get home from work until seven, so we're running late to dinner. It's really hard not falling asleep during the ride to his aunt and uncle's house. By the time he helps me out of his truck, he almost has to drag me to the front door. I keep thinking of Andrés's comfy bed in his old room upstairs, and how nice it would be to lie down for a little nap, although I'm so exhausted and my neck is sore from sketching ideas for my dress all day, I probably wouldn't wake until morning. Luckily, I'm so hungry my stomach feels like it might implode on itself. I know I need to eat something before I even think about sleeping.

I only hope his aunt made tamales. I don't know why, but I'm also craving coleslaw and tiramisu. Hopefully, Tia has them. If not, maybe she's got brownies and ice cream. I could go for that, too.

I wrap my scarf around my neck and hug my coat to my chest as an arctic blast hits me, burning my eyes and cheeks. I close my mouth to keep my teeth from chattering. Andrés wraps a warm arm around my shoulders and we walk to the house. The two story ranch is aglow in lights. A giant wreath with the words *"Feliz Navidad"* scrolled across the top in festive red ribbon hangs on the front door.

My senses are accosted by all kinds of good smells when we walk through the door, and I groan as Andrés leads me toward the dining room. When we pass through the living room, I smile at the tree. Every single branch is weighed down by what looks like homemade ornaments and Christmas crafts. I remember being shocked after Tio put it up a few weeks ago. Tia told me it took her an entire day to decorate it mostly with Christmas crafts her boys made when they were little plus several hanging bulbs imprinted with school pictures of Andrés and his cousins. Tia's tree isn't designer by any means, but I think it's possibly the best kind, one decorated with love. Tejano holiday music filters in from overhead. I'm not sure what they're saying, but the festive beat lightens my mood, despite the fact that my insides are churning.

Andrés's family is sitting around a large dining table, most of them with cleaned plates. His Tio and Tia are there, along with his other aunt and uncle, Arturo and Inez, and his cousin Marie.

I was hoping Christmas Eve dinner was just going to be with his Tia and Tio. I really didn't want a large audience when we told them our news, especially not the baby part, but I guess I should consider myself lucky the rest of Andrés's extended family isn't here. I fight the urge to run when they all turn in their seats to look at us. Andrés must sense my nervousness, because his grip on my hand tightens. I look up and when he winks at me, and I flash a weary smile. I have to remind myself everything will be okay. I've got Andrés, my rock, my pillar. He's been there for me through some difficult times, and I know he'll get us through tonight.

Tio leans back in his chair and pats his swollen stomach. "Sorry, mijo. We couldn't wait any longer."

Marie looks up at us with a scowl. "What took you so long?"

Marie is a few years older than me. She's, pretty, with large chestnut eyes slightly tapered and thick, wavy hair cut in a bob just below her chin. It always seems like she's in a pissed off mood. I don't know if she's normally a bitch or if she doesn't like me. Either way, she makes me uncomfortable, but since she'll be my family soon, I guess I'll need to learn to put up with her.

"I had to finish the timesheets." Andrés groans as he rolls his eyes at his cousin.

She answers with another sneer. Then she focuses her eyes on me, and I shift uncomfortably while she gives me the once-over before looking away.

Okay, she definitely doesn't like me. What the hell did I ever do to her?

"You're piling too much work on him." Tia arches a trimmed brow and then points a fork at Tio across the table. I like Andrés's aunt, whom he affectionately calls Tia. Andrés told me she has had some plastic surgery, but nothing I'd call excessive. Just a little tightening around the eyes and mouth. She looks to be in her early forties though she's almost sixty, and she carries herself like a confident woman. She raised four boys mostly by herself while Tio worked late hours, and her love for her boys is obvious. I hope I can be half the woman and mother she is.

"What are you talking about?" Tio shrugs before taking a swig of his longneck beer. "He took all morning off."

I have to remind myself to keep my tongue in my mouth as Tio swallows the cool beverage. No more beer for me for at least another eight months.

"Slacker." Marie laughs as she reaches across the table and stabs a steak with her fork.

I try not to get upset when I see she's taken the last steak off the platter, and she's already got a clean T-bone on her plate. I settle my hand over my hollow stomach as it growls in protest. I could have so gone for a steak right now.

Andrés squeezes my hand and leads me to the end of the table, next to Tia and across from the bitch cousin.

"He had to go to that military shrink," Tio says loudly and then belches into his fist.

I tense as I look up at Andrés. I think I feel his hand shake before he tightens his grip.

"Andrés, what's wrong?" Tia gasps as she drops her silverware onto her plate. "Are the nightmares back?"

Just when I think Andrés is about to crush my fingers, he releases my hand and pulls out a chair for me. "It's nothing, Tia," he mumbles.

"Christina." Tia looks at me with fear in her wide eyes. "Is he having the nightmares again?"

Andrés stands behind me and settles his hand on my shoulder. I look up at him and place my hand over his.

Tia screeches so loud I think she's ruptured my eardrums. "Omgiod! The ring!" She squeals as she jumps from her seat. "She's wearing the ring!"

She throws herself into Andrés's arms, jumping up and down as she squeezes him to her chest.

My chair is pulled back as Tio pulls me up for a hug. Before I know it, the rest of his family is hugging me, too. By the time Tia grabs me in a vice grip, her eyes are red and swollen from crying. After several more tearful congrats, Andrés and I sit down.

Marie gapes at us from across the table. "My cousin's getting married," she says in a monotone, cold and devoid of emotion, before she stabs her meat with a knife.

Andrés doesn't seem to be phased by her reaction as he scoops some enchiladas onto my plate.

"Have you set a date?" Tia pops open a bottle of champagne and fills our goblets to the top.

I warily eye Andrés as he smirks at me and pushes my goblet to the side. He hands me a glass of ice water.

"We think February first but we're not sure yet." Andrés piles my plate with guacamole and sour cream. My mouth waters at the heaping chunks of avocado and tomato. Andrés knows how much I love toppings.

"Why so soon?" Tio asks with a note of accusation in his voice.

I feel my face flush ten shades of red as I avert my gaze and reach for my water.

Andrés clears his throat as if to speak, but when I look over at him, he's got this deer-in-the-headlights expression I've never seen before.

"We were going to wait until spring, but we've had to adjust our plans." His voice cracks at that last part, and I am embarrassed for him. For us. I fight the urge to crawl under the table.

I knew telling his family I was pregnant wasn't going to be easy. I never planned for it to be this uncomfortable.

Tia clears her throat loudly, waving her champagne glass in the air. "The sooner the better. I've been bugging them to get married, anyway." She winks at both of us.

I raise my water glass as his uncle recites some sort of sappy congrats. I'm so numb from apprehension, I don't even remember what he says. When everyone says *"salud"* and clinks their glasses, I notice Marie sitting in her seat with her hands fisted by her plate.

She can't even toast us. What the hell is her problem?

Everyone downs their champagne and then the table breaks into a chorus of chatter. Tia leans across the table, saying something to me about wedding preparations. I know I need to tell her my mom is handling everything, but Tia is so excited, I hate to let her down, especially here in front of everyone… in front of Marie.

Andrés nudges me several times during dinner when he sees me picking at my enchiladas. I mumble that I'm not that hungry as I push food around on my plate. Then Andrés's gaze travels to his cousin, who's been shooting eye darts at me the whole time. My stomach churns when I see them locked in a stare-down.

Finally, Marie gets up, thrusts her chair against the table, and stomps away. Andrés doesn't say a word, but he squeezes my hand tight before leaning over and kissing my temple. That's his way of apologizing for his cousin. And though I appreciate him trying to soothe me, it doesn't change Marie's attitude. It's obvious she doesn't like me. I only hope she keeps her opinion to herself and doesn't try to ruin this wedding.

* * *

Tia and I clear the dishes, along with Andrés's other aunt Inez. The guys go into the den to watch football. I notice Marie follows them and doesn't offer any help in the kitchen. Andrés's aunts keep telling me to go with the guys, but I can't leave them with all these dishes. Besides, I've never been a fan of football. That's what I tell myself, anyway. It has absolutely nothing to do with the fact that I don't want to be in the same room with Marie. I suspect she's probably giving Andrés a hard time right now. The more I think about the way she reacted at dinner, the more my insides burn with anger.

I rotate my sore neck and set another platter on the drying rack. I shouldn't have sketched so long today, but I was so enamored with those little flowers, I couldn't stop drawing them. I can't wait until this dress is finished. I can already tell it will be beautiful.

"You should have Andrés rub that kink for you." Tia winks before bumping me with her hip.

"Ohhh, I like a good kinky rubbing," Inez says with a throaty growl as she fans her heavy breasts with a dishtowel.

Tia laughs so hard, she snorts.

Oh, gawd, I'm flanked by two horny old women. I can't help the blush that creeps into my cheeks, flaming my face like wildfire.

"Now that the dishes are finished, we'll open a bottle of wine and start planning this wedding." Tia smiles broadly at me as she nods toward a barstool at the counter.

"Arturo and I will do the catering," Inez says matter-of-factly as she stacks the last dry dish and wipes her hands on her apron. "You like Mexican food, don't you, Christina?"

"Of course she does," Tia says as she grabs a bottle of wine from the fridge and two glasses. "Haven't you seen the way she scarfs down my tamales?" She sets the glasses on the counter and pops the cork, then flashes me a knowing grin. "You can't drink, can you, mija?"

"No." I shake my head as I dry my hands on a towel. I didn't think I could get any redder, but I feel the flush all the way to my toes. Both of Andrés's aunts are looking at me with smirks and raised brows.

Inez comes up to me and places a chubby hand on my belly. When she leans over, breathing against my neck, I can smell the strong residue of wine on her breath. "Pssst," she whispers rather loudly to me before nodding her head toward Tia. "Her oldest boy was born seven months after she married."

"Inez!" Tia shrieks before throwing a towel at her.

"What?" Inez shrugs before slanting a sideways grin. "I didn't always pay attention in school, but I can add seven plus two."

Tia's tanned cheeks flush pink. "He was premature."

Inez rolls her eyes. "He was ten pounds!"

"Enough," Tia holds out both hands before picking up her glass and gingerly taking a sip. "We need to plan the wedding."

"Uh," I say as I anxiously eye one woman, then the other. "My mom hired a wedding planner, and I'm not sure who she's getting to cater the wedding."

Inez looks at me with an arched brow. "Find out who she's using and cancel them. The Cruz family caters all of our own weddings."

"I'll let them know," I say with a hesitant smile, though I already suspect what my mom will say. She was pretty adamant about those shrimp puffs.

Tia looks at me expectantly with one hand on her hip. "Your mom is planning the whole wedding?"

"Most of it," I barely manage to squeak.

I don't like the accusation in her voice, like I've done something wrong. If Tia only saw my mom take charge, the unstoppable wedding express, maybe she'd be more understanding. I heave a sigh as I lean against the kitchen counter. My special day has turned into a runaway train, and all the details are racing further and further away from me. Soon, I'll be reduced to a spectator at my own wedding, just doing what others tell me. Thankfully, I managed to wrest control over the dress—my dress. A smile tugs at my lips when I think of it. I might be forced to eat seafood pastries, but at least I'll look amazing while I'm retching up my meal.

"What about your dress?" Tia asks.

My mouth falls open at the expectant look in her eyes. No, she will not have any say in my dress. Nobody will. It's the one thing I've got left.

I swallow hard before averting my gaze. "We found a gown today."

"You got a dress? You didn't tell me."

I spin around to see Andrés standing in the doorway. He's holding an empty chip bowl, looking at me with a slack jaw.

I heave a frustrated groan. I'm tired. My neck hurts. What's the big deal about the dress? "You've been at work all day."

"You could have sent me a message." He flashes a crooked smile, one I guess could be considered playful, but I'm not in the mood to play right now.

"You *never* answer my texts," I say in an accusatory tone that sounds too severe even to my own ears.

I cringe when he takes a step back, looking at me as if I've wounded him with a verbal knife.

I know my fuse is short, and I fear it may get even shorter unless Andrés takes me home. It's been a long day and I want to go to sleep, so I can be rested for our drive to San Antonio tomorrow.

He shrugs. "I guess it doesn't matter. I'll see it when we get home."

Inez gasps and crosses her heart before muttering something in Spanish. "No, you can't see it. It's bad luck, Andrés."

"I'd like to see it." Tia steps forward, squaring her shoulders.

When I look at the hurt in her eyes I feel like a balloon has popped in my chest. I hate that Tia is upset, but I don't understand why she would be.

"It's at the apartment. You can come by and look at it anytime." I reach behind my head and rub my sore neck and shoulders. Why did I think planning this wedding would be fun? So far, it's turning out to be a big pain in the neck—literally.

"I'll come with you, Tia."

I stifle a gasp as Marie steps from behind Andrés. She leans against the wall in a casual pose, one leg crossed over the other. She's got this smug look on her face, and I swear the glare she gives me is hot enough to melt lead. Oh, this is so not good. I don't want Marie to come to my apartment. In fact, I don't want her anywhere near my dress.

The image of that bride pointing her cigarette at me flashes through my mind. And now I know exactly what she was trying to tell me: this runaway train is heading for disaster.

Chapter Ten

Christina

"What's wrong, mija?" Andrés grips the steering wheel as we drive down Highway 35. He keeps his gaze focused on the road, but I can tell by the way he works a tic in his jaw he's got a lot on his mind.

"I'm tired, Andrés," I say on a sigh. "I just need some sleep."

I know work has been stressful for him lately. The last thing I should do is unload on him, even though I feel like I may break under the pressure of this wedding planning. I lean against the headrest and massage the tension building in my neck. No matter how much I rub, it seems to get worse.

"You didn't look happy tonight. Did my family upset you?"

When Andrés takes one hand from the wheel and laces his fingers through mine, my thin thread of composure starts to unravel.

My throat tightens with emotion when I look over at him and see his eyes darken with concern. I don't want to burden him with my troubles, but he probably should know what's going on, anyway. I turn away and look out at the highway.

"Your aunts are hurt they don't get to help and your cousin does not like me." I hate the whine that slips into my voice. Damn. Why'd I tell him?

Andrés releases my hand and grips the wheel with white knuckles. "Yeah, Marie. I was hoping you didn't catch that."

"Uh, yeah." I definitely caught it. I was drowning in her venom the whole night.

"Don't worry about Marie." Andrés looks at me and winks. "She grew up with a bunch of boys. I think she likes being the only girl, and she's jealous you're getting so much attention.

"Great. So how do I get her to back off?"

"Just ignore her. She'll come around."

But I don't like the edge of doubt in his voice. I also don't like the uneasy tension that clings to him like a second skin. I can see the way his shoulders stiffen and the veins protrude in his neck. Andrés looks like he's got a lot on his mind, too, so I decide to drop the topic of Marie. Talking about her makes my stomach sour, anyway.

"You don't look happy, either, Andrés." It's a statement, not a question, and I wait with bated breath for him to answer.

If anything, the tension in the truck cab thickens, so much that I can feel his nervous energy snaking up my spine.

"I had a rough day at work." His jaw is so tight, I'm amazed he can even speak.

"Do you want to talk about it?"

"No. I want to forget it." His tone is clipped, firm, leaving little room for me to argue.

This pregnancy, this wedding, can't be helping his stress, and lately he seems very stressed. I admire how Andrés acts like a different man at work, focused, authoritative. But having worked with him so long, I'm starting to see through his tough guy veneer. Andrés is a strict boss, uncompromising with his employees. I used to think his style was a product of his military training, but more and more lately, I'm noticing the weariness in his eyes, the stoop of his shoulders every time something goes wrong at one of the shops. Andrés hates his job.

"So what's going on with the wedding?" Andrés cuts into my thoughts. I look at him with a weary gaze. His aunts weren't thrilled with my mom's wedding plans. I wonder what Andrés will think. After all, this is his wedding, too.

"We're still looking at February first." I pause as I summon the nerve to hit him with the latest news. I know he wanted the wedding at the ranch. "Nora is talking about having it at a hotel on The Riverwalk."

"We can't do it at Tio's ranch?"

Damn. He didn't miss a beat.

I try to keep my tone even, though my body and soul are weary. I don't feel like discussing this wedding anymore. All I want to do is curl up underneath my blankets, fall asleep, and pretend this wedding isn't turning into a nightmare. "My stepdad has a large family. My mom wants it someplace bigger, more formal."

"The ranch has a lot of room, and you can make it more formal. That's your job now, isn't it?" There's no denying the accusation in his voice. I want to get mad at him, to argue, but he's right. It is my job to decorate weddings. I know I could make the ranch look just as beautiful as any hotel. But my mom is so set on having it in San Antonio. She wants to give me an extravagant wedding because she's missed out on all of the other milestones in my life, and she feels if she spends a lot of money, she'll somehow make it up to me. I'd feel bad denying her that.

"I don't know. I think The Riverwalk sounds nice." I lean over and try to look into his face, but Andrés doesn't so much as blink, much less look in my direction. "That's where we went on our first vacation together, remember?"

"I remember, mija," he says, "but Tia's not going to be happy."

I stiffen my spine. "This isn't her wedding."

He finally looks over at me, and a knot tightens in my chest at the accusation in his gaze. "It's not your mom's wedding, either."

"I know," I say as I look away. The weight of this wedding is pressing so heavily on my chest I fear I may suffocate, especially when I realize there's no way I can make everyone happy.

* * *

After we get home, Andrés fixes me a virgin sangria. We climb into bed, and he asks me to fill him in on our wedding plans. I tell him all about Nora. I sense he doesn't like the idea of this woman planning our wedding. I try to emphasize that she and The Cobra are no longer friends, but somehow I get the impression he's not buying it. I don't blame him, either. I wish I could find a way out of using her.

We discuss the wedding party. I tell him I want my brothers to be ring bearers and he wants his little cousin Amelia to be the flower girl. I only want one bridesmaid, Grace, since I don't talk to my other sorority sisters anymore and, besides Andrés, she's my only good friend. Andrés is going to ask his cousin Cesar to stand up with him. He hints he wants to see my dress, but I think back to what his aunt said about it being bad luck. I'm starting to think this wedding doesn't need any more bad mojo, so I smile coyly and tell him he'll have to wait until the wedding.

As tired as I am, I fall into him and wrap my arms around his neck when he kisses me goodnight. I try to deepen the kiss, but he pulls back and plants a chaste peck on my forehead. What the heck? He doesn't even bother making a move.

"Goodnight, mjia," he says.

When he gets out of bed and pads toward the living room, I bite on my lip and squeeze my eyes shut, trying my best to stifle my tears. A few slip out of the corners of my eyes, anyway. I keep my eyes shut; I don't want to open them and see Andrés is gone. I squeeze my pillow as fatigue overtakes me. It's been a long day, and I fear the time between now and the wedding may prove to be even more demanding.

Chapter Eleven

Christina

"Merry Christmas, mija."

I stretch my arms above me as I slowly open my eyes. Andrés is lying beside me, and even though I know he spent the night in the other room, I try to pretend he was with me all night long.

"Merry Christmas," I say as I inhale the tempting aroma of warm butter and cinnamon. "Something smells good."

"Mmmm," he answers as he massages my lower back. "I made you breakfast."

I roll into him and wrap my arms around his neck, nuzzling that little patch of hair on his chest with my nose. He is warm and inviting, and as I press my ear against his chest, I can hear the steady and reassuring beat of his heart. I sigh into him. He kisses my temple and continues to rub my back. How nice it would be to lie here together all day long, but I know my family is waiting for us in San Antonio. Andrés is supposed to help my stepdad prepare dinner, and my mom and I are going to decorate the dining room. I can't wait to try out my new designer skills today. This is, after all, what I'm supposed to be doing for my new career.

Despite the stress from the wedding and the pregnancy, I have the feeling today will be my best Christmas ever. This holiday has never meant much to me, mainly because I spent most Christmases listening to my adoptive mother and father getting drunk and swearing at each other. But this time is different. This time I'll be surrounded by people I love who love me back. In some ways, it feels like I'll be celebrating my very first Christmas, and the excitement rises in me like effervescent bubbles. I have a lot to be thankful for. I squeeze Andrés's neck tighter, and giggle when he tickles my ribcage. I spring from the bed, feeling like a child anxious to open presents from Santa.

But my excitement is short-lived as I'm hit by a wave of dizziness. I fall back onto the bed and groan.

"Should I bring you breakfast in bed?" he asks, concern lacing each word.

"No, just give me a minute," I say as I close my eyes and will the nausea to subside.

"Your breakfast is ready, mija. I'll go get it."

Andrés rolls out of bed with an ease that makes me jealous and he returns a few minutes later with a tray of food. Mmmm. It smells even better close up. I can't believe the spread he's made: French toast, eggs, hash browns, and real pork bacon (not the fake crap). Best of all is the steaming cup of coffee, which looks to be twice the size of my daily limit, but I'm not complaining.

He props up some pillows behind me and my mouth waters as he sets the tray down. I scoot up against the headboard and reach for my coffee. I frown at the tea bag floating in the liquid.

"Got it at the vitamin store. It's supposed to help with morning sickness," Andrés says, as he puffs up his chest, looking adorably proud of himself. "I sweetened it with honey."

"Thanks," I say, stunned. "I guess it's worth a try." I try not to make a face as I swallow the bitter liquid. I've never been a big fan of tea, but since Andrés went through all the trouble, I know I'll have to finish it. Besides, the sweet honey makes the flavors somewhat bearable, and masks most of the funky aftertaste.

I close my eyes and take several sips, while I tell my morning sickness to piss off. After a few minutes, and nearly half the cup, I feel slightly better, so I open my eyes to see my smiling fiancé holding a forkful of French toast topped with syrup and whipped cream just below my chin. I open my mouth and gladly take a bite, groaning as I bite into cinnamon, warm butter and cream. Damn, he can cook.

I savor the flavors as long as possible before begging for more. Andrés and I share the rest of the meal this way, and morning sickness be damned, I eat until I can't fit in another bite. After I take a quick shower and get dressed, I find Andrés in the kitchen, cleaning the last of the pots and pans. I feel bad I didn't get to help, but I doubt I can work at his speed anyway. It is as if life is in slow motion, and I don't have the energy to do much in the morning.

Andrés hands me another steaming cup, and this time I smile in relief when I smell the aroma of roasted almonds and vanilla. I take a deep drink, savoring the richness as if it's the last cup of coffee I'll ever drink.

Andrés watches me drink with this expectant look in his eyes, and the nervous energy roils off his skin in waves. My chest tightens and my heart starts to race. It's present time!

He wordlessly reaches for my hand, and I follow him into the living room. My last thought before we sit beside the small tree sitting on top of a side table is I hope Andrés likes what I got him. But before I can give him his present, he pulls a small box, wrapped in red velvet and topped with a gold bow, from behind the tree. I gasp as I take it from his outstretched hand while looking deeply into his warm eyes, swirling with amber and honeyed gold flecks.

"I hope you like it," he says in a low raspy voice.

I bite my bottom lip as the warmth of his words coats my senses like rich, maple syrup. "I'm sure I will." I untie the bow and peel back the paper.

I gasp when I open the box. Inside is a bracelet and matching earrings. Each has the same diamond and emerald flower pattern as my engagement ring. I don't even have to ask if these are real; I know they are. I hold up the bracelet and the stones sparkle as they catch the reflection from the tree's glowing lights.

"Andrés. These must have cost a fortune."

He runs a hand down the side of my face. "You're worth it, mija."

I lean into him, relishing the feel of his touch as it sends ripples of pleasure across my skin. I'm so very tempted right now to postpone opening the rest of our presents and drag him into the bedroom. If only my mom wasn't expecting me.

After Andrés helps me put on the earrings, and I lavish him with many, many "thank you" kisses, we open less expensive presents, like jeans and scarves. He bought me a Spanish tutorial CD for the computer, and I can't wait to learn enough to have a conversation with him, even if I'm not able to master the accent. I love that smoky look in Andrés 's eyes when he opens the black lace nightie, that is technically a present I bought for myself, but more for his enjoyment. Finally, comes the last present, the largest one, and the one that makes my gut twist with apprehension. This present cost me my entire last paycheck, so I hope he likes it. If not, I've saved the receipt.

Andrés's face lights up when he opens the box, a collection of bronze pots and pans. The guy at the upscale culinary store told me it's what the professional chefs use.

He lets out a low whistle as he reads the words on the box. "You bought me bronze, mija? These are expensive."

He looks lost in thought as he stares at the box. He must be thinking I've spent too much, but his present couldn't have cost more than mine. Besides, he's such an awesome cook, he should have nice cookware.

"Your food deserves the very best. You should have been a chef, you know," I add, thinking he'd be more accepting of my gift with a little boost to his ego.

My heart sinks to my stomach as his face contorts into one massive frown.

"Don't you like them?" I hesitantly ask.

He pats the top of the box before setting it on the coffee table. I'm rendered speechless when he looks back at me. There's a sadness behind his smile I can't define. Why would pots and pans make him so melancholy?

He clasps my hands in his and kisses my cheek. "They're perfect, mija," he rasps into my ear. "I love them."

But his words lack conviction, fizzling like a balloon running out of air. I don't understand how my present could have soured his mood, but I definitely sense a change in him, like a dark haze has settled over his soul. And now my soul is hurting, too.

* * *

That big breakfast still weighs heavily in my stomach as we pack the car with presents and head to my mom's house. I end up sleeping the entire two hour drive. By the time we pull into my mom's circular driveway, I'm feeling rested and refreshed. I stretch my arms, relieved to see Andrés smiling at me. "Did you enjoy your nap?"

"Yesss," I say through a yawn.

My brothers bound toward me before I have one foot out the door. They're bouncing around the car like jackrabbits on speed, chanting something about "more presents."

"Yeah, I'm happy to see you, too, boys," I say wryly as I bend down and open my arms for a hug. Little Manny is the first rugrat to launch himself into my arms, followed by big brother, Gio. They cover my cheeks, in sloppy, sticky kisses and then tell me to hurry up inside so they can open more gifts. Have I mentioned lately my brothers are the cutest kids ever?

Andrés tells me to go with them while he unloads the car. I feel bad leaving him behind, but my brothers don't leave me much choice as they drag me toward the house. My mom is standing on the front porch, and my stepdad is beside her, dusting his hands on his apron.

"Merry Christmas," they sing in unison, beaming at me with infectious smiles.

It warms my heart to see how much those two are on the same wavelength. More than once, I've watched Doc and my mom finish each other's sentences and both laugh uncontrollably at the same jokes. I sure hope mine and Andrés's marriage will be this solid after we've had kids.

After sharing hugs and kisses with them, I'm anxious to get to work helping my mom with the decorations. She leads me through the tall foyer while Doc helps Andrés carry in presents.

My senses are accosted by the smells of warm cinnamon and nutmeg, and imagine my surprise when my stomach growls loud enough to rival a grizzly bear. My mom and I both stop and look down at my midsection.

"Didn't you have breakfast, dear?" she asks.

My jaw drops as my stomach growls again. "Uh, I had a *huge* breakfast."

"Well, you are eating for two." Mom winks and pats my stomach.

I scratch my head. "Yeah, but this baby is only the size of a peanut."

Mom's green eyes twinkle with laughter. "I gained most of my pregnancy weight early on with all you kids. My stomach was like a bottomless pit." She starts toward the kitchen and I follow. "Come on, let's get you something to eat."

My heart slams when we pass beneath a pale gossamer curtain and into the dining area. The place looks like a winter wonderland, aglow with twinkling lights and fake snow. The walls are draped in more gossamer curtains, and sparkly snowflakes of every size hang from the ceiling. It's breathtakingly beautiful, and my mom did it all without my help.

"Isn't it beautiful?" she asks with a lilt.

"I thought I was supposed to help." I hate that I sound like a petulant child, but I can't help but feel hurt that she'd left me out.

"Oh, dear, I know how tired you've been lately." Mom pats me on the hand, speaking in soothing tones like she's trying to quell a child on the verge of a tantrum. "I worked on this for the past two days. You would never have been able to finish it in time, especially in your condition." She nods toward my stomach, which, unfortunately, chooses that very moment to let out another loud rumble. Mom walks over to the buffet against the wall and picks up a big ball of clay. "I saved the sculpture for you. I figured you could make it look like a snowman. The boys would love that."

My shoulders slump when I think back to my junior year in college when my sculpting teacher told me my work had no depth. My assignment had been to mold the bust of one of my parents. I'd chosen to sculpt The Cobra, the lesser of two evils. I figured her image had no depth because it was a reflection of what was on the inside. Either way, I survived that course with a B minus, thanks to tons of extra credit.

I take the clay and let the weight of it settle in my hands. I've always loved the way it felt when I pressed my fingers into the soft, yet firm substance. Maybe I can sculpt something small, but I'm still terrified it will look like crap.

"I've never been that good at sculpting."

Mom frowns, and the pity reflecting in her gaze is so humiliating, I feel like hiding behind those gossamer curtains and never coming out.

"The boys don't care if it's not Michelangelo. Just maybe Frosty the Snowman or Rudolph."

"Okay." I barely mouth the word as I absently nod. My stomach rumbles so loudly this time, I feel like I'm caught in an intestinal earthquake.

"Let's get you some food." Mom tugs hard on my hand, pulling me through the kitchen doors without another word.

I heave a sigh. I had all of these designs in mind for the dining room, but mom's wonderland is pretty awesome. Still, I wish I could have contributed more than a clay snowman. Not only has this pregnancy rendered me a tired eating machine, it has rendered me useless.

* * *

Dinner is amazing thanks mostly to Andrés's homemade gravy and warm, buttery tortillas that practically melt in my mouth. Yes, our personal chefs decided to skip the biscuits and make homemade tortillas, which Doc said were far better than anything his Mexican grandmother ever made. I believe him, too. Andrés is an amazing cook.

My Frosty doesn't come out too bad either, even though he leans a little bit to the right. Andrés dubs him The Leaning Tower of Snowman and then Gio decides to knock off his head with a turkey leg.

I decide not to be bothered by it. Today is still by far my best Christmas ever, because the people I love most in the world are sharing it with me. The food is great, and my mom and stepdad bought me a beautiful winter coat and matching boots plus an awesome SLR digital camera, complete with zoom and a macro lenses.

My mom loves the personalized gift I made her, a scrapbook with all my childhood pictures that I "acquired" from my adoptive mom's house while she was at her weekly pluck and color appointment. I also give her a beautiful silk scarf, green to match her eyes. We bought Doc several kinds of exotic teas, since he's into that stuff. They give Andrés a San Antonio Spurs sweatshirt and a blue and silver daddy diaper bag packed full of bottles and newborn diapers. Andrés graciously thanks them, despite their hint that they want him to take an active part in raising the baby.

Then Mom winks at me while proclaiming loudly she hopes Andrés will get to use the bag often. I can feel the heat from Andrés's embarrassment radiating in waves. As I lean into him, I feel like I'm pressed against a furnace. I am only slightly miffed by my mom's hint. After all, Andrés does work way too many hours, and I've been worrying more and more that he may be too busy to help with the baby.

Afterward, Andrés takes my brothers outside and teaches them how to operate the remote control helicopters we bought them. Manny cries when Gio "accidentally" knocks his helicopter into a bush. Gio cries when Manny chases after his helicopter with a plastic baseball bat.

Doc finally comes outside and tells my brothers it's time for a nap. This makes them cry even harder. I kiss them each goodbye and tell them to stay off the naughty list or else Santa will take back their presents. That seems to do the trick, as they both clam up and let Doc lead them to bed.

Even though my mom is disappointed, we have to make our goodbyes. Since the dreams started back up, Andrés does not feel comfortable spending the night anywhere but his sofa. On the way home, we make one more stop. Andrés delivers presents to James's sons. James was Andrés's best friend in the Army, and his widow's home is not too far from my mom's house. Though the boys are about my brothers' ages, their personalities are as different as night and day. They accept Andrés's presents with a polite, "Thank you, sir" and play quietly in the other room while Andrés and I visit with James's wife and her new fiancé.

We're both shocked to learn she's remarrying. I think Andrés takes it harder than he lets on, as he's unnervingly quiet during the ride back to Austin. I don't know if it's because I'm tired of Andrés's pensive mood, or else I'm just tired, but just as we reach that half-way point, I take another nap. It's past nightfall when we pull into our apartment carport. I'm so exhausted, I can hardly heave myself out of the car. I'm relieved when Andrés sees me struggling and carries me to our apartment. He lays me down in bed, kisses my forehead and tells me he's got to go finish unloading.

That's all I remember before I fall back to sleep.

* * *

I jump up in bed, startled at the sound of Andrés's screams coming from the other room. I toss aside my sheets and hurry to the living room, cursing as I trip over the edge of a rug, nearly falling face first onto the floor.

His screams are louder, and it sounds like he's fighting with someone, but it's so dark I can barely see.

I rub my hands across the wall and hit the switch. I spin around to see Andrés turned sideways on the sofa, punching the cushion so hard, the stuffing is coming out.

"Andrés!" I cry as I rush to his side. I jump back when he thrashes about, barely missing his arm as it swings wildly at me. "Andrés!" I cry again. "Wake up!"

He thrashes about some more, only this time, less violently. Then he stills. He groans a bit and rubs the sleep from his eyes before finally looking up at me with a dazed expression.

It's only then I breathe a sigh of relief. I hadn't realized I'd been holding my breath, waiting, worrying he wouldn't wake.

Andrés slowly sits up on his elbows, his brow creases into a heavy frown. He rubs his hand through his hair and turns his gaze toward the battered pillow cushion. He reaches for a frayed end and then twirls a bit of stuffing around his finger. Finally, he heaves a sigh before looking up at me.

The pain in his glossy eyes is enough to make my heart break.

"See why I can't sleep with you, mija?"

His shoulders cave inward, and he pulls his knees to his chest and withdraws into himself. I lean down and reach for him, but he pulls away. This can't be happening. This can't be my Andrés, my strong, confident, hero. But as I watch him withdraw further and further away from me, there's no denying the truth. Andrés is falling apart. Guilt and self-loathing surge through me as he asks me to go back to bed. This wedding, this baby, has pushed him over the edge.

Chapter Twelve

Andrés

Cursing, I hang up with the scheduler at the VA hospital. She says Doctor Barnes is on leave and would I like to see some other shrink? Hell, no. I'm not waiting in line at some grocery store check stand for the next cashier. Do they really expect me to start over with a new doctor every time I need help? Oh, well. I guess it's for the best. Cars still need maintenance during the holidays, and I've got to train two new mechanics today.

I slip my phone into my pocket and refill my coffee before I check on Christina again. She's still sleeping. I feel bad that I woke her last night. She doesn't need the extra stress of worrying over me in her condition. Add to that the fact that my aunt and her mom are pulling her in different directions about this wedding. I've got the feeling that this wedding shit is going to get worse before it gets better. Hell, at this point, I'd be happy if Christina and I ran off to Vegas. It would be a lot less fuss and drama, plus I'd be able to get away from my job for a few days.

If only.

I hate to sound ungrateful, but I hate my job more and more each day. But what choice do I have? I need to support my new family. My mind keeps racing back to Christmas Eve when my Uncle Arturo pulled me aside and asked me to quit Cruz Automotive and go work for him. Uncle Arturo owns a popular Mexican restaurant chain in San Antonio, and he says he's expanding to catering. His only child, my cousin Marie, doesn't show any interest in working for the family. She's still set on going to law school. Arturo says he needs someone he can trust working for him. He says he can tell I'm unhappy and I'm missing my true calling.

What sucks is I know he's right. Even Christina has joked I should have been a chef instead of a mechanic. I'm so damned tired of the smell of auto grease on my hands. When it's my night to cook, and I'm immersed in the heavenly scents of garlic and cilantro, that's when I'm truly happy. Sure, I know how to fix cars. I'm good at it, but I don't enjoy it. It's something I learned to do spending summers at Tío's shops since I was a kid. I've always preferred cooking tamales and enchiladas with my aunts and Uncle Arturo to changing a fan belt.

But it's too late for wishing what could have been. I've committed myself to taking over Tío's businesses. He's the one who raised me, not my Uncle Arturo. How would Tío feel if I left Cruz Automotive? He'd be crushed. This man has done so much for me since my mother died when I was six years old. I can't turn my back on him now. Besides, Tio's businesses are a sure thing. This catering venture with Uncle Arturo could flop. Then where would that leave Christina and the baby? No, I've got to suck it up and learn to like my job, even if it kills me.

* * *

Christina

I spend the morning alternating between worrying over Andrés and painting cyclamen on my dress. These tiny pink and red flowers can be found on the perennial plants growing along the bank of the Riverwalk. I was so taken by them when Andrés and I first visited San Antonio, I knew I had to paint them on my gown. They remind me of that night we spent together, when he opened up about his past. Though it was heartbreaking learning about the death of his best friend in Afghanistan, it was a turning point in our relationship, the moment I realized I wanted to be with Andrés forever. And despite the difficulties we're facing right now, my love for him hasn't wavered. If anything, I love him more. Andrés told me he was going to call his doctor today. I hope this guy is able to help him.

After I finish painting, I take a shower and make myself a stack of pancakes. I practically scarf the whole platter. I can't believe how hungry I am, and I'm honestly thinking about making more, but I remember Andrés telling me I need to eat healthy. That's when I realize I have no idea what I should be eating. I sit in front of my laptop with what's left of my one cup of coffee and download several pregnancy books onto my e-reader.

The first book I open is huge, so I quickly scroll through the first month. Our baby looks like a little pea. I still can't believe he or she will one day grow into a human being. I skim through the advice about morning sickness. Luckily, other than a little nausea and fatigue in the mornings, I haven't thrown up since last weekend at my mom's house. I've figured out I'm okay as long as I don't eat breakfast too early. The book also says I should be taking prenatal vitamins, so I make a mental note to pick some up. Sadly, the author also advises I should limit my coffee intake to one cup per day. Damn. But there's nothing restricting my pancake limit, so I turn off my e-reader and make another batch.

Just as I finish licking my plate clean, I hear a knock on the door. I groan when I see Tia and Marie through the peephole. I remember Tia telling me she wanted to come see my dress. I wish she would have called first, so I could at least prepare for their visit, like go upstairs and hide in Grace's apartment until they left.

I slowly exhale and try to calm my frayed nerves as I unlock the door and swing it open. "Hi, Tia!" I lock eyes with her and intentionally ignore Marie standing behind her. She's not the only one who can play the bitch game.

Tia pulls me into a tight hug and pats my cheek before walking past me. I follow her gaze as she does a quick sweep of my compact kitchen. I haven't had time to clean my pancake mess, and I know it looks like a batter bomb went off all over my stovetop. Marie follows behind Tia, refusing to acknowledge me as well. I want to slap that smug expression off her face as she surveys my home. She looks at Tia with raised brows, and I can read the meaning behind her smirk. That I'm a lazy, pregnant slob.

"Sorry for the mess," I say as I brush past them and set my dish in the sink. "I just finished breakfast. If I'd known you were coming," I add with a touch of annoyance, "I would have eaten earlier."

"Christina, you're just finishing breakfast?" Tia makes a big show of checking her watch. "It's past eleven."

"I don't like eating too early." I shrug a shoulder and wipe down the stove with a dishrag. What I really mean to say is I can't eat early because of my morning sickness. I realize they know I'm pregnant, but I'm in no mood to acknowledge the elephant in the room. It will only incite more snickers from Marie. Not that I care what she thinks, anyway.

"What have you been doing all morning?" Marie asks me accusingly.

None of your fucking business, I say to myself. God, how I want to voice my thoughts aloud, if only Tia wasn't in the room. I plaster on another smile, this one so taut, I feel my face may break. "I was painting my wedding gown."

"Painting it?" Tia gasps.

"Yes," I say, puzzled by her reaction, "with little cyclamen flowers."

But Tia only stares at me with a look of horror in her wide-eyes. Marie looks away as she mumbles something in Spanish.

I lead them down the hall to the spare bedroom, which we turned into my art studio. I don't know why, but as I hear their footsteps behind me, a heaviness settles in my chest and I feel as if I'm marching to the rhythm of my own funeral.

I open the door and turn on the lights. A fan is propped up on an old dictionary in one corner of the room, blowing across the floor on full speed. The dress is laid out on the carpet, drying on top of plastic sheets.

"Aye Dios mio!" Tia shrieks.

"Red on a wedding dress?" Marie folds her arms and shakes her head. "Seems a little unorthodox."

I cock a hand on my hip and glare at her. "Good thing I'm not having an orthodox wedding."

Tia splays one hand across her heart and gapes at the dress with a slackened jaw. "How do I explain this to our priest?"

"He's not going to like it," Marie snickers.

"What priest?" I ask. Andrés and I have only gone to his family's church once, and that was for a baptism of one of his cousins. I vaguely remember meeting the priest.

Tia backs up a step, bumping into the door frame and then clutching it like a lifeline. "Don't tell me you're not having Father Navarro marry you."

"Are you even a Catholic?" Marie asks.

My gaze sweeps from Tia to Marie, and I get this sinking feeling in my gut. Why are they turning this wedding dress into a criminal interrogation? "My parents never took me to church."

Tia makes a sign of the cross and then clasps her hands in a prayer pose.

Marie waves a hand at me like she's shooing away a fly. "I don't think Father Navarro can marry her, anyway."

Tia purses her lips and regards me for a long moment. "There might be time to make you a Catholic before the wedding."

Make me a Catholic? "I'm not really into organized religion."

"This is not how I envisioned Andrés's wedding." Tia's shoulders fall as she sulks out of the room.

I follow her, the sound of Marie's laughter ringing at my heels. "My mom said she's hiring a minister. It will still be a Christian wedding."

"Yes, but it's not the same," Marie says behind me.

Tia nods toward Marie. "I'll talk to Father Navarro and see if there's anything that can be done." Then she gives me the once over, scowling at me all the way down to my toes. "I was about your size when I got married. I bet my dress will fit you."

My chest tightens. I have given up so much already. I am *not* giving up my dress. "I like my dress. Once it's finished it will be pretty."

Tia wags a finger at me, scowling. "Red flowers on a bridal gown? Do you know what that means?"

I shrug. "To me, the flowers represent love." Somehow, I don't think I'm going to like Tia's interpretation.

Tia looks at me with sorrowful eyes as if she's about to tell me I've got some incurable disease.

"It's like waving a red flag around announcing to everyone you're pregnant." Tia throws up her hands. "It means you're soiled."

I jerk back, feeling her verbal rebuke like a slap to the face. "I love those flowers."

Marie eyes me coolly. "Is there any way you can change the colors?"

I clench my hands and square my shoulders. There is no way they are interfering with my dress. No way. "It's permanent paint."

Tia waves me off with a flick of the wrist. "I'll bring my dress over tomorrow. Hopefully it will fit. And don't forget to call your mom about the caterer." She holds up her fingers and starts counting off orders. "Tell her we will handle the food. Also, we'll get the band. Better yet, give me your mom's number, and I'll call her."

I'm pretty sure my jaw hits the floor at this point. Tia didn't come over here to see my dress. She came over to assert control over my wedding. Anger boils up inside me and I swear my ears are going to start shooting steam any moment. Just as I'm about to give Tia a piece of my mind, Marie cuts me off.

"I need to use your bathroom."

I've gone numb from shock and anger, and I rigidly direct her to the bathroom in our bedroom. I think about taking her into the guest bathroom, but the sink is full of paints, and I know she'd love to make a snide comment about the mess.

I cringe when we walk inside my bedroom. Andrés's socks and underwear are balled up on the floor and the bed isn't made. I'm sure she'll report back to Tia that my bedroom is sloppy, too. Without saying a word, I point to the bathroom door next to my dresser and turn to leave.

"So when are you due?"

I slowly turn on my heel and lock gazes with Marie. I don't like the sing-song tone of her voice. Her artificial sugary sweetness is a lame attempt at masking her true feelings.

"I don't know." I shrug and examine the paint splatter stuck to my fingernails, pretending indifference, when I'd much rather wrap my hands around Marie's throat. "I don't go to the doctor until next week."

Marie turns up her chin and flashes her most dazzling smile. I'm not fooled. I eye her warily when I recognize the loathing in her eyes, the same gleam The Cobra would give one of her enemies right before she was about to strike.

She arches a brow while tossing her hair back. "How convenient that you get pregnant right before my cousin is about to inherit a fortune."

If I was angry before, it was nothing compared to the fury that infuses my skull now. "Excuse me?" I say on a hiss as I narrow my eyes at her. Marie has been dumping on me ever since Christmas Eve, and I'm about fed up with taking her shit.

Her brows dip beneath her bangs. "Cruz Automotive. My uncle's giving him five shops. Andrés will be rich." She says this as if it's supposed to be some big surprise. Yeah, I know about Andrés's inheritance, but I loved him way before I knew this, back when he was just a mechanic living in a tiny apartment.

"Are you saying *that's* why I got pregnant?" A stupid question, and I instantly regret the words as they pour from my mouth, but I'm so stunned by her rude accusation I don't know what else to say.

"Why else do girls get pregnant?" She bats her lashes and flashes a smug smile.

I clench my hands so tight, I can feel nails breaking skin. It's so hard, so very hard not to slap that fake smile off her face. "It was an accident."

She snickers and then bobbles her head around like a diva on crack. "So you're calling my baby cousin an accident?"

I'm tired of this word war with Marie. I'm so furious, my head is starting to spin, and I fight the urge to rub my aching temples. I don't need this kind of stress, especially not in my condition, but I don't dare show her how much she's upsetting me. She'll only think I'm looking for sympathy.

"You know what? You've obviously already made up your mind about me. Andrés knows I love him. That's all that matters." I turn on my heel and slam the bedroom door behind me as I march back into the kitchen.

Much to my dismay, Tia is at my sink doing dishes. I don't know what else to do but stand in the center of the kitchen, gaping at her back. My nerves are so frayed, it's starting to zap my energy. All I can think of is kicking them out of my apartment, so I can enjoy a nice soak in the tub and a nap.

"I just couldn't let these dishes sit her like this," Tia says over her shoulder.

I don't answer her as I sit down at the table and groan into my palms. How did I know she'd try to make me feel guilty about the mess?

"So how about you come to the ranch for lunch? We need to get your measurements, so we can adjust my old dress."

"I'm sorry," I say through a strained voice. "I've got plans already."

"Come by the ranch tonight then. We need to get my dress to the seamstress before it's too late."

I exhale a slow steady breath while straightening in my chair. I will not let her bully me into wearing some other dress for *my* wedding. "Tia, thank you so much for the offer, but I want to give my gown a try. I'm not even finished painting it."

Her spine stiffens and she clucks her tongue as she sets the last dish in the rack. I watch her rigid movements as she dries her hands on a towel. I know once she turns around, she'll keep trying to wear me down, and I'm so not in the mood to argue anymore.

Luckily, just as she opens her mouth to speak, there's a knock on the door. Grace! I'd nearly forgotten we were supposed to go shopping for her maid of honor dress today. I jump up so fast, I nearly topple the chair behind me.

I race to the door and swing it open. Grace is standing in the entryway, looking as polished and poised as ever. I have no idea how her wavy blonde hair and golden skin always looks so flawless, like she just stepped out of a fashion magazine.

"Hello." She smiles and turns up her pert nose. "You ready?"

I sigh as Tia comes up behind me. I can feel her breathing down my neck like a tiger ready to pounce on her prey. I open the door wide and nod toward my best friend. "Grace, you remember Andrés's aunt?" I sweep my arm toward Tia and they both smile at each other. Grace and Tia already met at the surprise graduation party Andrés threw me. Even though it was only a few weeks ago, it feels like ages. I was so happy at that party, maybe because Marie couldn't attend, or maybe because it was before the engagement and the baby news.

"So where are you two headed?" Tia asks while she eyes me suspiciously.

I look back at Grace, willing her to read the meaning behind my pleading gaze. *Please don't tell her where we're going.*

"Maid of honor dress shopping," Grace says with a little too much perkiness.

Damn. I cringe as I warily eye Tia.

She clasps her hands together and squeals. "Oh, you'll make a lovely maid of honor."

Grace beams at her. "Thanks."

Poor girl. She's totally oblivious to the fact that she's fallen into the snake pit of doom.

"Come in, dear. I was just finishing up the kitchen." Tia steps aside and motions toward the living room, as if this is her apartment. She smiles as my unsuspecting friend takes a seat on the sofa.

I sit beside Grace and nudge her knee. When Grace looks at me, I try again to warn her by making subtle overtures toward Tia as she sits across from us. Other than running out into the stairwell and pulling on the fire alarm, I don't know what else to do. I'm hoping Grace will understand my meaning and think of something to get us out of here.

Tia crosses one ankle over the other and eyes me pointedly. "Christina, did you notice Marie seems upset?"

I try to swallow the tension that clogs my throat like a lump of clay. "I noticed," I say dryly.

"You have to understand," Tia says with a dramatic sigh, "she and Andrés were very close growing up. I think she's hurt you haven't asked her to be a bridesmaid yet."

I gasp. "A bridesmaid?" She can't be fucking serious.

"Of course. She was the only girl cousin in their group. All of Andrés's other cousins are going to be groomsmen. She'll be left out if she's not in the wedding."

Grace clears her throat beside me, and I can tell by the way she fidgets in her seat that she finally understands the trap we've fallen into.

"Andrés and I discussed this." I try my hardest to keep my tone even, but I can't help the note of desperation that slips into my voice. "He's only asking Cesar to stand up with him. I was hoping for a small bridal party. Honestly, I don't want any bridesmaids other than Grace." I squeeze my best friend's hand, thankful when she scoots closer and squeezes back. " Besides, I don't think Marie wants to be in my wedding, anyway."

Tia gapes at me like I've grown a second head. "Of course she does."

As if on cue, Marie walks out of my bedroom. She smooths down her hair while fixing us all with a serene expression. She's not fooling me. I know the bitch that lurks beneath the façade.

Tia turns in her seat and angles her head toward her. "Marie, do you want to be a bridesmaid in your cousin's wedding?"

Marie shrugs, and I watch her knuckles whiten as she clutches a little black purse in front of her. "Sure."

My whole body tenses up when Marie looks over at me, a triumphant gleam in her eyes. I squeeze Grace's hand so tight, she gasps.

Tia turns back to me. "Then it's all settled. Should we follow you to the fitting or go in one car?"

Chapter Thirteen

Christina

Luckily, I'd forgotten to remove artificial flowers and other props from the back of my car, so Tia and Marie have to follow me in Tia's SUV. Tia says she's not good with her new navigation system and she tries to make us go with her. Thankfully, Grace makes up some story about getting motion sickness in big trucks. I fill Grace in on all the details as Marie and Tia follow us. By the time we get to the dress shop, Grace is seething with anger and ready to punch Marie in the face.

A physical confrontation is the last thing I need right now, so after I talk my best friend off the ledge, we get out of the car and walk through the parking lot to the bridal shop. That's when I notice Tia's truck isn't in sight.

"Oops," Grace says with mock innocence as she tosses her halo of hair over one shoulder. "I must have lost them."

But just as we're walking into the shop, my shoulders fall when I see Tia's big silver truck stopped at the light across the street. Mom and Nora have already taken over a corner in the rear of the store, leaning back in oversized chairs and drinking some bubbly concoctions while the saleslady piles sample gowns on a rack in front of them. Grace halts like she's run into a brick wall and makes a gagging sound while gaping at the dresses. I do a double take when I see the hideous array of gaudy colors, and I'm wondering if a rainbow vomited all over the dress rack.

"Christina, darling," Nora calls as she waves us over.

I trudge toward them, having to pull Grace along while she makes more gagging and choking sounds. Christmas music filters in from the speakers above, and I swear it's louder than last time. I thought Christmas was over already.

Nora doesn't bother standing up as she blows air kisses at me and Grace.

I offer a hesitant smile, but Grace pulls a face and turns her attention to her fingernails.

Nora doesn't seem to be affronted. Judging by the look in her hooded gaze, she's already three sheets to the wind.

"We've already found several fabulous dresses for your lovely bridesmaid." Nora's words slur together in a jumbled mess, as if all of them are in a race for the finish line and her tongue is tripping them along the way.

My mom eyes Nora through slitted lids. Maybe she'll see hiring her is a bad idea.

"What's in this stuff?" Mom asks as she frowns at her drink and then sets it on the little table beside her chair.

I introduce Grace to my mom and Nora, and then a bell jingles. I look over my shoulder to see Tia and Marie storming through the door. Eyebrows knitted together, they glare at Grace as they make their way toward us.

I cringe when Grace cocks a hand on her hip and locks gazes with Marie.

I can already tell this is going to be one fun wedding.

Before anyone can say anything, I decide to intervene. "Tia, you remember my mom from my graduation party?"

Tia stops glaring at Grace long enough to smile at my mom. "It's so nice to see you again, Mrs. Domingo." Her voice rises several octaves as she holds out her hand.

My mom stands, and rather than shaking Tia's hand, she opens her arms for a hug. "Call me Jenny." She pulls Tia into a hug. "Since we're going to be family," she adds with a wink as she pulls back.

The tight lines around Tia's mouth soften. "You can call me Rosa."

"Who do we have here?"

Mom smiles warmly at Marie, and it makes me want to vomit. Marie doesn't deserve a smile. What she deserves is a kick in the ass.

"My niece, Marie." Tia eyes Grace with derision. "Christina's *other* bridesmaid."

"Oh, how exciting!" Mom clasps her hands together, beaming at all of us.

"Yes, yes, very exciting," Tia says with a flick of the wrist.

I can already tell she's got another agenda, and my gut ties itself in a knot when I fear what it may be.

"So…" Tia says as she taps her chin. "Christina tells me the wedding will be in San Antonio."

"Yes." Mom sighs as her eyes glaze over dreamily. The poor woman is totally oblivious to the estrogen overload in the room, which I'm beginning to realize is toxic in large doses. "Nora has already booked the hotel. It's going to be beautiful."

I hear a small giggle, and then watch as a rack with gowns topples behind my mom, followed by another, and another. I cringe as the wedding dress dominoes continue to topple. The saleslady shrieks and rushes to the disaster. She must think Austin is having its first earthquake, but I know what force of nature could be capable of such destruction. My brothers.

Mom shrieks and spins around. "Gio, Manny, where'd you go?"

I gasp, and my mouth suddenly goes dry. "You brought my brothers?"

Mom heaves a frustrated groan as she climbs through the rubble. "The babysitter cancelled."

"I said it would be okay for her to bring them," Nora slurs, by way of drunken apology.

Mom finds them under the last toppled rack. They are giggling uncontrollably and flopping around like fish out of water as she hauls them up.

"What have you done?" Mom shrieks.

Manny, the youngest, squirms out of Mom's grasp and rushes to me. He clutches my leg, looking across at my mom with a trembling lip. "Sissy, save me!"

I reach down and haul him up on my hip. He reeks of tart cherries. His mouth is coated in a thin layer of grime and what looks like pink dye. When he wraps his arms around my neck, it feels like he's rubbing my skin with super glue.

"Ohhh, your hands are all sticky." Wincing, I set him back on the ground as I unstick his hands from my hair.

"You naughty boy! Where did you get that candy?"

Looking up, I see mom holding my oldest brother Gio at arm's length. Gio is kicking and squirming, acting like a mental patient trying to free himself of his restraints. His hands and face are covered in sticky paste, too, and I can only imagine the condition of the dresses.

"Christina, honey, I can't stay." Mom says apologetically as she wipes her hands down the sides of her pants.

"That's okay. I'll stay with her." Tia folds her arms across her chest. "I'd like to contribute *something* to this wedding."

I resist the urge to roll my eyes. I'm certain my mom is too frazzled to pay any attention to Tia's blatant sarcasm.

"Thank you, Rosa," Mom says as she pulls Manny from me and hauls the boys out the door.

I'm not sure, but I think I hear Gio say, "Miss Nora gave us the candy," but his little voice is drowned out by the sound of the bell.

I look at Nora, whose gaze is focused on the bottom of her champagne glass. Why would Nora give my hyper brothers candy? And at an expensive dress shop of all places? I had to have heard Gio wrong.

Grace is helping the salesladies as they try to stand up the racks. One of the staff cries out that a dress is covered in candy mess. They'll be sending my mom the dry cleaning bill, no doubt. A sneaky suspicion snakes up my spine as I eye Nora, who still hasn't taken her gaze from her glass. Her mouth is wrapped around the rim and she's staring down at it like a zombie in a trance.

"Those boys aren't going to be in the wedding, are they?"

Tia's sharp gaze is on me.

"They're our ring bearers."

Tia's eyebrows dip beneath her thick bangs. "Oh, because Andrés has a cousin who's slightly older and better behaved."

I shake my head. "I want my brothers."

"I know." Tia heaves an exaggerated sigh before she and Marie share a knowing glance. "I don't want them to lose the ring or ruin the wedding."

I fix each of them with a hard expression. "They're not going to ruin my wedding."

"The ring bearers don't carry the ring anymore. We put a decoy on the pillow." Nora waves a manicured hand with a flourish, flashing a lopsided grin before she holds up her empty glass. "Where's that girl with the champagne?"

The front door bell rings again, and Violet, Grace's girlfriend, walks through the door. She is dressed in her usual attire, faded denim jeans, western boots, and a flannel work shirt. She's recently cut off her spikes, and now her hair is cropped so short, she looks like she just got out of boot camp.

Violet waves hello to me before walking over to Grace and handing her a cellphone. "You forgot this in my truck."

"Did I?" Grace says as she pecks Violet on the cheek.

"Riding in trucks makes her sick, does it?" Marie grumbles behind me.

I cringe when Marie and Tia start firing off words in Spanish. They're bashing Grace, no doubt.

"I figured you'd need it." Violet lowers her voice, but her deep tenor carries far enough for me to hear. "Unless you were trying to avoid me."

"No." Grace's face flushes as she breaks eye contact with Violet. "I wasn't trying to avoid you."

Violet shrugs and turns to me. "Congratulations, Christina."

"Thanks, Violet."

I flash a weak smile, thinking how very much I don't want to be here. I can tell Grace and Violet are at odds. I just hope it isn't serious. The tension between Grace and Andrés's family is so thick it's stifling. I feel awkward while I watch Grace alternate between giving Marie and Tia icy glares and withdraw from Violet. And then there's my wedding planner, who's spread eagle in her chair while calling to the saleslady for more champagne. She's so drunk and disoriented, I have no idea how she's going to find her way home much less manage this wedding.

I join Violet as we help Grace and the salesladies put the dresses back on the rack. I hope the damage isn't irreparable. I cringe when I see a few of the white gowns marred by sticky candy. I follow a trail of pink splatter and discover an empty container of cotton candy beneath a mountain of white hoops. I quickly tuck the container underneath my jacket, thinking it best if I hide the incriminating evidence. Although I doubt it will matter. We were all witness to my brothers' trail of destruction. Who in the heck would give little kids cotton candy in a bridal shop?

It doesn't take long for us to get the store back to normal. I quickly slip outside and search out a trash can. When I can't find one, I throw the container in my car and go back to the store. My eyes bulge at Karri's familiar spiky pink hair as I see her get out of Violet's truck and wave me over.

Why did Violet bring my ex best friend here?

I pretend I don't see her, although that bright hair of hers shines like a beacon. I'm pretty sure satellites can pick it up from space.

I slip back into the store, grateful nobody threw any punches in my absence. Nora is piling Marie and Grace with dresses when she turns to me.

"Where are your other bridesmaids?" Nora asks impatiently, as if expecting my entourage of mythical best friends to arrive at any moment.

I shrug. "I don't have any other bridesmaids."

"This is it?" Nora sneers at Marie and Grace as if they've got a case of the plague. "Don't you have any other friends?"

"I wanted to keep the bridal party small." Speaking of small, I wish I was the size of my brothers, so I could disappear beneath a mountain of dresses for a while. I hate the way Nora and Tia are gaping at me, like I'm some friendless reject.

Tia clucks her tongue as she and Nora share a knowing look. "But Andrés will have all of his cousins standing up with him. You can't have an uneven number."

"How many groomsmen will he have?" Nora asks Tia, since obviously Andrés's aunt knows more about my wedding than I do.

"Four." Tia frowns at me. "But we were hoping for more."

"Can't you come up with two other bridesmaids?" Marie interjects in the same tone I use on my brothers whenever they get caught doing something naughty.

I look over my shoulder for Grace to come save me, but she and Violet are in the corner of the store, heads bowed toward each other. Grace's tone rises every so often, and I realize they must be arguing.

My shoulders fall. "No."

"Violet can do it." I gape at Grace, as she drags Violet toward us.

"Violet in a dress?" I blurt and then slap my hand over my mouth when Violet's cheeks flush a deep scarlet. I mouth "sorry" to Violet, but I don't think it helps. She casts her gaze to her scuffed boots as Grace tightens her hold on her arm.

Just then the front door chimes and I'm nearly blinded by Karri's hair.

"Hi, Christina." She smiles and waves, clearly oblivious to me rolling my eyes at her as she skips through the shop toward us, her heavy boots making a muffled thudding sound on the plush carpet. I'm surprised to see she's dressed much like Violet, in cowboy boots, worn jeans and a work shirt.

"Congratulations on your wedding," Karri says in a much too perky, and much too sober, tone. Before I can stop her, she pulls me in for a hug.

"Thanks," I say, baffled by this sudden change in my ex-BFF. I pull back and search her gaze for any signs that she's stoned out of her mind but her eyes are clear and vibrant.

Huh?

"Ahhh. We've found a fourth bridesmaid."

My heart stops beating for an eternal second when I see Nora's gaze fixed on Karri.

Karri takes a step back. "M-Me?" she stammers. "You want me to be a bridesmaid?" Despite Karri's incredulous tone, there's a wistfulness in her gaze. I don't like it one bit.

"I don't think so," I say as I square my shoulders and glare at Nora, then Karri.

"I remember you." Nora crosses over to Karri and settles her hand on her arm as if they're old friends. Then she flashes me a wide grin. "You two were practically joined at the hip when Christina was in high school."

Karri tilts up her chin. "We were besties."

"Things change," I groan as I cross my arms.

Nora's demeanor suddenly shifts, and I'm reminded of the way weather in Texas can go from sunny and calm to cloudy and stormy within the blink of an eye. "Beggars can't be choosers, Christina." Her mouth hardens as she points a finger at my chest. "You need a fourth bridesmaid."

* * *

"Are you coming out or what?" Grace is pounding on the fitting room door where Violet has barricaded herself.

I've got a wedding-induced migraine, so I'm nursing a ginger ale while I sink back in a cushy, oversized chair, wondering how the hell the day of my dreams is turning into my worst nightmare. Tia has just revealed to Marie the shocking news that she thinks Grace and Violet may be lesbians. Marie is sulking in a nearby chair. After she begrudgingly tried on the red dress we chose, Marie refuses to try on anything else, claiming the dresses Grace and I like are for *"putas."* I'm not sure what a "puta" is, and I get the feeling I don't want to know.

Grace has already changed back into her jeans and turtleneck, but she looked incredible in the shimmery red silk dress. It had a V neck, tapered waist, and just the right amount of swish when she twirled. Not to mention the fact that her long, lean legs looked absolutely stunning in it. The best part is I think this bridesmaid's dress will complement the red flowers on my gown. I can see why Marie doesn't like it. Like me, she's short, but she's got a much thicker build. When Grace twirled and the iridescent colors caught the light, she reminded me of a rose in full bloom. Marie looked more like a turnip that's been sprayed with a water hose.

Finally, the door to the dressing room creeks open, and Violet, or what was once Violet, hesitantly steps out. I jerk up and slosh ginger ale down my shirt, letting out a low whistle at the bombshell before me.

"I look stupid." Violet glares at Grace who looks as stunned as I feel.

The salesladies gave Violet a wig of straight goth-black hair with cropped bangs, hooped earrings, and someone even painted her face with mascara and cherry lipstick to match the dress. The red heels compliment Violet's mile-high legs.

She looks runway model perfect. If it wasn't for that pained, constipated look in her eyes, I'd say Violet makes a damn fine girl.

Grace's gaze travels the length of her girlfriend, and her bright eyes darken as she licks her lips. I know Grace is thinking about dressing room sex right about now.

"Babe." Grace stroke's Violet's slender arm. "You look good enough to eat."

I hear Tia whispering even louder to her niece. "I told you they're lesbians."

Violet's shoulders fall, and she hunches awkwardly while kicking the carpet with a spiked heel. "It's not me."

"But you're beautiful." Grace turns to the plump, thirty-something saleswoman, who's beaming from ear to ear as she hovers behind them. "Do you sell these wigs here?"

"We sure do," the woman says.

Violet tugs at the wig until it's sitting at an awkward angle on her head. "Can I take it off now?"

Grace gasps and swats Violet's hands while adjusting the wig. "Don't you want to look sexy for me?"

"Lesbians," Tia hisses again.

Oh, dear God!

I can only imagine Tia's panicking how to explain all of this to the family priest. First a "soiled" bride and then lesbian bridesmaids in "puta" dresses.

Violet jerks the wig off her head and storms back into the dressing room. Grace tries to stop her and nearly gets her hand caught in the door.

"I'm not wearing this damn wig," she hollers from behind the door.

"Stubborn jerk!" Grace punches the door and then storms toward me and flounces into a nearby chair. Groaning, she hangs her head in her hands.

I don't want to turn around, but I'm sure Tia and Marie are sharing disapproving glances.

Karri comes out of the adjacent dressing room. Sadly, the dress isn't doing much for her. The bright red only makes her pale complexion look more sallow and the circles around her sunken eye sockets more pronounced. And her cotton candy hair clashes with that bright apple dress in the worst way. She looks like a mutant circus snack.

I cringe when I hear Marie's raucous laughter behind me. I still can't believe I allowed Tia to bulldoze my wedding plans. That I allowed Marie to have any part at all in my wedding. The bitch should be lucky she's even invited, and now here she is making fun of my bridesmaid dresses, actually pretending she wants to be in my wedding? Now that Karri has been pulled into this, I feel like I'm about past my breaking point.

But what pisses me off the most is that I've allowed this wedding circus to continue. I didn't put my foot down from the start and demand to have *my* wedding *my* way. What the hell is wrong with me? Seven months ago, when I walked out on my domineering ex-fiancé and controlling mother, I vowed I'd never allow anyone to push me around again. Now here I am right back where I started, the wimpy pushover Christina. I don't know if it's the pregnancy hormones turning me back into the old Christina, but I don't like her one bit.

Karri flashes me a hesitant smile. "Isn't it pretty?" She says as she bunches the fabric in her hands and spins around. "I feel like we're back in high school, and we're prom dress shopping."

Those days are long gone, I want to tell her, but I don't. Something about Karri's half smile looks so pathetic, I actually feel more pity than anger toward the girl who screwed my ex-fiancé and then ran out on her family.

Kari spins another slow circle and her face falls as she stops to stare at herself in the mirror. I'm thinking maybe she doesn't like the reflection of a washed up druggie staring back at her, but she reaches across her body and settles it on one pale shoulder. The shoulder with Tyler's name scrawled inside a heart tattoo.

I remember the day she got it. It was our first night clubbing after she'd had Tyler. We hadn't stayed out late, mostly because I insisted she needed to get a good night's sleep, so she would be alert for her baby the next day, but she'd insisted on stopping off in that tattoo shop. I remember how angry I was she'd spent a hundred bucks on a tattoo when she was always complaining about the cost of diapers. But anger turned to empathy when she emerged from the artist's chair with a tattoo dedicated to her baby boy.

Nora, whom I'm pretty sure had been napping just moments earlier, sets down her empty champagne glass and rises from the sofa on wobbly legs. She walks up to Karri and slowly circles her, looking sideways at her like she's an errant dog who's been caught humping the pillow cushions. "You'll have to tone down your hair."

Karris' eyes bulge as her hands fly to her scalp. "My hair?"

Nora's collagen enhanced lips twist into a puffy scowl. "It's too pink. It will detract from the bride." She waves at me with an impatient flick of the wrist. "This is *her* day, not yours."

Really, Nora? Because it seems more like everyone else's day.

Karri's bottom lip turns into a pout. "But it matches the dress."

I fight to keep from laughing out loud. Karri's never had great fashion sense, and I've always suspected she was color blind, too.

Karri looks at me with eyes as big as a little lost lamb's. "What do you think I should do, Christina?"

Her question catches me off guard, maybe because it's the first time anyone other than Grace actually cares what I want.

"What do I think?" I ask as I clench my hands and slowly rise. "Does anyone care what I think?" I do a visual sweep of the room, disheartened by the blank stares. Grace pops her head up and rises to stand beside me. Just as I thought. Other than Grace, nobody else cares.

"Of course we care, darling," Nora slurs as she sweeps her arm with drunken flourish toward everyone.

Tia swears something in Spanish and Marie snickers. Karri drops her gaze to the floor and then sulks away. A distinct ripping sound comes from Violet's dressing room.

I cock my hand on my hip and glare at Tia and Marie. "What I think is I need a drink. A big, strong one."

Tia gasps and shakes her head.

This time I don't repress the urge to hold back my feelings. I roll my eyes so hard, I imagine the whites are scraping the ceiling. "But I can't drink because I'm pregnant, so I'll have to settle for some chocolate." I grab my purse off the chair and turn to Grace. "Are you ready to go to lunch? I'm hungry."

"Yes, please." Grace doesn't bother saying good-bye to Violet as she grabs my hand and we head out the door.

"Where are you going?" Tia calls behind us, but neither of us look back as we jump into Grace's car and peel out of the lot.

* * *

Grace and I are sitting across from each other in a cozy booth at a posh little café. Country Christmas music filters in from speakers all around the café. I actually don't mind it so much. George Straight's Christmas Cookies song is one of my favorites. It brings back a fond memory of Karri's mom baking sugar cookies with us when we were kids.

I like how they've decorated the place with pinecone wreaths and mistletoe hanging from the ceiling. We've already gotten our drinks, and I'm anxiously awaiting my order. Grace has promised me "The World's Best Brownie." I so wanted a double latte with an extra heaping of whipped cream and shaved chocolate, but I've opted for an organic green tea with stevia instead. Andrés would be proud of me…well, except for the brownie part.

Marie has already texted me three times asking if I'm coming back to the bridal shop. I have no idea how Marie got my number. I'm assuming Tia gave it to her. I don't need the added stress right now, so I choose to power down my phone rather than answer her.

"I don't want Karri and Marie as my bridesmaids, and no offense, but Violet really doesn't look happy in a dress." I take a sip of my tea, and try to swallow it without tasting. I've never gotten used to the odd flavor, and I suspect the tea gets its green coloring from runny diaper doo. I swear this stuff leaves a pungent aftertaste that's almost as bad as kissing Jackson.

Grace pulls a face, looking as if she's just swallowed a lemon wedge in her organic green tea. No, wait, maybe it's the tea. "I guess it's not her thing," she says with an exasperated breath.

Now I feel bad. I play with the string on my stinky tea bag and slump in my seat as I think about how this whole wedding is going down the toilet. Most of my bridal party is made up of people I don't want (or else people who don't want) to be in my wedding.

"Then don't make her wear it."

I think back to Violet as she came out in that dress and wig. Other than that twisted scowl, she makes a hot chick. Too bad she doesn't want to be in my wedding. Then again, maybe I don't want two lanky beauties outshining me on my special day. It's bad enough I'll probably be bloated and "soiled."

"I was trying to help you. I want you to have enough bridesmaids." Grace flashes a woeful smile, the kind of smile I'd give to a three-legged dog or a homeless baby. Okay, maybe I went a little overboard with the homeless baby part, but the smile oozed pity, and the fact that my wedding is turning into a charity case is over-the-top humiliating.

"I did have enough." I square my shoulders and turn up my chin. "I had you. I don't want anyone to do anything they don't want to do. I want my wedding to be happy and fun." Images of Violet ripping off her wig and Marie's smug smile flash through my mind. I pound the table with my fist. "I want red flowers on my dress. I want fucking tamales!" I cringe when I hear a gasp at the booth behind us, and I drop my voice to a strained whisper. "I don't want this wedding. Not like this."

Grace's blue eyes turn as dark as a stormy sea. "Do you want me to tell them to back off?"

"No." I groan as I push aside my tea cup. "That will piss them off even more."

"What are you going to do?"

"I don't know." I feign a smile. "Eat chocolate." I really wish the waiter would hurry up with my brownie. Maybe if I get enough chocolate in my system, I'll forget all of my troubles in a sugar induced haze.

Grace frowns. "You look terrible. Aren't you sleeping?"

"Just feeling a little under the weather," I mumble. I reach for my stinky tea and stare into the steamy green liquid. Truthfully, it's hard to sleep in that big bed alone, especially when I'm forced to endure listening to my fiancé's night terrors in the other room.

"You're rushing this wedding."

I jerk my head up to see my best friend eyeing me pointedly.

"It's a little too late for the lecture." Smirking, I pat my stomach.

Grace responds with a patronizing scowl.

I'm tired of pretending I'm drinking liquid vomit, so I set my tea down for good, grimacing as it sloshes all over my hand. "What about you and Violet?" I ask with a note of accusation in my voice. After all, she's got no room to criticize Andrés and me for getting married so soon when she and Violet started talking about marriage months ago. "You two have been dating as long as Andrés and I have."

Now it's Grace's turn to avert her gaze. Uh, oh. I was hoping their little argument in the bridal shop was no big deal.

When her eyes gloss over, I clasp her hands in mine. "What's wrong?"

"I think we rushed things." She sniffles. Oh, crap. Grace is one of the strongest women I've ever known. Other than the time her parents disowned her after she came out, I don't think I've ever seen her cry.

"You two used to seem so happy together."

Grace grabs a cloth napkin off the table and dabs her eyes. "The honeymoon's over. Now she's taking in all these troubled teens."

"But that should be perfect for you. Isn't that why you're studying to be a therapist?"

Grace dabs her eyes again and then blows her nose.

I jerk back at the sound that comes from her nose, a cross between a dying whale and a fog horn. Wow. That's something I've never, ever seen her do. Grace had been raised to be a prim and proper southern belle.

"Yeah," she says as she daintily folds the napkin and sets it to the side, "but Violet doesn't want my input on how to deal with them. It's like my opinion doesn't matter."

I look at the busboy cleaning a nearby booth, and I think about warning him to use rubber gloves for our table, but Grace needs me at the moment, so calling out the Hazmat team will have to wait. "Andrés and I went through that, remember? I didn't listen at all to him."

Grace sinks into the booth and rubs her temple. "You guys worked through that, but I don't know if this is fixable. And it's not just that. She's always so busy, we hardly do anything together anymore, unless it involves the ranch."

I think back to last night, and every other night these past few weeks, when Andrés has had to work late. I have been telling myself things will get better when he learns the ropes, but Andrés has been working there for almost a year. What if these long shifts are permanent? But I push those dark thoughts aside. Andrés will make time for us. He has to.

"What are you going to do?" I ask, when in reality, I know I'm asking myself the same question.

"I'm going to give it a little more time and try to see if she can understand my side, but we're definitely not getting married anytime soon." The hopeless look in Grace's eyes is enough to break my heart.

"I don't blame you," I barely rasp, choked up all of a sudden. I decide to blame it on the tea, and not the bad feeling I get about this wedding. I burp up the rancid taste of old stevia and pungent tea. Ew. Guess that's my karma.

I want to curl up into a fetal ball and roll away from this whole conversation when Grace looks at me again with that pitiful smile. "It was only a few weeks ago that Andrés walked out on you. Are you sure you're ready to get married so soon?"

I don't want to answer her question, so I look away, and then damn, I'm burping up tea again. I should have had the latte. Despite the café's noisy chatter and clatter of forks scraping plates, I feel like I'm trapped inside a glass bubble with Grace, and she won't let me out until I tell her the truth, but I'm not even ready to face the truth myself. Everything about this wedding feels wrong, and the bubble around me is closing in, cramping my space and making it hard to breathe. I'm forced to ask myself why I'm doing this. And I don't just mean the shrimp puffs and annoying bridesmaids. Why am I marrying a man who is clearly overworked and overstressed?

Because you love him, Christina, a voice inside me echoes. And it's true, I do love him more than life, but I still can't help but wonder if we're making a mistake.

Grace slaps a white envelope in front of me, startling me.

She flashes a crooked smile. "I'm sorry. We came to this lunch to celebrate right?"

"What's this?" I say as I pick up the envelope and dump the contents on the table.

"An early wedding present," she says with a wink.

I gasp when I recognize the airline printout. "Tickets to Vegas? Grace, these must have cost a fortune. I can't accept these."

"Too late." She arches back against her seat, tossing her blonde hair over her shoulder. "They're non-refundable. Besides, Violet helped me pay for them."

I'm completely stunned. Vegas. Wow. I've always wanted to go. That was my original dream for my twenty-first birthday. I'd hinted to Jackson more than once, but he said he didn't like to gamble, as if my twenty-first birthday was supposed to be about him.

"So is this for our honeymoon?"

Grace laughs out loud. "Would you listen to yourself? These tickets are for whenever you want. I'm not the one to tell you where to honeymoon."

I shrug half-heartedly. "Everyone's making all the wedding decisions for me, I guess I fell into habit. I've always wanted to go to Vegas, though." I clutch the tickets to my chest and smile. "Thank you. A Vegas honeymoon would be perfect."

"You're welcome. And if the wedding prep gets too out of hand, you can always screw it all and get hitched in Vegas." She tosses up both hands in the air, like she's on a roller coaster at Six Flags.

Oh, right. If only. "Our families would freak."

Grace grasps the edge of the table with her perfectly polished nails and leans forward. "Who cares what they think? Besides, you have your maid-of-honor's blessing. My opinion is the only one that counts." She laughs again, more like the unaffected Grace I know.

Wow. Just the thought of running off to Vegas with Andrés and screwing this whole wedding planning thing makes me giddy inside. The idea is too tempting, but I think again of the horror in my mom's and Tia's eyes when we get back from Vegas and announce we're already married, and that swelling inside my chest quickly deflates.

Luckily, I don't have time to dwell on my disappointment, as the waiter finally shows up with my brownie.

"Omigod," I squeal like an eighth grader who's been asked out by the hottest boy in school. "Have you ever seen a brownie like this?" Grace had warned me it was big, but this thing is monster enough for three people to share, which is exactly why I'm glad I ordered my own. Now I have something to snack on when I get a chocolate craving in the middle of the night.

I immediately stab it with a fork, but quickly realize I'll need a knife to cut through all those layers of fudge sauce and gooey dough.

Grace works faster than me, cutting through her brownie like a logger with a chainsaw. She moans as she takes the first bite. "It's perfection."

"Do me a favor and don't tell Andrés about the brownie," I say with a wink. I finally saw off a chunk and twirl fudge sauce around my fork before sinking my teeth into chocolate bliss. "Mmmm," I groan and don't have the mental facility for much else. All rational thought has completely shut down, and I focus all my brain cells on savoring the rich, chocolaty flavors that explode in my mouth. If I could get an orgasm from food, this would be the brownie to do it.

In fact this brownie is so damn delicious, its euphoric flavors are almost enough to make me forget about my problems.

Almost.

Chapter Fourteen

Christina

Grace and I spend the rest of the day bridal shopping. We hit at least ten different shoe stores and I can't find the right pair. I'm probably making this harder than it needs to be. All I need is a pair of white heels, right? I know it sounds crazy, but none of the shoes I try on speak to me, and after a while they all look like the exact same shoe, white satin heels with buckles, and sometimes pearly flowers.

Big whoop.

I'm not interested in the same old bridal shoe. I want something different. That bold voice inside me tells me I should be daring and go for something either red or pink to match the hues of the flowers on my dress, but then that wimpy Christina whom I thought I'd gotten rid of last year rears her timid head and warns me Tia would have a heart attack if I walked down the aisle in red shoes.

We finally give up shoe shopping and go to Hobby Lobby instead. I'm ecstatic when I find flowers that look almost like the Cyclamen on my gown. I've been thinking I want to design my own bouquet. That way I can keep it forever, and now I have the perfect flowers. I also spot these adorable little gossamer butterflies I'm going to sew onto the bottom of the gown once I finish painting in the flowers.

It's late evening when we finally drag our weary butts home. Tonight is my night to cook, which means I've got pizza takeout in Grace's backseat. I ask Grace if she wants to come inside, but she's going to Violet's ranch to patch up things.

Andrés is sitting at the kitchen table, tapping away at his laptop when I stumble through the door, steaming pizza in one hand and a big bag of crafts in the other.

As soon as he sees me, he jumps up and takes the box. "Where have you been?"

I jerk back, stunned by the harshness of his tone.

"I was with Grace," I say, shocked by the way he slams the pizza box down.

He leans against the kitchen counter, folds his arms across his chest, and glares at me like I'm one of his wayward mechanics. "I've been trying to get ahold of you for the past three hours."

"Oh." I shrug as I walk past him toward the bedroom. "I turned my ringer off," I say this in the same indifferent tone I would use to choose between pepperoni or mushrooms. I've had a rough day dealing with his family's shit, and I'm not going to deal with his anger, too.

Andrés's footsteps echo behind me, and I can practically feel him breathing fire down my neck. "What if I had an emergency?"

"Did you?" I heave my weary limbs onto the bed and start removing my heeled boots, not bothering to make eye contact

"That's not the point. Tia called me freaking out." His voice rises an octave with each word. "She said you took off today upset."

"Yeah." I laugh under my breath. "Major understatement." Why am I not surprised Tia would try to drag Andrés into this? As if he doesn't have enough stress to deal with right now. I slip off my socks and wiggle my toes as pain lances up the soles of my feet all the way to my ankles.

"What the hell is going on?" Our bedroom isn't big to begin with, and Mr. Angry Ogre's booming voice shakes the cramped space around me.

I resist the urge to cover both ears with my hands. "Don't raise your voice at me," I say through clenched teeth.

Again, I remind myself he's been under a lot of stress lately. I rotate my ankles to alleviate the soreness. That's when I notice they look bigger than normal. I'm only a few weeks pregnant and my ankles are already swollen? Crap! What are they going to look like when I'm nine months? I have this sudden horrifying vision of me wobbling around with swollen kankles that resemble monster truck tires. So not good.

"You could have at least called to tell me you were okay."

Ugh. He's not giving up, is he?

Tara West

"You never answer my calls when you're at work," I say dryly. I want to add something about how he's quick to answer Tia's calls, but I don't want to piss off the ogre even more.

"You could have sent a text."

"You never answer those, either."

Andrés steps into my personal space, hovering so far over me, he looks ready to topple at any moment. "I was fucking worried!"

Oh, no, he didn't just swear at me. Sore feet and swollen ankles be damned, I pull myself up and stand on the bed. Now I'm the one towering over him.

That throbbing temple above my eye swells like a raging river. I jab my finger in his chest. "And I was fucking fed up!"

Andrés's jaw drops and he takes a step back, holding out his palms in a defensive gesture. "Christina, don't get your blood pressure up. It's not good for the baby."

Really, Andrés? It's a little late to think about my blood pressure now. "Then don't upset me!"

Andrés's face falls faster than a pile of dominoes. Something about that wounded look in his eyes tugs at my heartstrings. He runs his hands over his cheeks, before flashing a sad smile. Now those heartstrings are about to snap, and I feel like a total bitch for hurting him.

"I'm sorry, mija." The rawness in his voice makes it sound like his chest has been split open. "I've had a stressful day at work and then this."

I slump back onto the bed and groan at the heavy discomfort in my feet. "You always have a stressful day at work." I lie down, thinking the pain will lessen if I elevate my feet.

"You don't know what it's like running five businesses at once." When Andrés looks down at me, his big, sad eyes remind me of a frightened child who's lost his mother.

My heart quickens, pounding out a painful staccato in my ears. I hate this. I hate knowing Andrés is dealing with stress all day and then coming home to more stress, and I fear the days ahead may not be any better. I don't even want to think about what we have to look forward to each night.

"Then quit." I drape my arm over my eyes, not just because I'm exhausted, but because I don't think I can stand to see his reaction.

I realize the significance of what I asked him to do; walk away from a thriving business and a good income. But Andrés is clearly not happy, and I don't see how we can go on with him coming home in a bad mood every day. Is this the life we have to look forward to? Because right now I'm thinking it's hardly a life at all.

"What?" he rasps, his voice barely audible above the din of my pounding heart.

"Tell your uncle you don't want to do it." I try to keep my tone even, which is in complete contrast to the quickening of the blood pumping through my veins.

"I can't do that. Who's going to provide for you and the baby?"

I sit up, resting on my elbows as I stare pointedly at him. Andrés is still standing by the bed, and though he's tall with a solid build, he appears to be shrinking. It's then that it hits me, just how much this job is stressing him. This is not the same strong, confident man I met last summer. This man, whom I once thought of as a tower of strength, is crumbling piece by piece, and now the pressure of the baby has to be making his stress worse.

My throat tightens at the realization. "There are other jobs."

"None that pay this well. We can have a big down payment for a house in a few more months. Don't you want our child to have a yard to play in?"

Again, it's all about the baby. Though I've had my suspicions before, I can no longer deny this baby is the underlying cause of Andrés's stress. He's letting this job break him down all because we got pregnant.

"I like our apartment." I try to sound hopeful, but my voice comes out flat. My gaze circles our small bedroom. Our home is barely big enough for the two of us. Where will we put a baby? The spare bedroom is my art studio, which means I'll either need to give up my passion or we'd need to get a bigger place. A bigger place means more money, more money means more work, and more work means more stress.

"So you don't want our child to have nice things?"

My heart stops beating for an eternal second as I look up into Andrés's accusing glare. How many more people are going to make me feel like shit before I crack? I'm so damn sick of being a passenger on the guilt trip express. When is this ride going to end, or will it be stuck in fourth gear for the rest of my life?

That throbbing in my temple returns with a vengeance, and I'm starting to feel nauseous. The swelling in my ankles is not going down. All I can think of is *Why me?*

Because of the baby, that nagging voice inside my head answers.

Panic seizes me and my limbs turn heavy as if my veins are filing up with concrete.

I jerk up and pound my fists on the bed. "I don't even want this child!"

Andrés crumbles before my eyes, like a cliff face caught in a landslide. He falls to his knees beside the bed, his eyes watering with unshed tears. He picks up my hand, squeezing it to his chest. "Do you mean that, mija?"

The pain in his eyes is harder to bear than staring into the blinding sun. I look away, feeling a familiar wave of shame wash over me. "Everything was fine until I got pregnant." I look down at my fingers as I twist them in my lap. "Now you're having nightmares, and we have to get married."

"You don't want to marry me?"

"I do but not like this. Everything is being rushed and forced."

"Would you rather wait?"

The sorrow that weighs down my chest is so heavy, I fear I may suffocate. "Yes, but the baby."

Andrés settles his hand on my belly. "Our baby, mija." He speaks with such tenderness, I feel as if my heart may burst into a million pieces. He's cherishing our unborn child, and I'm resenting it. I don't deserve Andrés, and I definitely don't deserve to be a mother.

I sniffle. "I know," I barely manage to say as my throat constricts. I lay back and close my eyes, even as tears slip out from beneath my lashes.

I sigh as Andrés tenderly strokes my cheek. He rubs my belly with the other hand, as if he's soothing our unborn child. The pain from my guilt is so severe now, I imagine it cutting a hole through my chest. I deserve it for admitting I don't want this child.

What's worse is that I'm not so sure I didn't mean it. Though Andrés is five years older than me, I still feel so young, like a baby myself. Now I'm going to be a mother, and the father is always working. Though he says he'll help me, I fear he'll be too busy. I don't know if I can do this alone. And what about my new job? Will I have time to get our design business off the ground? I also fear Tia will be visiting all the time. If she's this pushy about our wedding, I can imagine how she'll be when the baby comes. She'll be telling me how to raise my child, intruding on my life and my sanity.

"What did you mean when you said things are being forced?" My eyes fly open. Andrés's hands have stilled, and his dark brows are drawn together.

Because you're pregnant, Christina, a voice inside me echoes. *Shut up!* I tell the voice. I was going to marry him, anyway, but not like this. We were going to take our time and plan the wedding we wanted, not the one that's being forced on us. My mom has forced Nora and shrimp puffs. Tia has forced Marie plus more bridesmaids, and now she's trying to make me change my dress.

Andrés stares at me expectantly, waiting for an answer. My mom is my problem. I'm too ashamed to bring up the baby again, but he should know about his aunt. If anyone can get her off my back, he can.

I sit up and straighten my shoulders. "Tia says I can't paint flowers on my gown. It makes me look *soiled*," I emphasize the "soiled" part with as much venom as I can muster. "She's forcing me to have four bridesmaids. Marie doesn't even like me. Why would she want to be in our wedding? And now Karri...."

"Druggie Karri?" he interrupts.

I let out a slow and shaky breath. "Yeah, only I don't think she was on drugs today."

Andrés's shoulders stiffen. "I don't care. She is not going to be in our wedding. I'll talk to Tia tomorrow, mija, okay?"

Relief floods through me as I nod.

Andrés strokes my cheek again as the clouds in his eyes disperse. "So one bridesmaid and flowers on your gown, right?"

"Yes."

Andrés clasps my hands, and his thumb comes to rest on my ring finger. He strokes that diamond and emerald band with tenderness.

"So if I change it back, will you want to marry me?" The veins in his neck strain as he clenches his jaw. His voice drops to a shaky whisper. "Will you want to have our baby?"

The longing reflecting in his gaze is more than I can bear. I throw my arms around him and sob against his chest. "I'm sorry, Andrés. I'm just feeling overwhelmed."

He sits beside me and pulls me into his lap. "Shhh, mija," his says in a heated breath against my ear. "It's going to be okay."

But the more he tries to soothe me, the more the tears fall, and I'm not sure how I can stop up this dam of sorrow. I want to believe him, so very badly, but none of us acknowledge the words I left unspoken. *Do I want to marry him?* Deep in my heart I know I do, although I was hoping we could wait until this spring or even next year. But we can't. All because I'm pregnant, and though I loathe myself for feeling this way, I can no longer deny the surge of bitterness that has created a chasm in my heart. I do not want this baby.

* * *

After I cry my heart out for what feels like an eternity, Andrés fixes me a steaming bubble bath. He later dresses me in an oversized T-shirt, and we eat pizza on the sofa in unnerving silence. I can tell Andrés has a lot on his mind, and I'm afraid I may have said too much.

Does he resent me now for admitting I don't want his child?

Instinctively, I lift my T-shirt and settle my hand over my abdomen. The muscles there are still taut from all the sit-ups I do with Andrés almost every morning. I find it hard to believe a child is growing in there. I rub my fingers across the smooth surface, wondering what the baby is doing. Is it digesting the food I ate today? Maybe sleeping? Does it have a heartbeat yet? Can it feel me touching my stomach?

This whole pregnancy thing seems so surreal. Other than a little bit of morning sickness and swollen ankles (which have thankfully returned to normal size), there's not much evidence I'm growing a person. Hard to believe something so small is uprooting our lives in such a big way.

Andrés clears his throat, and I look up to see him staring intently at me. He sets our plates on the coffee table and scoots closer. He settles his hand over my abdomen, too. I'm surprised at how warm it is. Even though I took a hot bath, I'm chilled. I shiver and lean closer to him as he wraps his arm around me, his other hand still cradling my abdomen. I sigh into him, nuzzling his neck. He plants a feather-soft kiss on my forehead, and then another, and another. He kisses my brow, my eyes, the bridge of my nose. I gasp as his hand drifts down my abdomen and dips beneath the elastic of my panties.

I arch my head back, and Andrés kisses my neck as he lowers us onto the sofa. He deftly slides off my panties and cups my pelvis in his hand, dipping his finger into me and circling my clit with moisture. I groan as a wave of pleasure washes over me. I pull him down for a kiss. He tastes like tomatoes and beer, and something more. He tastes like mine. All mine. This man who is kissing me, fingering me, is my fiancé, my future, and I love him with all my heart. Renewed hope surges through me, and I think that as long as Andrés loves me, we will find a way to work it out. We must.

The tempo of Andrés's finger matches the urgency welling inside me. I love him. We *must* find a way to work it out. I can't live without him. "Please, baby," I cry against his mouth. "Please love me."

"I do love you, mija." He groans as he grinds his finger deeper into me. "Forever."

"Make love to me," I beg. "Please."

I cry out as he pulls his finger out. He jerks off his pants and throws them to the floor before he settles between my legs. He pulls my shirt over my head and I arch, wrapping my ankles around his waist, needing him inside me. Wholly. Fully. Mine.

I gasp at the intensity in Andrés's gaze, so dark and thunderous, he looks almost dangerous. His mouth is on mine, crushing me to him. He slips his hand beneath my ass, lifting me as he thrusts deep into me, so far that our hips are locked. He grinds his shaft against me, over and over, in slow, undulating circles.

I lift my legs higher and open them wider, until I feel him gyrating even deeper inside me.

His tongue spears into my mouth, possessing every part of me. Andrés groans as his tempo increases. The length of his engorged cock thrums inside me, as my channel hums with slick desire. My nerve endings are pulsing with need as desire nears its peak. He cries into my mouth, squeezing my ass beneath his bruising grip as his head explodes inside me. His orgasm pushes me over the edge, triggering my own climax. Spirals of ecstasy ripple through me, and I dig my fingers into his back, clinging to him as he stills deep inside me, bathing me with his seed. I pant into his mouth as more pulses of pleasure burst from that point deep inside me.

Andrés feathers kisses across my neck and collar bone. He suckles one nipple, then the other before he rolls off me. I already miss his heat when he disappears into our bedroom and returns with a bath towel.

I lick my lips as I stare at his large shaft. Andrés surprises me by shaking his head, snickering. He lifts me up and settles the towel between my legs. "You need your rest," he breathes into my ear.

"I need you, Andrés," I say as I nuzzle his neck, but my words have fallen on deaf ears. His burning skin cools beneath my touch.

He carries me to bed, lies down beside me, and wraps an arm around my waist. I sigh as I sink against him. Though I want to make love again, Andrés is right. I am tired. My eyelids are heavy,

and as his strong hands massage my neck and shoulders, my eyelids get heavier still. The next thing I know, I'm lying on my back and he's kissing my forehead, my cheek, and finally my lips.

"Goodnight, mija," he says before his weight lifts from the bed. He disappears into the living room without a backward glance. My drunken stupor of lust starts to wear off as reality sets in, and my heart, which was full of peace and love just moments ago, feels empty and cold.

Chapter Fifteen

Andrés

I love the smell of cilantro.

After a long, stressful day at work, and then dealing with my aunt, I need a release, and being surrounded by my new pots and pans full of steaming food is just the way to do it. I chop up spices, garlic, and onion, and add them to the butter before checking the rice. I look at my phone one more time. It's nearly seven-thirty. I'd wanted to start dinner earlier, but, as usual, I had to work late, and the phone call with Tia put me back even more.

I don't want to think about the shit storm I've created. Tia's heart is in the right place, but sometimes she can be too pushy. I know she loves us. I know she means well. I tried to explain Christina's side, but I only offended her more. Now Tia's saying she won't come to the wedding. There are times like tonight when I just want to book a flight to Vegas. We can get hitched there, hit a few buffets and spend the rest of the time in bed. Sounds like the perfect wedding to me. Fuck having something big and complicated. All that matters is that Christina will be mine.

Christina sent me a text she will be home soon, empty handed after shopping for wedding shoes. I'm not sure what it takes to find the perfect wedding shoe, but I guess it's a difficult process. I'm hoping she'll come hungry. Our baby needs proper nourishment, and chicken grilled in a creamy cilantro pesto sauce and topped with portabella mushrooms should do the trick. I've also made a hot spinach salad and warmed the tortillas my uncle Arturo dropped off today.

I shake my head when I think about my meeting with Arturo. He's still pestering me to work for his new catering business. He even promised to give me creative license. Arturo remembers how much I've always loved to cook. How I'd spend hours with him and Tia making tamales and buttery tortillas. I made the mistake of giving him a sample of my pesto sauce last month. Now he doesn't want to let this catering thing go.

What's killing me is I know I'd be good at it. I know I'd enjoy working for his restaurant more than the job I'm doing. Hell, any job would be better than the one I've got. But Tio's turning over all five shops to me next month, and I'll be making a mid-six figure income, something Arturo can't promise me. I've got a family to consider now, and I want to provide for them. Heck, even if I wasn't going to be a family man, I don't think I could walk out on Tio.

* * *

Christina

After another unsuccessful day of wedding shoe shopping, I'm relieved to come home to the smell of home-cooked Mexican food. Andrés kisses me on the cheek and gets back to making dinner, and I slip into the bedroom and take off my shoes, groaning at the pain in my swollen ankles. What the heck? I'd worn comfortable flats today. My ankles should not be this big, but after several hours of walking through the mall, my poor feet look like stuffed sausages.

I hobble to the kitchen, sink into a chair, and lay my head on the table.

"Rough day, mija?"

I prop my chin on my palm and eye the big bowl of guacamole dip in front of me. "Can I just walk down the aisle barefoot?"

"I don't care what you wear as long as you marry me." Andrés laughs and then fluffs what appears to be Spanish rice. He's using the new pots and pans I bought him, which makes me feel all giddy inside. Whatever the reason for his initial reaction to his presents, at least he's using them.

"I wish your aunt was as easy to please as you are." I search the table, disappointed to find there's only carrot and celery sticks to go with the guacamole. Bleh. If I wasn't so damned tired, I'd search the cabinet for corn chips. "Did you talk to her?"

I cringe, not knowing if I want to hear his response. His heavy sigh as he covers the pots isn't reassuring. I jerk back when I hear a loud grumbling noise coming from my midsection. I settle my hand over my stomach. My gut feels like a hollow drum, ready to implode at any minute. I guess that soup and club sandwich followed by the fudge brownie I ate today (yes, I went back for another World's Best Brownie) wasn't filling enough. I scoop out a big chunk of guacamole with my finger and lick it off. Luckily, Andrés still has his back to me.

"Yeah, that didn't go over so well." Andrés turns off the burners, grabs a half-empty beer off the counter and sits across from me. I don't want to say anything, but he seems to be drinking a few beers every night now. When we'd first started dating, he was just a casual drinker. Not that I'm bothered by a few beers each night, but I know a few can turn to several as the years progress. It's exactly what happened to my former parents.

"What did she say?" I ask, knowing now isn't the time to start nagging him about the drinking, but I know I need to address it soon.

Andrés levels me with a glum expression. "She's not coming to the wedding."

I gape at him for a long moment. "Omigod. Really? Over a dress?" I can't believe Tia would do this to us, to Andrés. She has to know this would crush him.

Andrés shrugs, his mouth tilted half-way in an apologetic grin. "She thinks you are shutting her out."

"This is ridiculous." My words are punctuated by a loud grumble from my tummy.

Andrés lays his hand across mine and squeezes. "Don't worry, she'll come around."

The grumbling gets louder. Apparently my stomach isn't convinced. Andrés eyes my gut with a smirk, pushes away from the table, and walks back to the stove.

"And if she doesn't?" I ask. "We can't have a wedding without your tia."

"I'll see if Tio can talk some sense into her." His back is to me, so his expression is unreadable, but I don't like the way his words lack conviction, almost like he doubts Tio will be able to sway her.

I slouch in my seat. "I feel bad, Andrés."

"Don't. This isn't your fault." His dark eyes sparkle with mischief as he sets two steaming plates of food on the table. "I still say it would be easier if we just ran off to Vegas."

"Then my mom would be mad at us, too." I pick up my fork and shove rice and vegetables around on my plate. I'm not in the mood to eat anymore. Too bad my growling stomach isn't on the same wavelength.

"This is *our* wedding, mija. *Our* future."

Tears well in my eyes as I look at my fiancé. I'm humbled and wracked with guilt at the sincerity in his gaze. "I wish it was as simple as that."

A shadow falls across his face before he takes another long drink of beer. "Me, too."

Chapter Sixteen

Christina

Two-thousand-five-hundred freaking dollars. That is how much my mom has to pay to dry clean all those wedding dresses. Shit! I feel so bad about all of this, but my mom writes the check without even batting an eye.

I glare at the bridal shop clerk as she smiles serenely while taking Mom's check. She doesn't present my mom with an official dry-cleaning bill, and my mom doesn't ask for one. Anger infuses my cheeks and warms my chest. And the old-fashioned Christmas music that filters from overhead does little to lighten my mood. It's not even Christmas anymore.

"I still can't believe you have to pay this," I grumble, standing beside her at the counter. "Considering it was Nora who gave them the cotton candy."

Mom waves me off. "Nora wouldn't have given your brothers candy in a dress shop."

But I'm not buying it. I've known Nora a long time, and I know beneath the sweet, tipsy façade, is the shriveled up heart of a calloused bitch, just like The Cobra. And even though she swears she's not my ex-mother's best friend any longer, I am seriously having doubts. What if my snake adoptive mother put Nora up to giving my brothers cotton candy? What if this is just the beginning of Nora's underhanded pranks?

"Then *who* gave it to them?" I ask.

"They probably found it," Mom mumbles as she slips her checkbook back into her purse.

"Who leaves a cotton candy container lying around?"

Mom doesn't look at me as she fiddles with the zipper on her purse, and I wonder if maybe she's starting to have doubts, too.

"Ma'am, I'm not supposed to say anything, but I think there's something you should know."

I narrow my eyes at the demure middle-aged woman behind the counter. She looks ready to disappear behind her black-rimmed glasses as she makes a quick sweep of the room.

"What?" my mom and I ask in unison.

She scans the room one more time and then leans forward. "Nora Richards dropped the ball on two weddings this month."

My jaw practically hits the counter, and my stomach sours—as if it needs any more incentive to rebel after this morning's turkey bacon and low fat granola. "What do you mean?"

"I mean the entire bridal party and guests show up to the wedding and there's nothing." Her eyes bug out, magnified by her thick lenses. "No caterer, no cake, and nobody booked the hall."

My mom clutches the leather straps on her purse until her knuckles whiten. "Why would she do that?"

The clerk's lips purse as she pushes the rim of her glasses up her nose. "Rumor has it her husband is getting the planning business in the divorce and she's trying to run it into the ground first."

The color drains from my mom's face. "Omigod." She stumbles back.

I grab her by the elbow and lead her to a nearby sofa. "Mom, are you okay?"

She mumbles something about finding her phone as she tears through the contents of her purse. "I need to call the hotel. Hang on." She taps the screen with shaky fingers. "I'm looking them up."

I sit on the edge of the chair beside her, waving away the clerk when she offers us champagne. "Hi. I'm calling about the Duval-Cruz wedding on February first. We should have the Grand Hall booked for that night." Mom rubs her hand down her face while she waits for a response. "What do you mean you don't have it listed?" Her spine stiffens as her voice raises several octaves. "Our wedding planner, Nora Richards, should have booked it. Martinez family reunion? No, that's not correct. It should be the Duval-Cruz wedding." Another long pause, and I swear I see my mom's youthful face age before my eyes. "Well, do you have another hall? You're booked until May? We can't wait that long." She throws her phone back into her purse and buries her face in her hands. "What are we going to do?" she cries.

I move over to the sofa and wrap my arm around her shoulders. "Don't worry. We'll figure something out."

She pulls a tissue out of her purse and dabs the corners of her wet eyes. "I can't believe Nora would do this to us."

Oh, but I can, I think to myself. But it's a little too late for the "I told you so," so I keep my opinion to myself.

"I'll call around." She sniffles and then blows her nose into the tissue. "There's got to be another banquet room in San Antonio. If not, didn't you say Andrés's aunt had offered her ranch?"

I make a face. "I don't think that offer is on the table anymore."

Mom shoots me a questioning glance.

I look away, pretending to pick imaginary grime out of my fingernails. "Long story." I don't want to drag my mom into my conflict with Tia. I fear it will only make things worse. Besides, I get the feeling Tia would either say no or make us grovel at her feet before she'd consent, and I already know the stipulation would include no painted flower bridal gown.

"I should have listened to you about Nora." Her lower lip trembles as she wipes her eyes again.

I exhale slowly as I summon the courage to tell my mom exactly how I feel. This conversation has been a long time coming. "I don't need a grand hall to make it special. Mom, I don't want to hurt your feelings, but I'm actually kind of glad this happened."

A look of shock crosses her features. "What? Why?"

"Because, mom, I'm just not happy with the direction of this wedding." I take her hand in mine and squeeze while searching her gaze. The hurt in her eyes makes my chest tighten, but still I go on. I was meek and mild for the first twenty-one years of my life. Even though I know it's not my mom's intention to make me a doormat, I refuse to be stepped on any longer. "It's supposed to be about Andrés and me, and it isn't."

Her hand goes limp in mine, and she slumps in her seat. "I just wanted your wedding day to be special."

I squeeze her hand tighter. "I know you do, and I appreciate all you're doing. I really do. I know that you feel guilty about all of those milestones you missed when I was growing up. I know you're trying to make it up to me now, but if you really want to make my wedding special, then let me have the wedding I want."

Though shadows fall over her face, she forces a smile. "What do you want, Christina?"

"I want one bridesmaid, tamales, and red velvet cake," I say on a rush of air, punctuating my words, as if I'm trying to make them stick in her memory.

She shakes her head. "But that's nothing."

"I already have everything: a loving mom, adorable brothers, and soon I'll have the perfect husband. That's what I want this wedding to reflect, a celebration of everything good in our lives. We don't need shrimp puffs for that."

She cups my cheek in her hand as her eyes gloss over. "What did I do to deserve a daughter like you?"

Freaking fantastic. Now I'm choked up. I swallow that knot of sorrow in my throat and stiffen my spine as I clasp both her hands in mine and pull her toward me. "You don't have to do this to yourself anymore. You were a baby when you had me. You gave me up to two people whom you believed would love me. And then, after all this time, you found me and invited me to be part of a wonderful, loving family. What you deserve, Mom, is my thanks, for having the courage to give birth to me, and then having the heart to find me again, because I know you had another option. You came at a time when I needed you most. Having you here with me, helping me with my wedding means so much."

Mom looks at me like she's going to say something and then her eyes start gushing like busted faucets. The fog of my mom's guilt settles over my heart like a heavy cloud. I feel bad that she feels bad, and not to sound selfish, but I don't need this kind of stress right now. I can literally feel my heart rate picking up, and even though I've been sitting around most of today, I'm starting to feel winded. This can't be good for the baby.

I muster my most reassuring smile. "Let's not stress about the wedding anymore today, okay?" I infuse extra enthusiasm into my voice, not just for my mom's benefit, but for mine. My stomach churns, leaving me with this queasy feeling like my body's a ship being tossed about in a violent storm. "We will work it out." I pat her hand harder. I remember the text message I received on my way to the bridal shop. "I'm having lunch with Mrs. James in a half hour. Want to come along?"

Even though it's early, she really looks like she could use a drink, or at the very least some shrimp puffs. I've been dying for her to see baby Ty, and I think his sweet little laugh will do just the trick to cheer her up. Besides, I've missed him these past few weeks, and I know he will certainly make me happy. I shift uncomfortably when I realize soon I'll be too preoccupied with my own baby to miss him. I should feel sad at this realization, but I'm not. In fact, for the first time ever, I actually get a warm feeling in my chest. I smile as I settle a hand on my stomach, which has thankfully stopped roiling for the moment. Even though my wedding is totally up in the air right now, I think for the first time in a long time, everything will work itself out.

* * *

Thankfully, mom isn't crying anymore. She's humming quietly in the passenger seat to Christmas music. Yes, she actually found a station that is still playing Yuletide songs. And though it's a far cry from my favorite country station, I put up with it because it makes her happy. By the end of the ride, I am startled to find myself humming along with her.

I do my best to try not to think about running into Nora or The Cobra as we get out of the car and I hand the valet my keys. I wish Mrs. James had picked a different place to have lunch, just in case Nora is there. I'm not sure I'll be able to refrain from bashing her face in. Then again, some twisted part of me wants to see her, so I can call her out on her two-faced behavior, but I know that won't end well. Confrontations with crazy, old collagen-enhanced women never do.

The more I think about it, the more I suppose it makes sense for Nora to want to ruin my wedding if her goal is to bankrupt her husband's company. I am also guessing those clients she gave us are bogus, which sucks because my mom was hoping Nora could help us jump-start Domingo Designs. Now not only will we need to plan a whole new wedding, we'll need to restart our business from the ground up.

I exhale a pent up breath of relief when my gaze sweeps the parking lot and I don't see Nora's or The Cobra's cars. Although, since they trade up their cars about as often as they change their hair color, that doesn't necessarily mean neither of them are here.

Mrs. James and Tyler are already waiting for us inside.

Tyler is munching on a fry when I introduce my mom to Mrs. James. My heart warms when Ty points a French fry at me and squeals, "Teeny!"

I kiss him on the forehead and pretend to eat the smashed up potato he offers me. I'm having a sense of déjà vu right now. It was just last month I was sitting at almost the exact same table with Jackson and playing the fry game with Ty. I steal a quick glance over my shoulder. I'd ended up having a confrontation with my adoptive mother. I sure hope I don't see her today. Jackson had told me his father would try to get The Cobra kicked out of the club, and I cross my fingers it worked.

"Thanks so much for meeting us last minute." Mrs. James beams at us as we sit down. Her long pale hair fans her face like a halo and her skin looks as radiant as ever. I've always been somewhat envious of her beauty. She makes it look so effortless, but I guess being married to a billionaire has is perks, like access to the best beauty products.

I woke up this morning with a monster zit on my nose, which I did my best to cover up with three different layers of concealer. Even though Blister Mountain now looks more like Blemish Molehill, I'm still feeling self-conscious about my complexion. I lay my napkin across my lap, trying to pretend my witchy wart doesn't exist and seriously resisting the urge to scratch it to oblivion. "Thank you for inviting me. I've missed Ty."

"Teeny!" Ty squeals again as he pelts me with a fry.

"No, no, Tyler," Mrs. James gently scolds him.

He flashes an adorable wicked grin and throws a fry at her.

"I can't believe he remembers me," I say.

"He was asking about you this morning. That's when I decided to call you." Mrs. James daintily picks the fry from behind her ear and wipes it on a napkin. Her soft curtain of hair, which is apparently impervious to projectile potatoes, falls back into place, taunting me with its smooth perfection.

I mentally kick myself in the ass for my petty jealousy. I could have nice hair, too, if I spent a small fortune at the salon each week. I narrowly miss another fry as it goes hurling across the table. My mom dodges it without even blinking and continues to peruse her menu. I guess she's been through this with Manny and Gio. I sure hope my baby doesn't act like this, but if he or she takes after my brothers or Andrés, I know I'll have my hands full. Ty tosses another fry before Mrs. James takes them away. He will make a nice quarterback one day, as long as he doesn't inherit his dad's derision to any activity that results in a mild sweat. I'm glad to see the color has returned to his cheeks. Last time I saw him, he didn't look well.

"How's he feeling?" I ask Mrs. James.

She shrugs while trying to pry the last remaining fry out of his little fist. "He had a chest cold, but he's over it."

I take a sip from my water glass, trying my best to pretend I'm not horrified as he lets out a wail and starts kicking his legs. He quiets down when Mrs. James gives him back the fries. I like Mrs. James, and I don't want to judge her, but rewarding Tyler for bad behavior isn't going to teach him a lesson. I steal a glance at my mom to gauge her reaction, but she's still engrossed in the menu choices. I'm assuming they have shrimp puffs here, because I think I see a bit of drool hanging off her bottom lip.

"That's good to hear," I say. "I was worried about him last week." *And now I'm worried for another reason,* I want to add. *I'm afraid he'll turn out to be just as spoiled and selfish as Jackson if you don't discipline him.*

After my mom sets down her menu and asks me to order her the shrimp cakes (probably the closest thing to shrimp puffs she could find), she excuses herself to go to the bathroom. Mrs. James watches her leave and then leans forward as if she's about to relay something top secret.

"You've always been so thoughtful." Her doe eyes light up as she nods toward my midsection. "You're going to make a great mother."

I gasp. "You know?"

"The whore told Jackson last night and he told us."

I assume by "whore" Mrs. James is referring to Karri. Though I'm not Karri's biggest fan, I'm not sure how I feel about Mrs. James talking about Ty's mother that way. I don't want Ty to grow up thinking that about his mother, even if it is true, but I guess it's not my place to reprimand Mrs. James for expressing her opinion.

"She didn't waste any time gossiping." I chew on my lower lip while I try to recall what I said to Karri during the fitting from hell. I don't remember telling her I was pregnant. Then I realize either Grace or Violet must have told her.

Her mouth tilts in a sideways smile. "I think she told him more out of spite. He still pines for you, you know?" she says with a wink.

I fan my face. My skin is so hot, I feel like I'm sitting under a heat lamp. I was so hoping we could enjoy the dinner without mentioning my ex-fiancé.

"I'm sorry." She pats my hand. "I'm making you uncomfortable."

"It's okay." I shrug, pretending it's no biggie I almost followed through with the worst mistake of my life by marrying that selfish, cheating bastard.

"Don't think I'm trying to push you two back together. I remember your Latin hottie. Can't say I blame you there." She rolls her eyes. "Especially if Jackson inherited his father's anatomy."

I pause with my glass at my lips and nearly spray my lemon water all over the table. I finally manage to swallow before I'm forced to cough out water lodged in my windpipe.

"It's just as I suspected." Mrs. James gives me that knowing look, as if I've been inducted into the teeny weenie penis committee.

I'm thinking she's going to follow up with a secret handshake. Maybe one that involves just our pinkie fingers. But as I listen to her baleful sigh, I realize beneath Mrs. James's beautiful façade is a very unhappy woman. I'm not feeling so jealous anymore.

"Mrs. James is everything okay?"

"Everything is wonderful," she says with forced exuberance. "My husband is married to his career, but at least I have that baby I've been wanting, and money," she adds dryly. "Lots and lots of money."

I have nothing else to say, so I gape at her like an idiot. I don't think this moment can get any more awkward, and I'm suddenly wishing I was somewhere else, like at my favorite coffee shop eating The World's Best Brownie.

I jump when I'm pelted in the side of the head with a French fry. I look at Ty, who's grinning like the Cheshire Cat.

"Ty really clings to you," Mrs. James continues before taking a sip of what I initially thought was tea, but now suspect may be something stronger. "That's why my husband hates you, you know?" She waves a disinterested hand in my direction, as if it's no big deal. "Jackson said you two were going to get married and take away the baby. My husband was furious. He loves Tyler as if he's his own son, even though he never gets to spend time with him."

"Uh, huh." I absently nod while peeling potato off my face. What the hell had Jackson been smoking that he would ever think I'd go back to him?

"But don't worry," Mrs. James says, her voice dripping with a tad too much sugary sweetness. "Mr. James doesn't hate you anymore. Not since Jackson and that whore agreed to the adoption."

"Adoption?" My mouth falls open. I know Karri's been a lousy mother, but would she really give up Ty for good?

Memories from the first day my real mom and I finally met replay through my mind. All of the tears we shed. All the regrets she shared. Even though I've forgiven her, she still wears her shame like an albatross around her neck.

Not a single day goes by when I don't regret giving you up, she'd cried.

No matter what I say, my mom won't forgive herself. As much as I don't like Karri, I don't want to see her have the same regrets, and I've got this gut feeling if Karri leaves Ty with the James family and walks away, it will be the biggest mistake of her life.

"So what does Mr. Tall, Dark and Handsome do for a living?" Mrs. James licks her lips while stroking her straw with the tips of her fingers.

Ew.

My spine stiffens, and I feel as if I'm looking at Mrs. James through new eyes.

I'm uncomfortable talking about my fiancé, especially considering her cougar smile. "He's inheriting his uncle's auto repair shops," I say mechanically as I choose to focus on Ty splattering ketchup with his fist.

"Nice," she drawls. "Are they profitable?"

I silently nod.

"Then he works long hours?"

I cast my gaze in her direction. One pale brow is arched as she continues to seductively stroke her straw.

"Yes," I say as an uneasy feeling makes its way down to my stomach.

"Get used to spending many nights alone. A few glasses of wine dulls the senses and makes it more bearable." As if to emphasize her point, she winks before taking a long sip from her "tea" glass. "So does a buff bodyguard."

I gape at her for a long moment. "Excuse me?"

But Mrs. James is too busy noticing something behind me to answer my question. "Oh, look who it is. Nora Richards and Vivian Duval."

And just like that, the uneasy feeling in my gut twists and turns until my stomach is one solid knot. The blood pumping through my veins solidifies like quicksand, making it impossible for me to turn around. I clench the linen tablecloth, bunching it in my fists as I stare out the restaurant's picturesque bay window. Golfers drive by on their carts, making me green with envy. I think how much being outside sounds more appealing than spending the afternoon inside this upscale prison with The Cobra.

"They're here just about every night," Mrs. James says. "We call them our resident drunks."

They just don't hide it as well as you, I want to say, but I keep my mouth shut as I turn my head in the other direction, scanning the room. There's a crowd of golfers blocking the nearest exit. Crap.

"Christina, are you okay?" Mrs. James leans forward and clasps my hand. "You're as pale as a ghost."

"I don't want to be here with her," I say through clenched teeth as I slowly unhook my fingers from the tablecloth. I've torn a hole in the fabric.

"Looks like they're leaving, anyway," Mrs. James says.

I take a chance and slowly turn. Nora's got her arm around my mom's shoulders, and they fall all over each other as they stumble out of the bar toward the large fountain at the center of the arched entry. I suppose that story about Nora no longer being The Cobra's BFF was just another line of bullshit. I exhale a sigh of relief when I see they are leaving the club. But my relief is short-lived when I hear an enraged shriek that sounds part predatory hawk and part tribal war cry. I feel like I'm watching a nightmare play out in slow motion as my mom descends upon them, and before I can stop her, my birth mother is shoving Nora and my adoptive mother into the fountain's basin.

I jump from my seat and race toward the entry, pushing through the throng of onlookers who crowd the scene.

My whole world implodes on itself as I get a good look at my mom. She's hovering over the fountain, hands clenched at her sides, while The Cobra and Nora flail in the water like drowning puppies. Mom points a shaky finger at Nora. "That's for trying to ruin my daughter's wedding!"

Nora stands up and swipes a strand of wet hair out of her eyes. "It was nothing personal, Jenny. My husband-"

"I don't give a damn about your personal life. I only care about my daughter!"

My heart slams when I see the rage in my mom's thunderous expression. She looks ready to spit fire.

"And that's for ruining my daughter's life!" she says to The Cobra who answers with a harrumph as she struggles to get out of the water.

Nora doesn't bother to offer her friend a hand up. I get the feeling their friendship isn't very solid. I still can't believe my mother, with her tiny five-foot-three frame, soft smile and easy-going nature, managed to knock both her adversaries into the water.

Though I'm terrified what will happen to my mom after publically assaulting these snakes in the grass, some part of me wants to pump my fist in the air and say, "Kick their asses!"

Instead, I decide on the sensible course of action—pull Mom away before security apprehends her, and then run like hell.

"Mom!" I raise my voice to get her attention. Imagine how awkward I feel when both my birth mother and adoptive mother turn to me. I purposely look away from The Cobra, after catching the venomous look in her eyes. I think I hear hissing coming from the water, and I imagine she's trying to turn us to stone right now.

The crowd is silent. Funny how nobody offers to help Nora and The Cobra out of the fountain.

My mom pulls back her shoulders, turns up her chin and walks up to me. Despite her show of courage, I note the haunted look in her eyes. It's enough to break my heart. I open my arms, and she buries her face against my neck, sniffling against my ear.

"I'm sorry, baby."

My throat tightens with emotion. "Don't be. I love you, Mom."

"And I love you," she says as she pulls back and flashes a radiant smile despite the sheen of tears in her eyes.

"You assaulted me!" An ear-piercing shriek resonates behind me. "I'm filing a police report, and you'll be hearing from my lawyer!"

I look over my mom's shoulder at The Cobra still standing in the center of the fountain. Her bony knees are shaking, and her short skirt clings to her wrinkled thighs. Her giant cone of hair plasters her head in saggy strands, exposing bald patches on her scalp, and her heavy makeup runs down her face in globs.

I stand shoulder-to-shoulder with my mom and entwine her fingers with mine, distressed to feel how badly her hand shakes. I narrow my gaze at the monster who raised me. "You sue my mom and I'll press charges against you."

She places both hands on her hips. "For what?" she slurs as water spews from her lips. "I was the one pushed into the water."

I take a deep breath and then slowly exhale as I try not to make eye contact with anyone, despite the multitudes of curious stares. "For being an accessory to child rape."

The Cobra gasps and stumbles backward. Nora, who's standing beside her, doesn't even try to break her fall as my adoptive mother hits her head on a spitting cherub.

My mom cries as her hand flies to her throat. "You don't have to do this, Christina," I hear her rasp.

The Cobra is groaning and rubbing her head. Nora finally lends a hand and helps her out of the fountain. I know I need to strike again, when my opponent is still down. The only problem is my sordid past will be known to everyone. But my adoptive mother needs to be held accountable for what she has done.

I turn up my chin and steel my resolve. "You knew my dad was raping me and you didn't even call the cops."

The Cobra looks like a wet rat, dripping all over the tile floor. The veins in her skinny neck stand out as her fingers curl like claws by her sides. "How dare you bring that kind of shame upon our family!"

"It's *your* shame, not mine." I lift my mom's hand, which is still clasping mine, and proudly show her. "Besides, you're *not* my family."

"I gave you my baby!" my mom shrieks, throwing me momentarily off guard as I stumble back, only to be pulled upright by her firm grip. "You promised me you'd love her, and you and your husband abused her! You heartless, cold bitch!" The crowd gasps and murmurs. A few of the women are hissing and the men are swearing. Whatever is happening, it's working.

"That's right." Mom pounds the air with her fist. "I have half a mind to bust open all that collagen in your face. I'll make those fat, ugly lips looked like popped airbags!" Mom shakes her fist at The Cobra and at Nora. "And I'll save one for your double-crossing friend, too."

"No, Mom." I tug on her hand, pulling her toward the exit. "Let her wallow in her shame."

The spectators part like the Red Sea when we walk out the door.

Even though my dad is six feet under, I hope now that I've exposed him to all his friends at the club he once held so dear, his corpse will be rolling in its grave for the rest of his miserable eternity.

Chapter Seventeen

Christina

I feel bad I didn't get to say goodbye to Tyler, but considering my mom and I were busy fleeing security guards, I didn't have much choice. I send a message to Mrs. James apologizing for skipping out on lunch. She writes back that she understands. She also tells me she's overheard several prominent club members calling for The Cobra's immediate expulsion from the club.

I don't know what tastes sweeter, the revenge my mom and I got on those two snakes or the warm chocolate fudgy perfection that practically sends my taste buds into orgasmic convulsions. Though my mom was looking forward to her fish cakes, I don't think she's terribly upset, as she moans with each bite of "The World's Best Brownie." Yeah, we're at my favorite café again. I'm honestly starting to think I've got a brownie addiction, but after the week I've had, I'd say I earned it.

My mom has earned it, too, after her performance at the country club. Have I mentioned lately she's my hero? If I were to rate her on the mom scale, I'd say she achieved rock star status today.

"Mrs. James seemed pleasant enough."

I look at her. Gone is the vicious mamma bear defending her cub. She smiles sweetly and dabs the corners of her mouth with her paper napkin.

"Yes," I say as I sip coffee. Yeah, it's my second cup, but it's decaf, so I don't think it counts. "But something about her is off. I think she's got a drinking problem."

She flashes a knowing grin. "That was a rather big Long Island Iced Tea for so early in the afternoon."

My mouth falls open. "Oh, is that what that was?" Geez. It's barely past noon, and she's already hitting the sauce. She also mentioned something about drinking wine at night. I wonder if her drinking is a habitual thing. That would mean little Ty has traded one addict parent for another. Now I understand why Tyler wasn't disciplined when he was throwing fries. She was probably too drunk to care. This is so not good.

"What's the matter?" I look over at Mom, who's frowning at me mid-bite, a chunk of brownie suspended on the faux silver fork in front of her lips.

I heave a sigh. "She told me Karri is letting her adopt Ty."

Mom sets the fork down as her frown deepens. "Why would Karri give up that beautiful baby?"

"They're probably paying her a lot of money. Mrs. James seems to love him, but I worry about the drinking. The Cobra was a heavy drinker." I think back to how my adoptive mom was drunk most of my childhood. As I got older, I realized her drinking wasn't just a way to tune out of her own life, but a way to tune out of mine. When she wasn't angry with me over something stupid, she was indifferent to my needs…painfully indifferent. "I don't want Tyler to be treated the way I was."

Mom folds her hands in front of her. She leans forward, her expression darkening. "No amount of money is more important than your child's happiness."

Though I agree with her, I also know Karri's addiction to meth is probably worse than Mrs. James's drinking problem. Plus, she'll never be able to provide for him like the James family. "Mom, I think Ty would be less happy with Karri raising him."

"Will he?" Her bottom lip trembles, and that haunted expression in her eyes is enough to turn my skin cold. "She's going to have regrets. Twenty years from now, she will. Trust me. I know exactly what I'm talking about. You *need* to talk to your friend."

I look away from her penetrating gaze. "She's not my friend."

"Do you still care about that baby?" Her tone is dripping with guilt so thick it rivals the gooey fudge on my brownie.

"Of course." I know she's right, but after the way Karri betrayed me and her family, I don't know if I can forgive her. I certainly don't want to have a heart-to-heart with her.

Those dark clouds in my mom's eyes turn thunderous. "He should be given the chance to know his birth mother. It's something I tried to negotiate in the adoption contract, but Vivian and your father refused."

"Why am I not surprised?" I ask wryly. My poor mom must have been terrified, pregnant at seventeen with no one to take care of her. I'm sure it was easy for my dad and The Cobra to manipulate her into any contract they wanted.

Mom shoots me a pointed look. "And how does that make you feel?"

"Angry." My brain feels like it's filling up with steam as I clench my fork so tight, the plastic gives way beneath my grip and breaks with an audible snap.

"How do you think Ty will feel twenty years from now? I know you don't like Karri, but you need to talk to her."

She pries the fork from my hand, and something about the gentleness in her smile reminds me of the rainbow and songbirds that come out after a storm. I'm not sure how or where she perfected her calming aura, but I hope I'm half as effective when I'm a mother.

I nod, letting out a slow exhale. "I will."

In an instant, the clouds reappear in her eyes as she drops the fork and squeezes my hand tight. "I wish I'd kept you. I really do."

"Don't do this again, Mom. Please," I say in the sternest voice I can manage.

She presses her lips together before wiping her eyes with a napkin. "I want you to promise me something."

"What?"

"Love your child with all your heart," she says through a sob.

Dear God. She could have sliced my chest open with a meat cleaver and it would have had the same effect. If she only knew how much I've been resenting this baby these past few days. Despite the knot in my gut which spirals up my torso and snakes a noose around my throat, I barely manage to clear my throat. "I promise."

* * *

I drop my mom off at her car in the bridal store parking lot, and then I cry my eyes out during most of the hour long drive to Tio's ranch as I think about how selfish I've been about this baby, resenting it for all the problems Andrés and I have had lately. None of this is my baby's fault. None of it. I'm the one who was so wrapped up in my life, I forgot to take my birth control pills. If anyone is to blame, it would be me.

But whose fault it is doesn't even matter. Andrés and I are going to be parents soon. Life is about to change in a big way for me. Maybe I won't be able to work as many hours as I'd hoped, but what matters first and foremost is that my baby will grow up in a happy, loving home.

I make a solemn vow to do whatever it takes to make sure my child feels loved and secure, unlike the way I felt growing up. I sniffle loudly and wipe my eyes. I will love my baby. I will.

And I will love my husband, too. After this weekend, I will start a hunt for a new therapist. I know Andrés can't always get appointments with the VA, and he deserves the very best attention. And if the stress from our baby is causing Andrés to have these bad dreams, I will do whatever it takes to make Andrés's transition easier. But I will never, ever again blame or resent my innocent child because he or she came at the wrong time. Maybe the timing wasn't right, but this child was conceived out of love. And just as I love the father of my child, I will love my child, too. Forever.

I swear when I pull into the gravel driveway and spy Marie's little BMW parked beside Tia's SUV. I grip my steering wheel, trying to channel all my pent up frustration into that poor, defenseless shiny leather. I straighten my shoulders and clench my jaw as I steel my resolve. I need to talk to Tia, but I guess I've got a few choice words for Marie, too. Might as well kill two birds with one stone.

I'm not shocked to see Marie open the door, leaning against the doorframe with her attitude locked and loaded. "What do you want?" she asks me in that bitchy tone of hers.

I march past her and into the kitchen. Tia's already elbow deep in tamales, probably preparing for the Cruz New Year's party. When she looks up, there's no mistaking the shock in her eyes. I hear the door slam, followed by Marie barreling down the hall toward us. I decide to make my move before Marie comes in and infects us all with her bitch virus.

I walk around the granite countertop and don't give Tia the chance to push me away as I wrap her in a hug. Tia holds her hands up as if I'm pointing a gun at her, and that's when I see her her hands are coated in yellow powder. I pull back and dust flour off my pants.

There's banging behind us, and I steal a glance over my shoulder to see Marie violently scrubbing a pot in the sink.

I do my best to not roll my eyes as I look at Tia. "I just wanted to say I'm sorry your feelings were hurt over this wedding. That was never my intention. But it was also never my intention to let anyone take over my wedding. I let my mom make a lot of decisions for me about the venue and the food. Honestly, I wanted the Cruz family to cater the wedding." I sweep a hand toward the uncooked tamales sitting in a shallow pan. "I love everything Andrés's family cooks." I flash a weary smile. "You know that." I think about mentioning that we might need to use the ranch for the ceremony, but I don't want to grovel. "All I wanted was a simple wedding with tamales and one bridesmaid." I nod toward Marie as she slams an empty pan in the drying rack. "Marie didn't want to be my bridesmaid, anyway."

Tia grabs a towel off the counter and wipes her hands. She looks at Marie with big, sad eyes and shakes her head. "Yes, she did."

Marie actually has the nerve to heave a sigh, acting as if I've just broken her heart. Really?

Anger as thick and toxic as black smoke infuses my skull. I really want to grab those pots and pans and smash them over Marie's head. I think back to those retro movies of Godzilla I watched when I was a kid, and I finally understand how he felt when he smashed up Tokyo. He must have had an annoying family member whose sole purpose was to make his life a living hell.

"Tia, before you asked Marie to be my bridesmaid, she cornered me in my bedroom and told me I was marrying Andrés for his money."

Tia's hand flies to her chest. "Marie!"

I tilt my chin and glare at Marie, who has the nerve to look directly at me with a scowl. "I fell in love with Andrés before I knew he was going to inherit. I am not marrying him for his money. I am marrying him because I love him beyond words. I guess I'm selfish, because I'm not about to lose him because you don't approve."

To my surprise, Marie casts a woeful look at Tia, who is now glaring at her niece with crossed arms. Then Marie's face twists into a knot before she turns her back on us and quietly washes dishes. Her arms and back are so rigid, she looks like a robot, but I don't care. I've made my point. She'll have to deal with it.

"And Tia," I say as I put a protective hand over my stomach, "I *am* pregnant, but I don't think that makes me soiled. I am not ashamed if anyone knows I'm carrying Andrés's child. This baby is a blessing. I am an artist. I put a lot of time into that dress. Those flowers are an expression of love, not just for my husband, but for our child. I am wearing *my* gown to *my* wedding."

Tia's scowl softens as she leans forward and places a hand over mine. "I understand, and I'm sorry."

I hug her a second time, and this time she hugs me back.

"I hope this means you'll come."

Tia looks at me with smiling eyes. "Of course. I wouldn't miss my *sobrino* and *sobrina's* wedding."

She bites her lip, flashing a pleading gaze. "So does this mean we can cater it?"

I laugh. "You know how much I love Cruz tamales."

Tia turns toward her niece, who is still busy ignoring us. "Marie, you need to apologize. That was a terrible thing you said to Christina."

Marie drops a pan into the water as her spine stiffens. "Sorry," she huffs without bothering to turn around.

If Tia's eyes were lasers, they would have burned twin holes into the back of Marie's head. "You will be working on a better apology than that. And you owe Andrés an apology, too, for insulting his bride."

She ignores Marie's groan and turns to me. "Are you hungry, *niña*?"

"I just had lunch with my mom. I have to go. I have one more stop, and I'm already exhausted."

"Don't wear yourself out too much." She winks and rubs my belly. "Our mama needs plenty of rest."

"I won't. Thank you, Tia." I leave without saying good-bye to Marie, not that she deserves anything other than a kick in the ass. I smile at the thought. Something tells me she'll be getting a verbal ass kicking after I leave.

I stumble on my way to my car as a slight wave of dizziness rolls through me. I think about what Tia said about rest, and I tell myself she's right. I need to slow down. But Violet's ranch isn't far from here. One more stop, and then I'm taking the rest of the day off. Maybe I'll read some more baby books. My first OB appointment is next week, and I want to be prepared.

I'm determined to put all of my troubles behind me and focus on having a healthy, happy child.

* * *

Violet's ranch is sprawling with teens. It's been a few months since I visited, and I can't believe how much the place has changed. Violet's grant money recently came through, and there's already a brand new bunkhouse near the main building, and the old run-down barn has new boards and is in the process of getting a fresh paintjob. Many teens armed with rollers and brushes are laughing and joking as they work.

I admire Violet for what she's trying to do here, and even though I'm still mad at Karri, I'm grateful Violet took her in, too. Violet does have a lot of work on her hands. No wonder Grace has become bitter. I can see managing a group of wayward teens would leave little time for romance.

I frown. Andrés seems to have a bigger workload each week, and has been coming home later and later. I wonder if his huge workload isn't the underlying cause of his nightmares.

I find Grace in the main house. She doesn't see me at first as I come in through a side door. She and a teen girl with Goth black hair and too many tattoos to count are bouncing around to Katie Perry while they set vases filled with flowers down the center of the longest dining table I've ever seen. It must seat at least thirty people.

"Hey, hummingbirds," I say.

Grace spins around, nearly losing hold of her vase. She sets it down on the table and holds her arms out for a hug. "Christina, you scared me," she laughs.

I'm surprised by her giddy tone. She's been so depressed over her relationship with Violet. I wonder if something has changed.

After we exchange an embrace, she asks the teenager to finish up. Then she loops her arm through mine and we go for a stroll through the foyer and out into her small herb garden. Only a few plants are blooming, but the place is even more beautiful than the last time I saw it. A little stone path, lined with several lattice archways, skirts the perimeter. In the center of the garden is a stone birdbath and a freshly painted white bench swing. A large oak tree is at the edge of the garden, and the canopy of branches adds just the right amount of shade to this surprisingly mild winter day.

I lean into Grace as we continue to walk arm-in-arm. "It's lovely."

"Thank you," she says with a smile in her voice. "It was my Christmas present from Violet."

We sit down on the bench, and I gaze into the house's large bay windows. "What a wonderful present."

"I know she loves me. I've been selfish to want all of her attention when she's committed to such a good cause."

Grace is smiling at a plant stem she twirls between the tips of her fingers.

A couple of kids nod to us as they skirt the outside path on the way to the barn behind us. They are covered in paint splatter and grinning ear-to-ear.

"Yeah, she is," I say, still in total awe at how much the ranch has progressed. "I can't believe how many kids are here."

"We've got teachers that come up during the day." Grace nods to the retreating kids. "School just ended, and now they have to finish their chores."

"What does Karri do all day?" I ask in as disinterested a tone as I can muster. I shouldn't care what Karri does with her day, but some part of me is hoping she's turning her life around.

"She's actually doing a lot more than I expected. Violet sent her grocery shopping today. One of the ranch hands went with her to supervise, and Karri came back with everything on the list." Grace's cheeks flush a rosy pink. "With the kids in school and Karri gone, Violet and I had a few hours to ourselves."

I nudge Grace in the ribs. "That's awesome."

She heaves a sigh before leaning back in a casual pose. Though she isn't the poised and polished Grace I'm used to, she most definitely looks happy.

"Thanks for listening to me gripe this week." Her voice is laced with shame, as if she's the only person on the planet who's ever had love problems. "How are you and Andrés?"

"Great, thanks." I laugh. "But his cousin is still a bitch."

Grace snorts and shakes her head. "Tell me something I don't already know."

I'm nearly tempted to address the fact that my poised and polished friend just snorted, but I like this new, casual Grace.

"Nora turned out to be an even bigger bitch." My cheeks flush when I think about Nora's betrayal, and I feel as if she slapped me in the face. I wish there was some way I could magically erase my memory, and forget those hours of precious wasted time I spent in that woman's company.

"I suspected something was up." Clasping my hand in hers, Grace fixes me with a penetrating gaze. "Tell me."

* * *

After I fill Grace in on the sordid details of Nora's betrayal and my mom's revenge, Grace offers me the most amazing solution, a wedding at Violet's ranch. Her garden, she says, will make the perfect backdrop. I think she couldn't be more right, but I don't want to put Violet and Grace out. Grace says she'll talk to Violet, but she insists the preparation will give the kids a meaningful project to work on. My spirits have lifted by the time I leave Grace's beautiful garden. She points me in the direction of the stables, where Karri is doing stall duty.

I'm not sure what that entails, but I suspect it isn't pretty. My eyes have to adjust to the dim light as I walk down the wide corridor flanked by stalls on either side. I remember these horses from my last visit. Violet comes from a long line of horse breeders, and when she inherited this ranch from her parents, they left her a profitable champion bloodline.

I can see the tops of two kids' heads as they talk soothingly to a horse and brush her shiny chestnut coat. I don't know much about animals, but I do know Violet's horses are beautiful, and I admire her for sharing them with these troubled teens.

I fight the urge to plug my nose. I forgot how badly manure smells. Though it's well past morning sickness time, I get an uneasy feeling in my stomach, and I hope I can keep my lunch down long enough to talk to Karri.

I think I spot a blast of pink hair disappearing into one of the stalls toward the back of the stables, so I continue on, apprehension settling in my gut like a lead ball. I still don't know what I'm going to say to her or if she'll even listen. I pause when I hear Karri talking to one of the teens.

"I took your advice and didn't get that tattoo," a girl who doesn't sound older than sixteen says.

"What did your boyfriend say?" Karri asks.

"He was pissed. And then I told him what you told me; if he really loved me, he'd understand.

Then he broke up with me."

"What an ass." I can almost see Karri rolling her eyes.

"Good thing I didn't get his name tattooed on my back." The girl laughs. "Thanks, Karri."

"No problem." The heartfelt note of sincerity in her voice reminds me of the Karri I once knew, the Karri who talked me off the ledge in high school after my dad's rape sent me into a spiral of depression and self-loathing.

I feel weird intruding on their tender moment, and almost decide to turn around and leave, but then the stall door opens and Karri comes out clutching a bucket filled with horse-shit in one gloved hand and a shovel in the other. She's got brown gunk smeared on her forehead and neck. I can tell by the bright freckles smattering her nose and cheekbones she's not wearing any makeup, but her skin has a natural rosiness and her eyes have a healthy glow. Despite the crap blemishes, I'd say this is the best Karri has looked in a long time.

"Hey." I hold up a hand and make some sort of half-assed wave, and I suddenly feel awkward standing here in my designer jeans and shoes, attempting to have a heart-to-heart with Karri looking like this. Not that I'm bothered by her appearance, but I can tell by the way she flushes all the way to her brassy pink roots, she's embarrassed.

"I already heard from Violet I'm not in the wedding, if that's what you were going to tell me." She drops the bucket on the ground, and debris flies out and scatters at her feet. Yuk.

That queasy feeling in my stomach rolls through me in a nauseating wave. I steel my resolve. I will not lose my lunch until I've at least talked to her about Ty.

I look away from the bucket of shit and turn my focus on Karri. If I don't look at it, maybe I won't get sick. "No, that's not what I came to talk about." She arches a brow before removing her gloves and wiping a bead of sweat off her brow. "What's up?" Her tone is a mixture of disinterest and irritation, and I wonder if she's embarrassed because of her appearance or if she really wanted to be in my bridal party. If she's pissed, she'll have to take a place in line behind all the other people determined to dump all over my wedding plans.

"My mom and I had lunch with Mrs. James today."

"How nice." Karri flashes a smile that looks more like a snarl. "She refuses to be in the same room with me."

That unsettling feeling in my gut increases, so I try my best to brush off her attitude. "My mom wanted me to give you a message."

Karri folds her arms across her chest. She's got this look in her eyes like she's an angry bull preparing for an attack. "What is it?"

"Don't give Ty up for adoption," I say on a rush of air. "She says to trust her you'll regret it later."

"Look at me." Karri laughs bitterly before waving a hand toward the bucket of shit at her feet. "What do I have to offer him?"

Again, I force myself to ignore the bucket, as I center my gaze on Karri's eyes. "A mother's love. That's more than what I had when I was growing up." My heart clenches with the admission, and I resist the urge to press a hand to my stomach and hunch over as my morning sickness worsens. Gah. It feels like someone is playing jump rope with my insides. Only a few more minutes, and if I can't convince Karri to change her mind, I'm running for the nearest toilet, or bush if I can't make it to the house.

Her eyes widen. "You don't think his grandparents love him?"

I heave a sigh as I think back to my lunch with Mrs. James. She seemed to care for Ty, even though she wasn't paying much attention to him. Still, I know it isn't fair of me to judge her parenting skills after just one lunch. "I do," I answer honestly. "I just think there's room for you in his life, too, and if you cut yourself out now, you're going to regret it."

Karri drops her hands as she stares down at her worn pair of boots. "They're giving me two million dollars." She looks up, her eyes glossy with unshed tears. "I can start a new life with that."

"Looks like you're already starting a new life." I motion behind her. I can still hear the teenager she'd been counseling shoveling inside the stall. Though Karri's life might not be glamorous, I can see she is still capable of helping others. "Why don't you give this one a chance first? I bet Ty would love to visit you on the weekends. There's so much up here for kids to do."

Karri smiles and blinks back tears. "One of the teen's little sisters came for a visit yesterday. We took her on the pony, just around the pen. You should have seen how happy she was. That's all I want for Ty, you know." She sniffles loudly before averting her gaze. "For him to be happy."

I swallow the rising tide of emotion that clogs my throat. At that moment, I realize I can forgive Karri for everything she's done. She may have made a mess of her life, and she has hurt many people who loved her, but she's still got some good in her. Maybe if she cleans herself up, and stays off drugs for a while, the thoughtful Karri I once knew will resurface.

"My mom told me, 'No amount of money is more important than your child's happiness,'" I say, hoping Karri will listen to my advice this time.

"Maybe she's right." Karri nods, flashing a weak smile. "Thanks."

I try to return Karri's smile, but the wave of nausea that overcomes me, nearly sends me tumbling onto the floor. I turn to find someplace to vomit, but I only make it a few steps before this morning sickness spirals out of control. A cyclone of dizziness spins inside my head, and it feels as if my whole world tilts and falls over.

"Christina, are you okay?" Karri echos behind me.

"I need to go to the bathroom," I mumble, but my voice sounds hollow, distant, as if someone else is talking for me and I'm miles away. I clutch my stomach as a sharp stabbing pierces my insides. I fall to the floor with a thud and pain lances up my shoulder.

"Christina! Hold on!"

I'm barely aware of Karri screaming, and then the soothing sound of Violet's voice before I succumb to darkness.

Chapter Eighteen

Andrés

I check the calendar on my computer, though I'm not sure why I care what day it is. I rarely get a day off, anymore. Tomorrow will be the last day in January. We were supposed to get married this weekend. Christina hasn't mentioned setting a new wedding date, and now I wonder if she ever will. Despair hangs over her like a dark cloud. I swear It stifles me every time I walk through our apartment door. She says I've forgotten about her. She says I'm staying late at work because I don't want to be with her after we lost our child. No matter how many times I tell her Tio has added to my workload, she doesn't believe me. She just retreats into this dark place inside her soul, and each day I feel her slipping further and further away from me.

This new business she's working on with her mom isn't keeping her busy enough. I've offered Christina her old job back, but I get the feeling she'd rather sit home and drown in her depression. Most days I find her in her studio, painting stark landscapes and images I don't get, like a chair alone in a hallway, or a rainbow buried beneath thunderclouds. I keep telling her she needs to see a therapist, but she refuses. I guess I should be relieved she still talks to Grace and her mom. I just don't understand why she's shutting me out. What did I do? I have told her too many times to count that I don't blame her for losing the baby. The doctor says these things happen, that nobody was to blame.

Words that fall on deaf ears, because Christina definitely blames herself. I don't know how to convince her I love her beyond life. Add that to the fact that I'm still getting these damn dreams about every other night, and you could say my life sucks right now. The dreams are consistent. I'm back in the Humvee crying for help, but no one hears me. I lie there and cry and cry and nobody comes to my rescue. This time my Army buddies aren't with me. It's just me, broken, scared, and alone. Kind of like how I've been feeling since we lost the baby.

I sit at my desk, staring at the monitor, stressing over all the parts on back order, all the responsibilities I have to fulfill before I can leave, and it's already five-thirty. I know I won't get out of here for another few hours, which means Christina will think I'm avoiding her again.

I feel so helpless, and I just don't see a way out. I fire off an email to my subordinate, asking him one more time to try to find another supplier, so we can get those parts in on time. Then I see the message from my Uncle Arturo. It's been a while since I've heard from him. Most of my family, even Tia, has kept a respectful distance since Christina lost the baby. I don't know if I should read his message. I really don't have time right now, but curiosity wins out, and I open it.

Hey, sobrino. Just wanted to let you know the catering business is going well. I've got several weddings and quinceañeras booked, but I could use some help. My offer still stands. Also, I'm sorry about your baby, mijo. I hope you and your pretty señorita are doing well. You are a good boy and deserve to be happy.

I lean back in my chair and stare at his message for a long while, even though I know I need to get back to work. The line that gets me is he thinks I deserve to be happy. The thing is, I can't recall what happiness feels like anymore. I close my eyes and try to remember, try to recapture that feeling. The memories are there, but distant, as if they happened a lifetime ago: images of when Christina and I first met, and me holding her while she stumbles over my feet, of the time the A/C went out in my old apartment, and we cooled off in my pool and then made love in the moonlight, us chasing her brothers around the yard, laughing and pulling celery out of their pants, and all the many, many times, we'd take baths together and then make love well into the night.

Christina and I have shared some wonderful times, but we haven't even been together a year. I know there are more memories we need to create, if only we can find a way to be happy again. I ignore at least a dozen unanswered emails and open up that travel site I've been hearing about on TV. I know I need to do something about us now, before it's too late. I grab my cellphone and scroll for Grace's number as I formulate a plan in my head.

* * *

Christina

The only happy memories I have of my father were the times he used to take me fishing. He usually let me bring my sketchbook, and I'd draw pictures of fish jumping through the water. I even drew one from memory once of him hauling in his catch. My dad said it was my best work of art and he'd hung it in his office.

The dried salt from the water felt rough on my skin after we'd come in from a long day of fishing, and the dock smelled of pungent fish blood as seagulls swooped down and devoured discarded entrails. I'd usually turn my head when my dad filleted each fish. Even though they were long dead, I still felt sorry for them. The meat was raw and grey as blood ran down the cutting board and onto the concrete beneath.

When I think of those fish now, I think of my heart. Raw and bleeding. Despite all the hardships I've dealt with in my life, nothing has even come close to the pain I feel from the loss of our child. Nothing.

And I don't know how I can recover from it.

The guilt that overwhelms me is so powerful it's crippling. I hardly have the energy to build my new wedding design business. I don't have the desire to do anything anymore except paint pictures that convey my feelings of darkness and despair. Otherwise, I spend way too much time in bed, thinking maybe the miscarriage was God's way of punishing me for resenting an innocent child. All the while, thoughts about what I should have done differently run through my head. I should have insisted my OB see me right away, rather than be satisfied with a two week wait time. I shouldn't have eaten all those brownies and pancakes and other sugary foods.

But I guess none of those regrets matter now that the baby is lost. Inconsiderate people try to console me, telling me I was only four weeks pregnant, and these things happen. Andrés and I can try again, they say, but after that miscarriage, I don't know if I want to risk the heartache of losing another child. Besides, don't they understand I need time to mourn? Four weeks or not, that was still my baby. I didn't even know if it was a boy or a girl. I never even got to see my little peanut on an ultrasound, and now our child is gone forever.

Andrés's depression makes mine even worse. At first I thought he was mourning the miscarriage, too, but after talking to Arturo on the phone yesterday I'm not so sure. I knew Andrés hated his job, but now that I know about Arturo's offer, it all makes sense. Now I understand why he was so melancholy when I bought him professional cookware for Christmas, and why the only time he seems happy anymore is when he's in the kitchen. I wish Andrés would open up and tell me if he's truly unhappy at his job, but I'm such a mess of emotions right now, I don't know how to help him when I can't even fix myself. If only I could find some way to bring us both out of this funk. My misery feeds off his, and we're dragging each other into an endless pit of depression.

I jump at a knock on the front door. Even though I'm in bed, the loud banging resonates through the apartment. Only one person I know knocks like that: Grace. I throw off my covers and grab my sweatpants off the floor. I catch a glimpse of myself in the mirror as I slip them on. I run a hand down my ribs, which are showing through my tank top. Andrés keeps telling me I need to eat, but I don't have the appetite.

The banging grows more insistent.

"Coming!" I close my eyes and groan. The sound of my booming voice does little to ease my migraine. It feels like Grace's knocking is echoing inside my head.

My legs are deadweights as I trudge to the front door.

Grace scowls at me, an impatient look in her eyes. "Hey, what are you doing in your pajamas?"

I rub my hand through my hair, pulling straggly strands out of my eyes. "I didn't have to work today."

"You look like shit." She leans forward and inhales, then makes a face. "Have you showered?" She fans her nose as her scowl deepens, reminding me of my reaction whenever I drive past a dead skunk on the highway.

I shrug as my irritation grows. "Not yet."

Her jaw drops. "Not yet? Christina, it's six o'clock." Her voice rises with a sense of urgency. "Andrés will be home soon."

"I doubt it." Ever since I lost the baby he's been working later and later. There are times when I'm already in bed when he gets home. Not that it matters, since he never comes to our bed anymore, anyway.

Grace pushes past me and stomps toward my bedroom. I slam the door and follow her.

"What are you doing?"

She's already in my closet, dragging out an empty suitcase from the back. She shoots me a pointed look before hoisting it on my bed. "Packing."

"For what?"

"Andrés finally cashed in those Vegas tickets I got you. Now go get in the shower while I pack." My arms and legs ice over, and I gape at her for a long moment, my feet rooted to the floor.

"Why are you just standing there?" she snaps as she grabs a handful of panties from a drawer and throws them into the bag. "Your plane leaves in two hours!"

"Vegas? We're going to Vegas?"

"That's what I said. Do I need to throw you in the shower myself?" She points a finger at the bathroom door. "Go!"

Chapter Nineteen

Andrés

Though it's midnight Vegas time by the time we reach our hotel, it's 2 a.m. in San Antonio, and Christina is dragging her feet when we walk through the door. If this had been our honeymoon, like it should have been, I would have carried her across the threshold, but I settle for carrying all of the luggage instead. I'm not sure why Christina needed such a huge suitcase for a four day getaway.

My cellphone buzzes against my hip, but I ignore it. Tio wasn't happy when I told him I was taking Friday through Monday off. I feel bad for leaving him, but I don't have a choice. Christina needs me more than he does.

Christina eyes the two queen beds like they've got bedbugs or herpes. Heat creeps into the back of my neck when she shoots me a sour look before trudging toward the bathroom. It's been over a month since I refused to share a bed with her, and she's still giving me a guilt trip about it.

I don't bother unpacking my things. We'll only be in this hotel for one night, then tomorrow we're going to do something a little different. I'm taking her to a mountain resort a little over an hour's drive outside Vegas. I checked the weather report and it snowed there a few days ago. Christina once told me she's never seen snow, so I hope she likes it. I don't know what else to do to make her happy, and I'm at my wits end trying to make this relationship work.

Christina is already sleeping by the time I get out of the shower. I kiss her on the forehead, telling her I love her, even though I know she can't hear me, then I climb into my bed and stare up at the ceiling. I lie there for several moments, trying to piece together how our relationship went so wrong, and what I can do to fix it. We haven't had sex in over a month, not since before she lost the baby. I climbed into bed with her last week, nibbling on her ear and whispering words of love in Spanish. She started crying and pushed me off of her. I felt like a total pendejo after that and haven't tried since. I close my eyes and pray that the nightmares don't come tonight, and if they do, that I don't wake her.

* * *

Christina

"Snow. I'm touching snow." I stare down in awe at the white crystals as I rub them between my gloved hands. I look up at Andrés. His cheeks and nose are a healthy pink, and his chestnut eyes sparkle like quartz jewels. I take another deep breath of crisp mountain air. Everything feels so alive here, even me, which is odd, because it was only yesterday when just the thought of getting out of bed was overwhelming. "It feels so different than I imagined."

He lifts my hand to his lips and blows the crystals back onto the ground. "That's the hard stuff." He nods behind us. "We need to wander off the road and find fresh snow."

I stare at the white slope, crowded with so many tall trees, I fear we may get lost and never find our way out if we venture too far. But I take his hand and follow his lead, slipping a few times, despite the fact that Andrés bought me the best snow boots money could buy when we were down in the valley. It's a chore just putting one foot in front of the other. These heavy pants I'm wearing make me feel like I'm wrapped in cellophane. But the weirdest thing is the way the ground crunches beneath my feet. I can't help but giggle with each step as he leads me off the path and toward deeper snow.

Hearing me, Andrés turns with a questioning look.

I nod toward the ground. "It crunches when I walk on it. It's like frozen corn flakes."

Andrés's jaw drops and he looks at me as if I've grown a second head.

"What?" I ask.

He reaches up and cups my chin, which is already numb from the cold. Then Andrés does something I haven't seen him do in a long time: he smiles. "I love you, that's what."

My throat tightens with emotion, and it takes all of my willpower to keep from turning into a blithering heap of sobs. He's told me he loves me a thousand times. Why do I feel like crying when he says it now?

"Stay close." He turns his back and holds his hand out behind him. "Those snow banks can get deep. I don't want to lose you in a corn flake avalanche."

We walk farther away from the lodge and then off the beaten path. I gasp when the frozen fluff reaches the tops of my shins. It's not compacted like the snow close to the lodge, but it's still thicker than I was expecting and it takes a lot of energy just to trudge through it. I don't know why I thought snow would be the consistency of clouds. Luckily, I'm able to walk in Andrés's footsteps, but it feels like forever before the mass of hanging branches thins and we reach a clearing.

The snow is even deeper here, and some of it reaches to my knees. Andrés takes me to what looks like a plateau. The afternoon sun beats down on us as I survey our surroundings. It's breathtaking. Even though Andrés says these mountains are small in comparison to the ones he's seen in Afghanistan, I've never seen real live mountains before, and I'm in awe of the Sierra Nevada's tall pines and snowcapped peaks. There are barely any clouds in the pale sky, and I can hardly believe they had a winter storm here a few days ago.

Andrés tugs on my jacket sleeve, pulling me toward him as he bends down on one knee. "Lie down with me. We'll make snow angels."

A refusal is already forming on my lips, and the sad thing is I don't even know why. When I catch a glimpse of that boyish smile, I can't refuse.

I follow him down to the ground, and a chill races up my spine as I'm enveloped in snow. I've made sand angels at the beach, so I think I already know what to do, but I soon discover there's a big difference between the two. My head feels numb from frost by the time we're finished sweeping our arms and legs up and down. Unable to stand another minute of the hard, cold ground, I sit up, and Andrés dusts off the back of my head. I'm glad he convinced me to wear that knit hat, even though I protested that it plastered my hair to my head.

I look over my shoulder, at the two angels touching wingtip to wingtip. I smile when I see the impression of us, but then my smile fades when dark thoughts invade the moment.

I look into Andrés's eyes as he brushes crystals off my cheek. "Do you think our baby is an angel?"

"I know it." He taps my nose, flashing a smile that doesn't quite reach his eyes. "No more sadness, mija. Okay?"

I swallow what feels like a wad of cotton and nod. "Okay."

He leans closer, until our lips are nearly touching, his minty breath tickling my skin. "And no more sad faces, or you get an ice wedgie."

I sway toward him, like the branches of a pine bending beneath the weight of heavy snow. Something inside me tells me I should resist. I should hold back. But why? Why have I been trying to put distance between us this past month? Why have I been fighting our desire? Our love? Am I trying to punish Andrés or me or both of us? That small voice inside of me grows louder, telling me it's okay to feel again. It's okay to stop torturing us.

I cup his chiseled jaw in my hand and brush frozen flakes off the two-day stubble. "What's an ice wedgie?" I ask with a playful smile.

"Something my cousins used to do to me when we'd go skiing. You don't want to know what it feels like." Andrés leans back, smirking.

I sigh, missing his body's warmth. I have no idea why, but this evil plan formulates in my head, and I act on it without thinking. I imagine that little devil on my shoulder is doing a victory dance while the angel on the other shoulder is sleeping on the job.

"Does it feel like this?" I press a hand against his chest and brush my lips across his. My mouth is so frozen, I can barely feel what I'm doing, but when he presses deeper into me for a kiss, instinct takes over and I welcome his mouth's invasion. I pick up a handful of snow and dump it down the back of his jacket.

He yelps and swats my hand away. I jump up with surprising speed when I see him grab snow. I try to run back the way we came, but my feet get stuck in the frozen quicksand before I have time to dodge his snowball. He tumbles into my backside, bringing me down with him. Somehow, he manages to spin me toward him, so he breaks our fall. I land on his chest, and we both burst out laughing.

How long has it been since we've laughed so hard? Since we've pushed aside all of life's problems and just enjoyed each other's company? When his lips find mine again, I don't push him away, and I don't reach for another snowball. I moan as his frozen lips soften and form against mine, thawing as he deepens the kiss. Our lips meld together, two parts to a whole, and for the first time in a long time, I feel complete, body and soul.

My extremities are numb from the cold, despite the warmth from Andrés seeping into me. I shudder and squirm on top of him.

Andrés pulls away, his eyes darkening, and I can't tell if his hungry gaze is fueled by lust or something more.

He stands and pulls me up, then wraps strong arms around my waist. "I want to take you back to our room, mija, and make love to you all day long."

Some part of me, whether it be instinct or guilt, tells me I should resist. But I'm tired of pushing him away. I'm tired of suffering all alone. I need Andrés. I need his love to chase away my sorrow, if just for one day. I answer his request by wrapping my arms around him and ever so softly kissing that hollow point on his neck.

* * *

We take off each other's clothes, slowly, gently, savoring each touch and caress as if it will be our last. When Andrés finally pins my nude body beneath his, he lavishes kisses across my collarbone and breasts before trailing kisses of fire all the way down to the juncture between my thighs. He kisses me tenderly there, as if my body is an altar and he is paying homage. He licks my folds with long, languid strokes before delicately suckling my swollen clit with agonizing tenderness. I arch my hips against his mouth, running my fingers through his thick hair and grasping it by the roots. It has been too long, and my willpower is weak. I know I will not last long before I fall apart. As if Andrés senses my needs, he pulls back, releasing my bud before lapping up my wetness once more. He trails kisses back up my abdomen, stopping to worship each breast, then my neck and an ear. Finally, he presses his mouth against mine, coaxing my lips open. I taste my essence on his tongue as it darts inside my mouth, spearing me in conjunction with his thick erection, as he drives it inside me.

Instinctively, I lift my legs, wrapping them around his waist as he slides deeper. He groans into my mouth as he buries himself to the hilt. My throbbing core is just a breath away from exploding in a cataclysmic orgasm. My need for release is strong, and yet, my need for Andrés is stronger. I hold tightly to him, relishing the feel of our joined bodies, wishing this moment where we are both hovering on the precipice of bliss could be suspended for an eternity. Andrés deep inside me, holding me close, is my nirvana, my spiritual and physical perfection.

And then he begins to move again. Slowly and torturously, he slides in and out of me, my slick channel molding around him like a wet, tight glove. I let go of that last thread of control, arch my neck and cry out toward the ceiling when the rhythm of his thrusts increases. He latches onto my neck with his lips, holding me still with a gentle tug of his teeth as he drives in harder. And then I unravel, surrendering to euphoric ecstasy as it washes over me.

He grunts through a groan and I can feel his throbbing head bathing me in fluid as he presses into me and then stills. We lie like that for several heaving breaths, our bodies locked together tightly. I feel my body sinking into the soft mattress as my insides continue to pulsate against him.

Andrés finally rolls over, pulling me with him, refusing to let me go or pull out of me. He holds me close, lavishing my forehead and cheekbones with kisses while we lie on our sides. He speaks words of love softly to me in Spanish, and I heave a sigh of contentment while snuggling against him, burying my nose against that light patch of hair on his chest.

I'd forgotten how wonderful making love to Andrés was. I've missed this. I've missed us. And as I wrap my arms tighter around his neck, I realize how badly I want our love back.

Chapter Twenty

Christina

"Where are we going?" I ask as Andrés navigates our rental SUV up the narrow, windy incline. I force myself to stop looking out the window. The drop off the narrow rails is so steep, it's making my chest tighten with anxiety. I've never liked heights much. I'm hoping Andrés doesn't see how much my nerves are frayed as I clutch the door handle, though I'm not sure how holding onto a door will help me if we were to skid off the road and go careening off the cliff.

"The guy at the front desk said there's a lodge at the top of the hill," Andrés says as he, thankfully, keeps his eyes on the road ahead.

I'm wishing I would have gone along with Andrés and stayed in bed all day, but since it was still afternoon, I had this crazy idea I wanted to go outside and play some more in the snow.

When we turn a bend, we leave the drop behind us, and both sides of the road are now flanked by blessedly solid ground and snowy pines that stretch toward the heavens and spread out as far as I can see.

I heave a pent up breath as that knot in my chest slowly unwinds. "It's beautiful here. This isn't what I was expecting when Grace said we were going to Vegas."

He clenches the steering wheel, as a shadow falls over his face. "Is this okay?"

My heart bubbles with joy when I think how wonderful this trip has been so far. "It's more than okay. Thank you."

We drive past what looks like a big Bavarian lodge. Several cars are parked out front. "I think that's the place," I say as we continue up the road.

Andrés flashes a sideways smile. "Not there. You'll see."

We drive for about another mile and pull to the side of the road beside a few trucks. When we get out of the SUV, the crisp, cool air assails my senses and chills my windpipe. I can hear screaming and laughter coming from beyond a copse of trees. Andrés lifts open the hatch in back and pulls out a long, bright yellow plastic rectangle with a rope tied to one end.

"What is this?"

"It's a sled." He drops it on the ground, and I watch it slide across the slick surface as if it's got invisible wheels.

I narrow my eyes. I sure hope he doesn't expect me to get on that flimsy contraption. "Where did you get it?"

"I bought it off some teens in the parking lot. I probably paid three times what they paid for it." His wide grin practically stretches ear-to-ear. "But it looks like fun, right?"

I grimace and take a step back as Andrés kicks it toward me. "You're not expecting me to ride this thing."

"Do you love me?"

Andrés's question catches me off guard, and even though his tone is playful, I sense an underlying desperation in his rigid shoulders.

"You know I do."

He bridges the distance between us in two strides, cupping my chin in his gloved hand. "Then make memories with me." He swallows and then fixes me with such a penetrating stare, I feel like I'm drowning in the depths of his dark eyes. "Happy ones."

Unable to speak through this tightening noose around my throat, I silently nod.

I take his hand and follow him as he drags the sled behind us. He helps me navigate a ditch beside the road. We walk toward the sound of laughter, and I am comforted knowing other people are nearby. After we walk through a copse of trees, I see the long slope rising at the end of the wide clearing. I watch as people climb up the side of the slope, mount their sleds, and then slide down the center, laughing and screaming all the way.

When we reach the base of the hill, my limbs ice over, and not from the cold, but from fear. I guess I've lived a sheltered life, because as I watch a kid on an inner-tube barrel past me, the notion of racing down the hill on an object without breaks terrifies me. I blame my fears on my adoptive parents, who were always too drunk or pissed off at each other to take me anywhere, with the exception of the few fishing trips my dad took me on, but even on the boat he usually drank a twelve pack.

I'm wishing I had a beer or two right now, so I can get up the nerve to get on that sled. Two kids on what appears to be a garbage can lid fly by us, nearly taking out my kneecaps before Andrés jerks me out of the way.

"Watch out for crazy drivers, mija," he gently scolds before he starts leading me up the slope.

Why I follow him, I have no idea. I feel like I'm stuck in a never ending dream as I trudge up the steep incline. By the time we reach the top, my chest is heaving and I'm straining for breath.

Andrés turns to me with a smirk. "It's a good workout."

"I'd rather be drinking rum at that lodge."

"This will be fun," he says with a wink. "I promise."

I only manage to slip and fall on my ass once as he's trying to help me get onto the sled. I don't know why my feet have to be so uncooperative before my butt finally makes contact with the plastic. Andrés tells me to fold my legs in and I stifle a scream when the ground slides beneath me. I don't even have a second to change my mind before he mounts the sled behind me and we are off. I'm so terrified, I think I forget to scream. Or maybe I do scream, but nothing comes out. Wind slaps my face, biting into my skin and chapping my lips as we zip down the slope at what feels like jetliner speed. That same kid who almost took out my kneecaps jumps out of the way as we careen toward the plain. We hit a bump and catch air before landing on the hard ground with a thud. I moan as pain winces up my tailbone, and this time I do scream as our little plastic rocket of doom continues its downward ascent. Even when the ground levels off, our sled propels us forward. I gasp when I see the tree line ahead. Andrés sticks out his leg, and we're spinning, over and over, until we come to a stop and topple to the side.

Andrés lands on top of me, clutching my back to his chest, and laughing hard in my ear. I'm too stunned to make a sound, but then Andrés is pulling me up against him, asking me if I'm okay. I turn to him with a slackened jaw, and see his eyes are wet with happy tears.

"Wasn't that fun, mija?" Laughter rings in each word.

And just like that, I forget about my holy trip of terror. I forget about the biting wind and the pain in my tailbone as I lean into him and plant a kiss on his frozen lips. Seeing Andrés this happy is like a balm to my soul. I wish he could laugh like this always.

* * *

The lodge is packed by the time we heave our exhausted and sore bodies into chairs later that day. We rode down the hill for what felt like hours until we were both so tired, we could hardly stand, let alone walk. I've never had so much fun in all my life. Andrés orders me a coffee with Bailey's Irish Cream, and I down most of it by the time our nachos arrive. I'm feeling pretty good after my second cup and a full stomach.

Andrés and I are sitting next to each other at the end of a long community table, and I lean back in my chair and watch the band set up as he reaches for my hand. He flashes a long, languid smile and winks at me when I look up into his soft eyes. I don't resist when he leans in for a kiss. Mm. I relish the feel of his warm lips on mine. He tastes like spiced rum and *queso*. And now that I'm exhausted, full and tipsy, I want very much to go back to our hotel and make love the rest of the night.

Andrés breaks the kiss when the band starts up. He kicks back his chair and extends a hand.

"May I have this dance?"

I look up at him and laugh. "I don't know if I have the energy."

"This is the best time to dance, mija," he says with a gleam in his eyes. "When you are loosened up."

I let him help me out of my chair, and then I follow him onto the dance floor.

The music sounds like German Polka. I vaguely remember hearing it on an elementary school field trip to the German settler town of Fredericksburg. I'm not quite sure how to dance to it, so I follow his lead, relieved when he two-steps us around the floor. And here's the amazing part. Despite being tired, sore and tipsy, I don't miss a step. I remember how humiliated I was the first time we danced together. I've never been a great dancer, and I was so nervous around Andrés the first night, I was stiff and clumsy. My raging hormones and his pure male sexiness had me so much on edge,

I'd felt like he was trying to sweep the floor with a broken broomstick.

Now, I feel like I'm gliding, and I imagine the soles of my feet are like that plastic sled and the floor is made of ice. We laugh and smile and he twirls me again and again, and I don't fall over my feet once. I think this magical day filled with crunchy cornflakes, sledding, dancing and passionate lovemaking, might just end up being the best day of my life. The only thing I can think of that would make it even better is if we ended it with more lovemaking. As I look into his darkening gaze, I notice his slow, seductive smile and feel the warmth from his hand seeping into mine, I know that's exactly how our day will end.

* * *

Andrés

I can't believe how easy it is to dance with Christina. We glide together as if we've been doing this for years. The truth is we've only been back to Dylan's a few times since the first night we met. I could tell dancing wasn't Christina's thing, and I didn't want to make her uncomfortable. But tonight her feet slide across the floor with ease and she sways in perfect timing to my rhythm. When the band strikes up a slow country song, I move my hand off her shoulder and settle it on her lower back, just above that sweet round ass I love so much. I pull her closer, pressing her soft body against mine.

I kiss the top of her forehead, whispering into her ear. "You look happy."

"I am." She flashes a radiant smile that nearly takes my breath away. "Because you are."

I falter and nearly stumble at the sincerity in her emerald eyes. Is that all it takes to make her happy? To see me happy? I'm humbled, grateful, and saddened as the realization washes over me. She's been mourning the loss of our child all this month, and what have I done to comfort her? Not much, because I've been wrapped up in my own miserable problems. I think about this job, and how much I hate it, and how I carry that stress home with me each night. If her happiness depends on mine, she will never, ever be happy unless I quit Cruz Automotive.

"I love you."

I look down at Christina. Worry lines are etched into her brow and her rosy lips are turned down. She must have sensed my unhappiness. I swallow hard and then force a smile. I will not let anything ruin this day. "I love you, too."

I wrap her in my arms, pressing more kisses on her temple as we move slowly to the gentle rhythm of the music. We dance a few more slow songs and drink a few more drinks. By the time we finish dancing to "The Cotton Eyed Joe," her cheeks are glowing with radiance. I've never seen her more beautiful.

Another slow song starts, and when I press her sweet little body against mine, she responds by "accidentally" grazing my groin with her hand. When I grab her wrist and flash a warning glare, she smiles coyly.

I lean down and growl into her ear. "Are you ready to go back to the hotel?"

Her answer is a breathy whisper. "More than ready."

* * *

Christina

Despite my exhausting day, I find my second wind as Andrés strips off my clothes and lies me down. When he slowly slides into me, burying his shaft deep inside my wet channel, I lift my hips, grinding into him. I melt into his body's heat as his lips seek out mine. I cup his face in my hands, relishing the feel of his rough skin on my palms. Our lovemaking is a timeless dance, our bodies, hearts and souls moving as one. He brings me close to climax several times before we both finally give into the powerful release that washes through us. We come undone, and then Andrés makes love to me again.

When he finally rolls off of me and pulls me against his chest, whispering Spanish words of love into my ear, my heart and soul sing with happiness, and my sated body hums in satisfaction. We fall asleep in each other's arms. The perfect ending to the perfect day.

Chapter Twenty-One

Christina

Last night marks the first night Andrés slept in bed with me since the nightmares began. I've forgotten how wonderful it feels to wake up in his arms, but that good morning kiss is pure heaven. The best part was he slept soundly beside me, no bad dreams at all. I'm hoping this little vacation was just what he needed to unwind and escape the nightmares, and he will return to our bed from now on. I strongly believe his recurring nightmares are associated with the pressures from his job, and maybe a change in employment would put an end to them. Even though I know Andrés doesn't want to let Tio down, my fiancé's mental health is more important than hurt feelings.

Though I'm sad to leave the mountains behind, Andrés reassures me we will make winter in Vegas an annual event, and next time we'll plan to spend more time in the snow. Andrés wants me to see the downtown lights tonight before we fly back to Texas tomorrow. He's been to Vegas a few times with his cousins and he says the lightshow is unlike anything he's ever seen. Though I'm sure he's right and I'll be impressed, after the way we made love last night, I'd be perfectly content to spend the rest of our vacation in the hotel room. We're staying at a hotel called The Golden Nugget, which Andrés says is at the heart of the light show.

I'm unpacking and trying to find just the right dress for dinner, although I already have an idea what I want to wear. Grace packed a sequined little black number in my suitcase. It must be one of her dresses, because I'd never be bold enough to buy something like this. As I eye the thing with a frown, I wonder if it's supposed to be worn with tights underneath. It barely covers my ass. Then I remember some of the girls I saw in the smoky casino downstairs. Their dresses were cut so short, their crotches were practically hanging out of them. I heave a sigh as I toss the dress on the bed. What would Andrés say if I wore it tonight? A smile lights up my face as I think I know exactly what will happen. He'll rip that dress off me and make love to me all night long. Okay, maybe I *will* wear it. I'll have to remember to thank Grace later for packing it.

Then I remember that *other* dress she packed. I should have known why my suitcase was so heavy. She actually had the nerve to pack my wedding gown, minus the train, of course, which I'm sure would never fit. The heavy silk skirt takes up nearly my entire suitcase. I can see the material bulging from beneath the luggage divider. I know it's getting wrinkled, but what the hell am I supposed to do with it? After all the stress Andrés and I have been through this month, I'm not sure now is the right time to get married. Besides, I never found the right shoes, and a girl can't experience the most momentous day of her life without the right footwear. I'd have my girl card revoked for sure.

Andrés is still in the shower, so I hurry and slip into the black dress and patent leather and rhinestone wedge heels. I sit at a pretty vanity table with a lit mirror and quickly apply mascara, blush, and lipstick. Andrés doesn't like my makeup too heavy. He says I'm beautiful without it. I'm running a brush through my hair when he comes out of the bathroom.

The steam from the shower eddies into the room, carrying the scent of his spicy aftershave. I love the way he smells. The heat from his musk sets my pheromones ringing like alarm sirens in a natural disaster. As I look at his clean-shaven face and slicked back hair, I realize my little black dress has nothing on Andrés's pure male sexiness.

My legs wobble as I slowly stand, and I can feel moisture pooling between my thighs.

He comes to me in a few long strides, his gaze traveling the length of my body as he lets out a low whistle. The look in his eyes is like a predatory cat preparing to pounce on his prey. "You know better than to wear a dress like that around me, mija," he growls into my ear before nipping at my neck.

A soft moan escapes my lips as he alternates between biting and kissing the soft curve of my neck all the way to my shoulder.

He cups the globes of my ass and hikes the flimsy fabric up over my hips. "Turn around," he commands in a tone that leaves no room for argument. I spin and watch as he hikes the dress up to my waist, balling the fabric in one hand and squeezing my breast hard with the other. I cry out when he pinches my nipple through the fabric. I gasp when he bends down behind me and rips my panties to the floor. He presses a hand against the back of my neck and pushes me forward. "Hands on the table," he commands.

I eagerly obey, and then he's kicking the stool forward and lifting my knees onto the padded bench. I'm on all fours, watching him in the mirror. Twin thunderstorms brew beneath his gaze as he unzips his pants and drops them to the floor. I lick my lips at the sight of his large erection springing from beneath his button up shirt. I shudder at the mischievous tilt of his smile as he hikes up my skirt again, licks his fingers, and then drives them into my slick channel.

"Naughty girl," he teases. "You're already wet. Did you start without me?"

"No." I shake my head.

Before I can say any more, he pulls out his fingers and buries the entire length of his erection in me, pounding against my swollen center like a battering ram. I suck in a sharp breath as he slides back out and then slams into me again and again. The vanity table rattles beneath me, banging against the wall as Andrés digs his fingers into my hips and drives in deeper, harder. And even though I'm still sore and tender from last night, my core weeps with wetness, savoring each achingly erotic thrust. I can feel that point of pleasure swelling inside me like a bubble ready to pop.

When Andrés cries out, burying himself deep inside me, my own release comes swiftly, bucking against his throbbing head as his juices spill inside me. After the wild pounding of my heart slows down to a heavy thud, he slides out and then quickly returns with a towel.

"See what happens when you dress like that?" He playfully swats my ass before wiping between my thighs.

"I'll have to wear it again," I tease, wiggling my hips.

Andrés lifts me and turns me toward him. He's got this look of pure satisfaction in his glazed over expression. Cupping my chin with his fingers, he feathers a soft kiss across my lips. "You make me very happy, mija."

My chest swells to near bursting as I wrap my arms around his neck and deepen the kiss, and for the first time in weeks, I feel as if all those broken pieces of my heart are fusing back together.

* * *

Andrés

"Wow. This has to be the best steak I've ever eaten."

My fiancé closes her eyes and groans as she bites into her steak. I'm suddenly jealous, and though I want to deny it, I know the reason why. I've been so busy, I haven't been able to cook for her lately, and she's enjoying that steak a little too much. I feel like her taste buds are cheating on me. I could probably make a steak that tastes just as good, if not better. I make a mental note to fix her one when we get home.

"What is in these mushrooms?" She leans forward and feeds me a bite. "Do you think you could make these?"

My mouth is awash in flavor. Marsala, and a mixture of Italian herbs. I nod as I open my mouth for another bite. Wow. If I ran Arturo's catering business, I'd definitely put mushrooms like this on the menu. Then I mentally kick myself in the ass for planning for a career I know I can never have. "I'm sure I can."

"Omigod!" she squeals. "I'll love you forever if you do."

I give her my best sideways glare. "You'd better love me forever, anyway."

She sets down her wine glass, bats long lashes and flashes a coy smile. "You know I will."

God, she looks so beautiful tonight. Her emerald eyes sparkle from the glow of the candlelight, and after spending the day in the snow, the color has returned to her face. But it's her smile that stops my heart, so wide it illuminates her entire face. I've missed that smile.

I've missed everything about her. I've been so absorbed in my job, I haven't made enough of an effort to spend time with her. After this trip, I intend to change that.

I stare down into my glass, at the mixture of rum and Coke and circular ice cubes, and though I don't intend it, I voice my thoughts aloud. "I need to make more time to do the things I love, like cooking and being with you."

Christina takes a sip from her wine, eyeing me skeptically. "Your Uncle Arturo called me a few days ago."

Why would he do that? Is he using her to convince me to work for him? I set my silverware down and push aside the grilled salmon plate. I have to force myself to unclench my jaw as I wait for her to finish.

She downs the rest of her wine, and then exhales slowly. "He wanted to offer his condolences about the baby and then he started telling me stories about how you used to follow him around in the kitchen. How whenever he would come over, you'd run and get your apron. How you'd rather help him cook than go outside and work on something for Tio."

I force myself to ignore the increasing tempo of my heart and try to keep my expression even. "That was a long time ago."

Biting on her lip, she runs a finger across the rim of her glass. Her expression is erotic, distracting. I realize the stakes must be high if Christina is using her sexual charms this early. "He thinks you've missed your true calling. He said something about his new catering business."

I shake my head. "I can't leave Tio."

She slumps in the booth, sighing. "It's obvious you're unhappy with your job, Andrés. Tio wouldn't want you to be miserable for the rest of your life."

"Catering doesn't pay enough, mija."

"Arturo said he offered you eighty thousand a year."

She says this as if I'm supposed to be impressed. Actually, the bills we have now don't exceed that income. Considering Christina was raised by a rich

253

bitch, she's pretty low maintenance, with the exception of the money she spends on paint. I know we could be comfortable on eighty-thousand plus whatever she makes. But I also can't forget she broke up with a billionaire's son to be with me. Ten years from now, when she doesn't have a luxury car or mansion, I don't want her regretting her decision.

"I've made almost two-hundred thousand this year working for Tio," I say. "I'll make double that next year."

I'm expecting her to be shocked by this news, but she doesn't so much as bat an eyelash. We haven't discussed how much I'll be making, other than it will be a lot. It was only last week, as Tio and I were going over the books with his accountant, that we discussed what I might expect to make in the coming years. They said I could easily pull in half a million a year.

Frowning, her gaze searches mine. I tense up, wondering what she's searching for. Finally, she folds her hands, staring at me with those penetrating eyes, as if she's trying to melt away my layers of resistance.

"But will you be happy?" she asks.

No, I think to myself, but I'm still unwilling to admit it. "We could buy a house. A nice house, maybe even a ranch of our own."

She strokes my hand with her delicate fingers. "How nice will it be if you're never there to share it with me?"

* * *

Say Forever

Christina

We walk hand-in-hand beneath the colorful, flashing lights on Freemont Street. A video plays on a large canopy screen above us. It's like the whole ceiling is a rock video, and hot music filters in from the loudspeakers surrounding us. The street is teaming with vendors selling all kind of goods, from chocolate to personalized license plates. And the entertainers on the street are hilarious. After growing up in Austin, the weird capital of Texas, I should be used to strange, right? But I don't know how to classify some of the people I meet in downtown Vegas. There's the topless woman who's somehow managed to avoid being labeled a flasher by painting giant strawberries on her Double-D, saggy breasts. Not quite sure who she's pretending to be other than a middle-aged woman with delusional Strawberry Shortcake fantasies. There's the old guy in a diaper, wearing cupid wings and a bow strung across his back. My favorite has to be the bronze cowboy. That's right. He's painted every part of his body, from his boots to his hat, bronze , and he stands as still as a statue while people pose for pictures. Of course, none of them do it for free, so Andrés hands three Elvises some bills and we snap a few pictures with them.

We're strolling arm-in-arm, eating cotton candy and enjoying the odd attractions, when I stop suddenly, as if I've run into a brick wall.

Omigod!

I break into a run until I reach the storefront window. I place my hands on the glass, and I think my jaw hits the concrete as I stare at the shoes the mannequin is wearing. And when I say *the shoes*, I mean *my shoes*.

These red, strappy heels with pretty shimmery flower bows match the flowers on my wedding gown perfectly.

"What is it, mija?" Andrés asks as he joins me.

I point at the window and jump up and down. "The shoes!"

He looks at me as if I've gone loco.

"My shoes," I squeal. "The shoes that match my wedding dress. I gave up looking for them and here they are."

Understanding dawns in his eyes, and then his full lips break into a slow grin. "We need to buy them."

* * *

I walk out of the store with my brand new shoes strapped to my feet. I know they totally don't go with the black dress I'm wearing, but I don't care. These beauties were practically screaming through the window for me to put them on. And as I sway my hips in front of Andrés before twirling around on my toes, I think these dazzling heels are the perfect fit.

Andrés smiles and whistles at me as we continue to walk down the street, past shops with high dollar clothes, noisy pubs, and blinking slot machines. I'm not quite sure how we end up standing in front of that wedding chapel, but as Andrés laces his fingers through mine, my feet propel me forward, and I'm drawn to the little white church like a moth to a flame.

That's when I realize the shoes, the chapel, the dress Grace packed for me has to be fate. As I look up into Andrés's soul-filled gaze, I know the one thing that would make this already memorable vacation absolutely perfect. As if we are both of one mind, we wordlessly walk inside. We reserve the deluxe Elvis wedding slot. Why we decided on Elvis, I have no idea, but I figure if we're going to get married in Vegas, we might as well go all the way. We rush back to the hotel and Andrés helps me into my gown.

I smooth down the fabric as I admire my reflection in the mirror. The dress isn't too wrinkled now, and the flowers and butterflies I added along the bottom are beautiful, but I think my shimmery red shoes make the gown, which reaches just above my ankles without the heavy train. I sway my skirt a few times, admiring my reflection.

Andrés comes up behind me, placing his strong hands on my hips. He pulls back my veil and plants a soft kiss on my neck. "You're beautiful, mija."

My eyes flutter shut as I savor the way his lips tickle my skin. When he takes a step back, I open my eyes and admire my handsome groom. He's changed into a suit jacket and dress pants. Not too formal, but not too casual, either. Although, Andrés could marry me in jeans for all I care. What matters is he's going to be my husband.

* * *

Andrés

I feel like the luckiest man in the world right now. Christina is so fucking beautiful. As I take her arm in mine and lead her through the hotel lobby, I still can't believe the girl of my dreams is about to become my bride.

I feel like I'm floating in a dream as we walk hand-in-hand across the crowded downtown sidewalk. Lots of people stop to congratulate us, which makes the trip take longer than it should. I nervously check my watch. We've got ten minutes before our scheduled appointment, and we've still got two more blocks to go. I summon what I learned back in Army training, square my shoulders and dodge, (sometimes push) people out of the way. I jostle that religious nut who says Revelations is upon us. I "accidentally" elbow the guy trying to sell us tickets to a strip club. We narrowly escape the old lady who wants to read our fortunes.

"Don't you fear what your future may hold?" she calls at our backs.

I pretend not to hear her.

The problem is, I do hear her. Because her voice is the same voice of worry that has been running through my head. I do fear what my future may hold. I fear it so fucking much, because once I make Christina my wife, my future will be her future, too. And the thought of it almost makes my knees go weak.

Considering how I buried myself in my job all last month while she mourned the loss of our baby, I know I've already failed her once. I should have insisted on time off. I should have been there for her.

Once we make it to an opening, I pull her along faster, but I don't know why I'm hurrying anymore. I realize we've got to make it to our wedding, but I feel as if something else is propelling my feet forward.

The word takes hold of me like a vice: *fear*. I'm fucking scared.

"Slow down, Andrés."

Christina sounds frustrated.

"Sorry, mija, but our appointment is in"—I check my watch—"four minutes."

She releases my hand and bends over, adjusting a strap on her shoe. "They won't care if we're a few minutes late."

"I don't want them giving away our slot." I pace the sidewalk while I wait for her. I can feel the tension mounting, pressing down on my shoulders like a two-ton sack. "I'm marrying you now before you change your mind." That last part comes out on a rush of air, and I'm not even aware what I say until it's too late.

She stands up, bunching up the sides of her dress in small fists. "Why would I do that?"

I heave a groan as I look from her penetrating eyes to the concrete. Might as well come out and say it. It's only fair she knows what she's getting into. "Because I'm not worthy of you."

Christina grasps my shoulders, pulling herself up on her toes while craning her neck to look up at me. "Don't say that. Don't ever say that." Her bottom lip trembles.

Damn. I've upset her. Now I feel even less worthy of her.

Shut up, Andrés. Take your beautiful bride and make her all yours. Don't fuck this up now.

But there's this aching in my chest, not strong, not enough to weigh me down. It feels like my heart has been punctured by the smallest hole, and it will never close until I come clean. Until I tell her how I feel, and I know I have to do it now. Before she commits to me for a lifetime, she needs to know this man she's marrying is not worthy of her. Not at all.

I look into her face and swipe a tear form the corner of her eye. "You don't have to be marrying me. You could be marrying a billionaire's son."

She shakes her head, biting down on her lip. "I don't want him. I want you."

I can see it's taking all her willpower not to break down and cry. I'm feeling less worthy of her by the second.

"I might have to quit my job, mija. If this catering thing doesn't work, then I won't have a job at all."

Christina settles back on her heels and crosses her arms. She was on the verge of sobbing just moments ago, and now she looks ready to bite my head off. "We haven't said our vows yet, but I'm pretty sure there's a part in there about for better or for worse, and when I say it, I'll mean it." She jabs me in the chest. "There's nothing that life can throw at us that will be any worse than the life I lived before I met you." Her expression softens as she splays her hand across my heart. "As long as we're together, we'll deal with whatever the future holds."

My heart pounds like a drum beneath her touch. I can still feel that hole, that fucking stupid hole, and though I know she's trying to reassure me now, all her forgiveness does is drive home the fact that I'm definitely not good enough for her.

"I wasn't there for you when you lost the baby." My throat feels so tight, I'm surprised I can speak at all. "I stayed too late at work. You needed me, and I wasn't there."

She frowns and looks at those red shoes of hers. She twists her feet for a moment, as if she's examining the flowers on her toes. And while she's contemplating flowers, I'm holding my breath, because I know it's not flowers she's thinking about. I know she finally realizes she can do better.

She lets out a slow breath of air, punctuated by a soft moan. When she looks at me, my heart stops. In fact, everything around me stops. I don't hear the noise from the crowd behind us or the blaring music. I don't see the flashing lights, either. All I see are those big, soulful green eyes staring at me.

"I did need you, Andrés, but you had a lot to deal with, too."

I shake my head, hardly believing she's trying to justify my behavior. "Don't make excuses for me, mija."

She flashes a weak smile while tracing a pattern on my chest. "You'll do better next time."

"I'm never putting my job ahead of you again. I'm sorry."

"Apology accepted." She leans into me, wrapping her arms around my neck. "Can we get married now?"

The impatience in her tone makes me laugh out loud. My fear and guilt seem to melt away as I bend her over and capture her lips in a soul crushing kiss. Yeah, maybe I don't deserve this amazing woman, but goddam, I'm making her mine.

We spend a half an hour filling out marriage certificate paperwork and picking our photography packages before Elvis will marry us. Christina gets offended when the woman at the front desk says she looks as old as her high school daughter. She checks over Christina's ID carefully, as if we've forged it. I stifle a laugh as Christina rolls her eyes at the woman. Christina doesn't bring a ring for me, but since the chapel is nice enough to have wedding rings on hand for an extra three hundred dollars a pop, we buy me a simple silver band. When Christina asks about bands for herself, I hold up a hand, telling her not to worry about it, and then I shrug off her questioning look.

Elvis really plays his part well as he saunters up to us, swaying an ass that is probably thirty years too old and forty pounds too much for those polyester pants with multicolored rhinestones sewn into the seams. He knocks his knees a few times and waves his hands around in an awkward circular motion before pointing at my bride.

"Rhythm is something you either have or don't have, but when you have it, you have it all over." He waves his hands down his body as if he's trying to fan paint fumes off his pants.

I try to pretend that's what he's doing, but I groan when he starts going on about us not stepping on his blue suede shoes.

Fuck. Why did we have to get the Elvis wedding?

But my bride giggles, so for her, I guess he's worth it.

We follow Elvis inside the little chapel and up to the rhinestone studded podium. Elvis's pianist, a woman who's either in her early fifties, or else in her seventies and bursting at the seams, (literally) from cosmetic surgery, plays "Here Comes the Bride" on the piano. I'm thankful it's not an Elvis song.

The ceremony passes in such a blur, I hardly remember what's happening, but I remember saying "I do" plenty of times, especially the part about cherishing her forever. That part is easy, because cherishing my amazing bride is second nature.

I like the look of shock on Christina's face when I pull out the diamond and emerald wedding band I brought with me. No, I wasn't planning on getting hitched, but I thought I'd best come prepared, just in case Christina lost her mind and agreed to be my wife.

I'm vaguely aware of saying our final "I dos" and then I cup my wife's beautiful face in my hands and stifle her gasp when my lips come crashing down on hers. I kiss her long and hard, until I feel the tension ease from her, and she melts like butter in my arms. Elvis clears his throat loudly behind us, but I don't give a damn. I keep kissing my wife, until we both finally come up for air, nearly out of breath and chests heaving.

My prick is rock hard. I can't wait to carry my bride across the threshold to our hotel room and fuck her every which way until she's begging for release.

Chapter Twenty-Two

Christina

"Good morning, Mrs. Cruz." Andrés is sitting up against the cushioned headboard. With a yawn, he stretches muscular, tanned arms toward the ceiling.

I stretch my arms out too, admiring my new diamond and emerald band as it catches a ray of light that slips in from behind the heavy window curtain. I still can't believe I'm a married woman.

"Good morning, sexy husband." I climb into Andrés's lap, and we share our first good morning kiss as husband and wife.

I taste the champagne on his breath from last night. Yeah, we had a few too many glasses after we said our "I dos" in front of Elvis, but it was our honeymoon night, after all. And what a night it was. After he carried me across the threshold into our room, my husband made slow, tender love to me all night long. My heart warms just thinking about it, so does that juncture between my thighs, and I think how very much I'd like to make love to my husband all day long.

He pulls back, brows drawn together. "You ready to catch that plane?"

I shake my head and then shift in his lap, as I not-so-subtlety grind against his erection. "Not really." I bat my lashes and bite my lip, hoping he'll lock me up in this hotel room a few extra days for bad behavior.

Andrés laughs as he nibbles my ear. "Maybe we could put off leaving for a few more days."

"Mmmm," I groan as I toss my head back while he tickles my neck with feather soft kisses. "What about your job?"

"Tio will have to understand we need a honeymoon," he says as he courses his fingers through my hair. "Besides, I'm quitting when I get back." He tenses up beneath me as he speaks with an edge to his voice. "If that's what you want."

I pull back and look into his gaze, which was reflecting love and adoration only moments ago. His frozen features can only be described as a look of pure terror.

I cup his face in my hands, kissing his full lips, until I feel his body relax beneath me. "I want you to be happy," I murmur against his mouth. "I want you to do what you love."

"Even if I have to give up all that money?" When his voice cracks, I think I feel my heart breaking, too.

I kiss him again and again, trying to drive away his fears with my affection. "I didn't marry you for your money. I married you because I love you."

* * *

The wedding reception is simply stunning. Mom enlists the teens, and they transform Violet's ranch into a winter wonderland, complete with popcorn snow, cotton ball snowmen, and thousands of papier-mâché snowflakes. Hundreds of little lamps hang from the oak trees surrounding the courtyard, giving the place an ethereal glow. They even built a beautiful hardwood dance floor in the center of the courtyard. Facing the dance floor is a large buffet table loaded with tamales, fajitas, and the most delicious red velvet wedding cake ever, plus a chocolate fountain loaded with fresh fruit and cookies, which is why my little brothers' faces are coated in brown sticky sauce every time my mom turns her back on them. I'm happy to report the buffet doesn't include a single shrimp puff.

Tia invites her priest to bless our marriage, and I think it's kind of funny that he looks exactly like the Elvis impersonator who married us. Since I put so much work into that train, I wear it attached to my dress for about the first five minutes of the reception, but then I get tired of stepping on it, and my mom hangs it like a tapestry behind the buffet table.

I think my favorite part of the buffet is the hot cocoa topped with marshmallows and spiked with Bailey's Irish Cream. I clutch my mug like a lifeline, letting the hot, sweet liquid warm my insides as Andrés keeps a strong arm wrapped around my shoulder.

Our guests go all out and dress for cold weather, with snow boots, jackets and knit caps, something Andrés suggested they do to go along with our winter theme. Good thing, too, because Texas is having an unusual cold spell. It even snowed north of Dallas. We all huddle in our seats, leaning into the warmth from the gas lamps and laugh while sipping cocoa. Everyone turns around when we hear a loud dinging sound. Tio is beaming ear-to-ear, standing in front of the buffet table, as he taps his mug with a spoon.

"A toast to the lovely bride and groom," he says and winks at us. "Salud!"

The crowd responds with a "salud" and we all drink.

"Sobrino," Tio says to Andrés as his voice takes on a wistful tone, "those first few months you lived with us, I never thought you'd come out of your shell. Now look at you, an Army hero, married to a lovely young woman, and I know you'll do a terrific job running Arturo's catering business."

Andrés's eyes have a glossy sheen as he tips his mug toward his uncle. I think he wants to answer back, but the look he shares with his Tio is worth more than a thousand words.

I'm so relieved Tio is supporting Andrés's decision to work for his Uncle Arturo. I sat beside Andrés when he broke the news to Tio and Tia last week. They both took it better than we'd expected.

"How could you ever think you'd disappoint me?" Tio had said as he clasped Andrés on the shoulder. "If you spend the rest of your life miserable because you care too much about what I think, then you'd disappoint me. Don't worry about me," he added with a sheepish grin. "I'm not ready to retire yet, anyway."

He told Andrés he'd give him a year to work for his Uncle Arturo, and if things didn't work out, Andrés would have a position waiting for him at Tio's automotive shops. Although, honestly, I hope Andrés never has to go back to Cruz Automotive. He's been so happy this week planning the wedding menu with his uncle and getting the catering business ready for another wedding next weekend.

I look up at my husband and smile as he squeezes me to him. A few relatives step in front of the buffet table and make their toasts. I cringe when Marie taps her glass, but she surprises me by wishing us the best and then apologizing to us both for judging me too harshly.

When my mom walks in front of the table, a hush falls. I lean into Andrés for support, and he braces me by holding tightly around my shoulder.

"My sweet baby girl," she says with a watery voice and red-rimmed eyes. "I held you in my arms for just a moment before they took you away, but I've held you in my heart forever." She pauses to wipe her eyes. "And I always will. I'm so happy that, despite the odds stacked against you, you've grown to become a caring, loving young woman, and you've found a wonderful husband who returns your love."

Unlike Andrés, I'm unable to hold back my tears. Andrés releases me when my mom walks up to me with open arms. We hug while crying onto each other's shoulders.

Then the band strikes up the first tune. I recognize it as the slow song Andrés and I danced to when I met him at Dylan's. They alternate between Tejano and country music after that. Everyone joins in the dancing, and we all make quite a sight when we circle around the floor to the "Cotton-Eyed Joe."

After over an hour of dancing, I fall into a nearby chair, exhausted. These little red shoes sure are pretty, but they're killing my feet. I was worried it would be too cold outside for our guests, but now, despite the fact that I'm wearing Andrés's suit jacket, I'm the only one who's freezing. Though the temperature was in the high forties earlier, it's steadily dropping, and I'm about to ask Grace if we can all move into the house when Andrés pulls my snow boots and heavy pants from beneath the buffet table. I eye him skeptically as he flashes his signature half-smile and tells me I need to go change.

When I come back outside, I can hear deep roaring engines, muffled by the sound of several high-pitched motors. The guests are no longer in the courtyard; they are cheering and laughing beyond the walls.

Andrés is waiting for me by the back gate with an outstretched hand and a devious gleam in his eyes. "Are you ready for your wedding present, mija?"

I smile at my husband, who's also changed into a downy jacket and snow boots. "What did you do?"

Imagine my surprise when I follow him through the gate and see several big trucks unloading fluffy white stuff onto a grassy slope behind Violet's house. A few guys come from behind the trucks and start blowing the snow, until it cascades like a giant slide down the hill.

Andrés sweeps his hand in front of us as he calls to the crowd. "Fresh snow imported from north Texas for my lovely bride."

The crowd breaks into applause. My little brothers are squealing and running around like puppies chasing their tails, begging my mom and stepdad to take them down the hill.

I'm too stunned to say anything as one of the teens comes up to us, handing Andrés a yellow plastic sled.

Andrés turns to me and arches a brow, his dark eyes looking far too sexy beneath that black woolen cap. "You ready to go riding?"

At the moment, I think I'd much rather be riding my new husband, as I bat my lashes and smile seductively up at him. "I can't believe you did all this."

His eyes light with desire as he strokes the side of my face with a gloved hand. "I'll do anything to make you happy." When he cups my chin and plants a tender kiss on my lips, I lean into his warmth, wrapping my arms around his neck. The plastic sled hits the ground as Andrés places his hand on the small of my back and bends me back while deepening the kiss and setting my body on fire.

I think I hear cheering and whistling behind me, but it's soon drowned out by the sound of the snow blowers and the wild beating of my heart.

* * *

Seven years later

Christina

"Again, Daddy, again!" James squeals as he and Andrés come to a stop at the bottom of the hill.

It's only after my husband lifts our son off the sled and sets his little feet on the ground that I breathe a sigh of relief. Andrés says I worry too much, but I can't help it. Though he's only four years old, James is quite the daredevil. Doc finally removed his arm cast last week after he fell out of that tree while trying to catch my brothers.

"I wanna be like Gio and Manny," he tells us. But my brothers are ten and eleven-years-old, and poor James can't keep up with them.

"Broder go down." Victoria giggles and squirms on my hip.

"Yes, he did go down the hill, sweetie." I kiss my baby angel on the brow, my lips lingering on her skin for a few extra moments. I've been so worried she'll come down with another cold. Though she's been a healthy child, that virus she caught last month was enough to scare even my big bad husband. In fact, the night her fever peaked was also the only night he's had a bad dream in seven years.

But I remind myself for at least the hundredth time that kids fall down. Kids get sick. It's part of life. The best I can do as a mother is love my children unconditionally. And I do love my family, more than I ever thought was possible.

I think back to the night it all began. The night of my twenty-first birthday. Andrés was my knight in shining armor after my friend's car engine blew up, and he's been my hero every day since. He saved me, not just from a bad home life, but from myself. Not only did I refuse to believe I was incapable of loving a family: I refused to love myself and let myself be loved the way I deserved.

"Me go with Daddy!" Victoria kicks her legs against my side.

"Oh, no, pumpkin," I stroke her tanned cheek and look down into her vivid green eyes. "I don't want you getting hurt."

"Pease, Mommy," she begs, batting thick lashes.

Andrés comes up to us and peels Victoria from my grip. "Just one time, Mommy."

"Andrés," I cry. "She's too little."

Andrés flashes a reassuring smile and kisses me on the cheek. "We'll only go half-way." Then he leans down and purrs in my ear. "But I'm taking you all the way tonight, mija."

A blush creeps into my cheeks, and damn my traitorous body for leaning into him, my senses craving the rich scent of his musk like a drug. I nip at his ear as he turns from me, our daughter pressed against his chest. James follows them up, and my heart goes with them. James hops on the back of Manny's sled and Andrés settles our little girl between his legs, holding her tight as they soar down the hill. My heart doesn't stop pounding in my ears until Andrés places our giggling girl back in my arms.

My mom trudges up to us in her pastel pink snowsuit, matching pink scarf, boots, and gloves. She looks like a vat of cotton candy, and I think she's adorable.

"Here, I think you could use this."

I take the steaming cup from her as Victoria launches herself into her grandma's arms.

I clutch the cup tightly, savoring the taste of Bailey's Irish Cream. I wonder who told my mom I needed alcohol. When Doc comes over to us with a sheepish grin, I have my answer. I usually only drink alcohol on special occasions, and I think stressing all day over the safety of my children is "special" enough. After I finish the whole cup, I think I'm finally relaxed enough to ride down a few times with my husband.

It's late by the time we settle in our cabin for the night. Andrés decided the family needed to spend Christmas in New Mexico, and I think it's a brilliant idea. His catering business is doing so well, he refused to take any money from my parents for the cabin.

It's been seven years since we moved to San Antonio and Andrés started working for his Uncle Arturo, and in that time, Andrés managed to complete culinary school and turn his uncle's venture into a thriving business. In fact, they are doing so well, his uncle closed all his restaurants, made Andrés a partner, and now they cater full time. Andrés and I sometimes get to work the same events together, which is fun. One time, we even managed to sneak into a utility closet and have sex while a bride and groom were saying their vows. Terrible, I know, but I'm fairly certain that was the day Victoria was conceived, so the risk was worth it.

My mom and I love working together. Our designs have now been featured in many major fashion and wedding magazines, and we've grown another side business off Domingo Designs. In addition to custom furniture and party designs we now sell home décor, and a few reprints of my paintings have been picked up by major retailers. One painting in particular, an abstract of a loving husband and wife holding a newborn baby, is our biggest money maker. It's already been reprinted several times and featured in prestigious art magazines.

Andrés was worried about money when we were first married, but last year we cleared seven figures. I'd say we're doing pretty well for ourselves. And to think, my adoptive mother thought I was throwing my life away when I told her Andrés and I were serious. Speaking of The Cobra, she made the San Antonio nightly news a few weeks ago after she and her best friend, Nora Richards, were caught trying to blackmail a state senator. Now they're looking at time in prison. Ouch.

My mom insists on taking the kids upstairs for bath time, and I don't argue. My legs and arms are so sore from climbing up and down that hill, I can hardly put one foot in front of the other. I fall into a cushioned sofa by the fire while Andrés fixes us drinks.

I slip my phone out of my pocket when it starts buzzing, and open up a text from Karri. It's a picture of Tyler and his horse jumping a barrel. I cringe when I see how high that horse is flying. Good thing Ty is a natural horseman. He's already won several races, and he's only eight. I'm so glad Karri finally got full custody of her child. Although after Mrs. James ran off with her bodyguard and Mr. James moved to France, it wasn't hard. She just had to convince Jackson to let her have him. Jackson was still drowning in sorrow after his latest fiancé dumped him. Seems she was so angry when she found out her engagement ring had initially belonged to me, she posted a public Facebook rant about his tight wallet and itty, bitty penis. Now he's tied up in a defamation lawsuit with his former fiancé, and too wrapped up in his own problems to worry over Tyler. Tyler still seems like a happy, well-adjusted child, and he loves living with his mom at Violet and Grace's ranch.

When Andrés sits beside me and hands me a cool glass of Bailey's and milk, I'm about to show him the picture of Tyler, but one look in his smoky eyes, and I know he's got another idea in mind. I only get a small sip of my drink before his very warm, very virile body is pressing into me. He sets my drink on the counter and lays me down, stretching across me. He reaches between us and rubs my hand up the length of his erection.

His heated breath tickles my ear, sending a shiver down my spine. "It's time for our bath, too, mjia." Feeling the rough pad of his thumb circle my palm, I soften against him.

"No, Andrés." I push against his chest. "What if they catch us?" But even as I'm pushing him away, my legs spread like melting butter.

"That's what you said when we made Victoria," he laughs.

He gets up from the sofa, pulling me with him. When he nods toward our bedroom on the bottom floor, I swear I see horns sprout from beneath his thick hair as his eyes twinkle with a devilish gleam. I repress a shudder and lick my lips as I follow his lead and lock the door behind us.

A few useless things you don't need to know about Tara West

1. Like Tyler, if I eat gluten, I will get very, very sick. I turn into a cross between a gremlin, Godzilla (only the flames come out the other end) and a rabid dog. It truly is an ugly sight.

2. I am married to the world's most awesome, supportive man and we have a sweet little girl. They are my everything.

3. I love my fans and writer friends. They give me purpose and keep me grounded.

4. I taught high school English, journalism and photography for eight years.

5. The World's Best Brownie is in Houston at a place called Ruggles Green. It is made from hemp flour, covered in gooey chocolate, and truly is an orgasmic experience for your taste buds.

6. I have written trashy parodies under the name PJ Jones. If you'd like to give PJ's books a try, just be warned; if your laugh-o-meter is set to prude, not crude, and you have high literary standards, or ANY standards at all, you will be sadly disappointed. My favorite PJ books are Driving Me Nuts!, Romance Novel, Attack of the Fairytale Zombies! and Melvin the Dry Cleaning Zombie. Now that you know I'm PJ, please don't throw rotten tomatoes at me or burn a Jane Austen effigy in my yard. Thanks.

7. Unlike Grace's Chihuahua, my little Chi is a ball of cuddly, cute sweetness, except when she sees a cat or a squirrel. Then she's seven pounds of fluffy terror.

8. I was born and raised in Las Vegas. We lived in a few different cities when hubs was in the military, but San Antonio is where we call home.

9. I wrote and published five books in 2013, and have many, many more book ideas in my head. In 2014 I hope to publish two fantasies, two YAs and a few sexy, funny paranormal chick-lits. I'm also planning a hilarious new adult roller derby girl story with a writing partner, who just so happens to be a former derby girl.

10. I work for a romance publisher and freelance as a book cover artist. I designed all of the covers for my Whispers books and my Something More series. I have designed close to a thousand book covers since 2005.

11. My editor cut 2500 useless words from this book. I have no idea why, but I guess I really, really, like useless words.

12. Please come hang out with me on my Facebook page: Facebook.com/TaraWestAuthor

My website: www.TaraWest.com

Or send fan (not hate) mail to tara@tarawest.com

BOOKS BY TARA WEST

From the Something More Series

Say When
Say Yes
Say Forever

From the Whispers Series

Sophie's Secret
Don't Tell Mother
Krysta's Curse
Visions of the Witch
Sophie's Secret Crush

From Keepers of the Stones

Witch Flame, Prelude
Curse of the Ice Dragon, Book One
Spirit of the Sea Witch, Book Two (releasing 2015)

From Eternally Yours

Divine and Dateless (releasing spring 2014)
Damned and Dateless (releasing summer 2014)

ALSO CHECK OUT THESE

EXTRAORDINARY AUTHORS & BOOKS:

Alivia Anders ~ Illumine

Cambria Hebert ~ Recalled

Angela Orlowski Peart ~ Forged by Greed

Julia Crane ~ Freak of Nature

J.A. Huss ~ Tragic

Cameo Renae ~ Hidden Wings

A.J. Bennett ~ Now or Never

T.G. Ayer ~ Skin Deep

Lizzy Ford ~ Zoey Rogue

Ella James ~ Selling Scarlett

Heidi McLaughlin ~ Forever Your Girl

Melissa Andrea ~ The Edge of Darkness

Kelly Walker ~ No One's Angel

Komal Kant ~ Falling for Hadie

Melissa Pearl ~ Golden Blood

Alexia Purdy ~ Ever Shade (A Dark Faerie Tale #1)

L.P. Dover ~ Love's Second Chance

Sarah M. Ross ~ Inhale, Exhale

Brina Courtney ~ Reveal

Amber Garza ~ Falling to Pieces

Anna Cruise ~ Maverick

Rebecca Ethington ~ Kiss of Fire

Made in the USA
Charleston, SC
14 September 2015